6

The Death Mage

Densuke
Illustrations by Ban!

Summary

In his second reincarnation, Vandal was born as a dhampir. After humans killed his mother, Dalshia, Vandal swore vengeance on High Priest Goldan and the others who killed her.

Vandal made new allies, enhanced his undead, took his first steps toward revenge on Evbejia, and then took to the road. Vandal and his party encountered the ghoul elder Zadilis and made contributions to the advancement of the ghoul grotto, becoming friendly with the ghouls. When Vandal decided to help fight off the incoming Noble Orc Bugogan and his army of orcs, Vigaro and the other ghouls begged him to became their Ghoul King. With Vandal as their king, the enhanced ghouls managed to defeat the orcs. Rather than face an oncoming conflict with their human pursuers, however, Vandal decided to lead his new companions away in search of fresh pastures.

This led them to the giantling city of Talosheim, known as the City of the Sun. Here Vandal was able to add many new allies to his forces, including the mighty Sword King Borkz, and power-up his followers through dungeon exploration.

As Talosheim continued to recover and grow, vampires secretly arrived in the city with orders to kill Vandal. However, Vandal acquired the skill Soul Crusher and took his revenge on Sercrent — the noble vampire who killed Vandal's own father — by eradicating his soul. He then crushed the soul of a divine artifact found beneath the castle of Talosheim, the magical spear Ice Age.

After becoming the king of Talosheim, the next threat arrived in the form of an expedition army from the Milg Shield Kingdom, led by Goldan and Raily — two of those responsible for the death of Dalshia. After defeating them and driving off a potential invasion of Talosheim, Vandal's allies desired that he strengthen the nation as a whole. Vandal, however, has his own plans to achieve noble rank and schemes a trip to the domain of Duke Heartner in the Olbaum Electorate Kingdom in order to finally register as an adventurer…

Character — Death attribute Magician

VANDAL

Hiroto Amamiya after his second rebirth. A dhampir born from a vampire father and a dark-elf mother, he possesses massive magical power and a command of Death Attribute magic. He finally achieved the Job change that he had almost given up on and became a true Death Mage.

DALSHIA

Vandal's mother. She suffered a terrible death, but Vandal used his Death Attribute magic to bind her to one of her own bones, keeping her in the world as a spirit.

ZADILIS

The elder of the Ghoul Grotto. She appears to be a young woman but is 290 years old. Perhaps held back by her physical appearance, her mental age is not as advanced as her years.

BASDIA

Zadilis's daughter. A female warrior with an athletic, honed frame that also features feminine curves. She has taken a liking to Vandal.

VIGARO

The young chief of the Ghoul Grotto. Trusted implicitly by the young male ghouls and adored by the females, he's a ghoul with everything going for him. He is also Basdia's father.

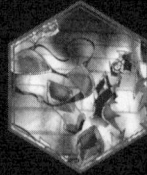

SARIA & RITA

Sam's daughters. They received living armor found in a dungeon treasure room to use as their bodies. Since obtaining the Spirt Body skill, they now have more of a visible outline.

TALEA

A former human, now a ghoul, who hitches her wagon to Vandal's after his rise as king. Has significant skill with making armor and weapons.

BORKZ

Giantling undead who was one of the heroes of Talosheim, known as the Sword King. Has incredible faith in Vandal.

ELEONORA

A former underling of the progenitor species vampire Vilkain, she attempted to assassinate Vandal. After witnessing his strength, she became smitten and swore her fealty to him.

CONTENTS

Chapter One
OLD ENOUGH!
007

Chapter Two
SAVIOR OF THE PIONEER VILLAGES
043

Chapter Three
THE GUY WHO WANTS A FOURTH LIFE
091

Chapter Four
KING. THE ADVENTURER?
175

Chapter Five
THE GUY WHO FINISHED ON HIS THIRD LIFE
231

Special Chapter
INTO THE DUKE HEARTNER HOUSE TREASURE VAULT!
301

Afterword
Glossary

The Death Mage
Written by Densuke | Illustration by BAN

The Death Mage

CHAPTER ONE
OLD ENOUGH!

Documentation. It goes without saying, but documentation would never exist without stationery. Functional materials could be made from tree bark, wood, and animal hide, but the pile of documents sitting in front of Vandal was made from paper—paper from a golem factory production line that he had established himself.

Examining the prodigious pile, Vandal was starting to regret having brought such high-quality paper into this world.

"Deskwork is a part of adult life," he said, trying to convince himself. If he became accustomed to it now, life would only be easier in the future. A man who got his work done efficiently would command the respect and admiration of others—or so he hoped. Admittedly, a muscleman who could hunt monsters would probably be a smidge more popular on Ramda.

In any case, he had to deal with these documents. He looked over them and used the official seal he had recently created to stamp his approval onto those that passed muster.

"Phew! Finally done," he breathed.

". . . Your Majesty."

Vandal looked up. It was Chezale, the undead of the commander from Milg.

"Perhaps you could impart your methods for handling paperwork to me?"

In life, Chezale had surely handled reams more documents than Vandal had ever seen. Him asking Vandal to instruct him likely had something to do with Vandal increasing his number of arms and heads to do his work.

"I might be able to give you some tips," Vandal mused, "but in your case, we'd get faster results if I physically grafted on more arms and heads. Shall I schedule a surgery for later today?"

"No, thank you. Maybe another time." Even though he was a zombie, Chezale seemed to be resistant to body/corpse modification.

"Do you have something new for me?" Vandal asked.

"Not new, Your Majesty, but it is time to reconsider the currency issue."

"Currency, huh?"

Chezale was currently creating all sorts of systems within Talosheim. Vandal hadn't ordered him to do it, but Chezale was taking the initiative to come up with new systems for the young nation. They now had an eclipse-inspired flag featuring a white and black circle, and templates for filling out various types of documents.

When it came to laws, those were based on the ones used in the lands of Duke Heartner—a region in Olbaum called the Heartner Domain—with which old Talosheim had often traded. At the moment, however, new Talosheim had little use for laws.

That same Chezale was the one to suggest the introduction of a currency.

"Your Majesty. I understand that simple trade is serving due purpose at the moment. But the introduction of a currency is vital for the expansion of our nation—especially if your future desire for trade with the Electorate Kingdom comes to fruition!"

"I've got an idea," Vandal countered. "If we're going to be trading with them anyway, why don't we just use their currency? I'm not really planning on making Talosheim an independent nation anyway."

"What's this?" Chezale exclaimed. "You're already planning on selling out your nation, Your Majesty?!"

"I was thinking more an autonomous country within Olbaum, without independent diplomatic rights."

"Your Majesty!" Chezale was only getting more worked up. "We have no intention of becoming a mere attendant nation! Please, you must rethink this!"

Vandal sighed and shook his head. His original plan had been to become an honorary noble in the Olbaum Electorate Kingdom. What happened to Talosheim after that would depend on whether human rights for undead and ghouls were approved and how things turned out with the progenitor species vampires. If everything went well, he planned for Talosheim to become an autonomous part of the Electorate Kingdom.

The possibility of everything working out wasn't high. But if he could pull it off, that plan seemed to have the best rate of return.

If it didn't work out, they would remain an independent nation, trading with what he presumed would be the skilled diplomats of the Electorate Kingdom while managing their own country. *Just how many veteran undead politicians am I going to need for that to work?*

"That's all for the future, anyway. Let's set it aside for now," Vandal said. "The issue is the currency, right? I'm going to be setting out for the Heartner Domain today. Can we think about this after my trip?"

Vandal had already turned seven. Summer was in full swing. He was supposed to be well on his way to Olbaum already.

The purpose of the trip? Guild registration.

Minors could only operate as adventurers if they graduated from the adventurers' academy. But minors could still register without attending school. Grade G adventurers who had only registered at the guild could take on quests like daylaborer work. However, those who wished to become Grade F or higher, proper adventurers, had to graduate first.

That was how it had worked at the adventurers' guild in the Electorate Kingdom 200 years ago, at the very least.

In the future, Vandal did plan to become a full-on adventurer, making a name for himself and becoming an honorary noble. But for now, once he got his guild card, he was planning on coming back to Talosheim rather than entering the school system. The reason was simple.

"I need to register before my status gets any more . . . provocative."

That was the entire issue. Registering with the guild provided a certificate of registration, generally called a "guild card." Upon issuance, the staff member would see the full status of the individual registering. In Vandal's case, that would mean his Aliases of Ghoul King, Eclipse King, and Unspoken Name, his previously unknown jobs such as Undead Tamer and Crusher of Souls, his previously unknown Death Attribute Magic, his undeniably absurd unique skill, God Smiter, and all the curses Rodocolte had left him with would be put on veritable display.

That was a bad look even at the moment. And there was nothing to say they wouldn't keep multiplying. He needed to register before things got any worse, and then hurry back to Talosheim before there were any consequences.

Of course, he was also planning on trying to find out what happened to Lebia, the first princess of Talosheim who had fled along with Borkz's daughter and the other giantling refugees to the Heartner Domain 200 years ago.

Like ghouls, giantlings lived for about 300 years. That meant he could probably ask around among any giantlings he found in one of the towns there and get some answers. He hoped they were doing okay—but maybe not so okay that they were campaigning to restore Talosheim. And he very much hoped they had some sympathy for undead.

"I'll bring some Olbaum Electorate Kingdom currency back with me. We can take a look at them then," Vandal said. All the currency in the Amidd Empire was issued by the Empire itself, meaning they had a single currency. In the Olbaum Electorate Kingdom, however, the individual lords and dukes issued the currencies, so they had fourteen different types.

There was the unified currency called the baum, which could be used across the Electorate Kingdom, but that was all mixed in with the currencies issued by each domain. While Olbaum was all one nation, there were currency exchanges on the borders between each domain, and merchants who were active in multiple domains had to keep an eye on the exchange rates at all times.

In addition to all of that, new currencies had replaced old ones throughout history on multiple occasions. It wasn't just about changing the face of the king carved into the coins; the metallic composition was also changed, in turn changing the value. It was quite possible that the currency would be completely different from 200 years ago.

"After a war six years ago, there's one fewer domain, but

it's still very complex. If we're going to make our own currency, we'll have to proceed with care," Vandal stated. They didn't want the composition of the coins created in Talosheim to cause issues at a later date, such as inflation. Vandal recalled learning about something like that once happening in Japan.

Chezale was looking at Vandal in surprise.

"You still plan on going to the Heartner Domain?"

"Sure, I do," Vandal replied. "Of course I do."

"You've already delayed departure by seven days."

"There are reasons for that." Vandal scratched his ear. "Lots of reasons."

He couldn't deny that he had put off his departure seven times in a row. The party headed for the domain would be himself, Zulan and Braga from the ninja unit, and Eleonora due to her superior infiltration skills. They would also be taking Lefdia, to provide a little living (if that was the word) proof to Princess Lebia, as Lefdia was the left hand of her younger sister, Zandia.

The idea was for Vandal to proceed to a town in the Heartner Domain and check things out. If Detect Danger: Death didn't pick up anything of note, he would call in the ninjas and Eleonora with Lefdia. He had been discussing this plan with everyone for a number of months. But when it finally came time to leave . . . .

Day one.

"No, no, no, I'm going!"

"Grrhing!"

"I wanna go, pwease I wanna go—no, that's not gonna woooork!"

"Pauvina, I'm only going and coming right back. I won't be

gone ten days. Rapie, I can't take you near a human settlement; you'd cause a panic. And Zadilis, please, can you stop that? It's embarrassing!"

Vandal got held up by Pauvina, Rapieçage, and—for some reason—Zadilis. Pauvina and Rapieçage were quickly placated, but Zadilis fell into a deep hole due to her own childish behavior, considering her advanced years. It ended up taking the best part of the day to cheer her back up. Vandal had given up on departing that day and played with Vabi, Jadal, and the other kids.

Day two.

Vandal headed outside, sure that today would be the day. Then, a shadow fell over him, and in the next moment, he was snatched up into the air.

An ungodly screech racketed off his ears. The one abducting him was none other than Knochen, the Union Bone.

"Excuse me, I really do need to set out today!"

"Raaagh! Ooohn!"

"I really can't take you, either!" Vandal insisted. Knochen was a Rank 8 Union Bone, meaning any sightings near human inhabitation would throw people into a mass panic. It was a disaster-level monster. "Once I register at the guild, I'll get you certified as my subordinate monster!"

"Raaaah!" It still took the rest of the day to talk the beast down, while being forced to ride around on his bony back up in the sky.

Day three.

Vandal headed outside, sure that today would definitely

be the day. Then he heard the sound of a horde of wings approaching, the sky darkened, and in the next moment, he was snatched up into the air.

Bzzzzzzzzzzzz!

"I thought this was déjà vu, but nope. Cemetery Bees." Dozens of the bees had grabbed onto Vandal and lifted him up, carrying him to the hive they had created. It was basically an extension to the castle. There, they offered him an assortment of honey and bugs. It seemed they were telling him to take these gifts and not leave.

"I'll be back, okay? Don't worry."

Bzbzbzbzbzbz.

"I promise! Please, I don't need to eat bug-based confections. At least let me cook them first!"

Vandal proceeded to do so, and the roasted bug balls with honey sauce actually turned out pretty great—crunchy on the outside, soft on the onside. Swap out the honey for a sweet-and-sour sauce and they might go well as a side dish, or with some alcohol.

Day four.

"Are you sure? I really think you should level up a little more. You said it yourself! You're not getting many levels recently!"

That morning, it was Dalshia who held him up, worried about him going off into the world.

"It's fine, Mom. I've hit a bit of a wall, sure, but I'm not getting weaker either," Vandal assured her.

She was correct in that his level had suddenly stopped growing—what was generally called a "wall." It was some cause for concern, but everything he could do yesterday, he could still do today. Furthermore, his growth wasn't going to be stunted forever. A wall could be climbed. Kachia was an example of someone he knew who had hit her own wall, but she had overcome hers and was currently leveling up again. The timing of hitting the wall and the size of the wall one faced always varied. Some decided it was too much and gave up, but many managed to clear the wall and keep growing. Hitting a *second* wall was much more likely to cut an adventurer's plans short.

According to most adventurers, they generally hit a wall around Grade D. Those who quickly overcame that would proceed to Grade C, while those who didn't manage it right away—like Kachia—often experienced a slump. Former Grade A adventurer Borkz had overcome three walls in his career and had been facing a fourth when he was defeated by Mikhail.

Vandal tried to explain this context to Dalshia. "So I'm actually as strong as a Grade D adventurer," Vandal concluded. "I won't have any trouble popping into town and coming back."

Certainly, every Grade D adventurer in the world would have something to say about such a claim. Dalshia was right there with them.

"No, Vandal!" Dalshia shouted. "I don't want to be separated from you! You have to take me with you!"

"I would like to, but it's a little dangerous for that." When entering the town, guards might inspect his belongings. They could find the piece of Dalshia's bone and realize that it was possessed. It was unlikely but still a possibility. If the guard called someone in to try to purify Dalshia's spirit, Vandal could see himself having to kill some people to escape. "Think about what would happen if I started firing off MP Shots, Mom."

It would be a nightmare scenario. Forget about killing a few guardsmen—he would leave holes in the gate and the castle in rubble. Maybe worse.

"Okay . . . if you say so. But you'd better come back to me."

"I will, Mom; don't worry."

But he had already missed his window that day.

Day five.

"Aaaaaaaagh!" Vandal was grabbed and carried off by an Immortal Ent, screaming as he went. He was later sighted slumped in the branchy arms of the monster, seemingly having accepted his fate.

Day six.

"Mnnnnnh!" Lefdia, upon learning that they would have to split up during the journey, was now clinging tightly to Vandal's face. He was trying to persuade her to let go when Borkz and some others showed up.

"Child, I know I gave you a letter for my daughter, but if she's having a hard time of it, please give her this too."

"Child, if you meet Lady Lebia, please give her this!"

"Please, take this too, Your Majesty!"

". . . You do realize my packs are already three times my size," Vandal said.

It took a long time to reorganize and repack things, which meant—yes—another delay.

This brought him to today—day seven.

"I've finally gotten everyone to accept my brief trip," Vandal stated. "The miso and soy sauce and fish flakes and smoked products and mayo and ketchup production lines can run for 100 years without me. Everything is ready. I just need to start walking."

"I'm sorry, Lord Vandal, but we have a bit of a problem." The speaker was Eleonora, just on queue to pour cold water over Vandal's enthusiasm.

"A problem?"

"Braga led the ninja unit out to a dungeon yesterday," Eleonora said. "It might be a few days before they return." It sounded like Vandal had kept them waiting for too long, and the impatience led them to head out and train.

"Enough delays," Vandal said decisively. "We can go ahead. If I leave communication undead behind, they'll be able to find us easily enough. Instead of Zulan, Eleonora, you can take care of Lefdia."

Vandal had found an additional use for familiars as communication undead, which could be used much like a mobile phone. They only worked over a short distance, and the voices were transmitted via the ears and tongue of the involved undead, meaning the speaker was not heard directly, but these were still a revolution when it came to Ramda technology. They looked like shrunken goblin heads, so the design side could use some work. Using human heads would have increased functionality but would also cause all sorts of difficult-to-answer questions, and so Vandal had given up on that.

"All right. Let's get moving."

"Yes, Lord Vandal! Ah, to travel the road, just the two of us!" Eleonora enthused.

"Don't forget Lefdia," Vandal pointed out. "And once we leave the tunnel, I'm continuing alone." It seemed unlikely, but there was a chance the town gates would have anti-vampire measures in place. In Eleonora's case, they also had to be careful about the progenitors who worshipped the Demon God of Living Pleasure, Hihiryu-Shukaka—both their information network and tricky things like magic items that could track individuals using their blood.

In this case, though, Vandal had decided neither of these would be a problem. He didn't know the full scope of the vampire's surveillance network, perhaps, but they probably didn't expect Vandal to have reopened the tunnel. Vandal also knew that they weren't such a massive secret organization that they would have agents hiding in every single town and village. Their primary bases would have numerous informants in place, but unless they had particular leads, other settlements would be outside of their notice. As far as Eleonora knew, their information network was restricted to the Amidd Empire.

In terms of the magic item, they had gotten ahold of the one previously used to track Eleonora. Even if there were more of the item, they probably didn't have much of Eleonora's blood left to use. To top it off, Vandal was pretty sure he could deal with a random progenitor servant if they did bump into one.

"We're finally leaving," Vandal said.

"See you in a few days, Lord Van," said Talea. "Please, make sure you come back to me."

"Van will be coming back to all of us, thank you," Zadilis added.

"Young Master, I hope you will choose to use my wheels next time," Sam wept.

Most of the nation seemed to have turned out to see him off. With that, Vandal and Eleonora departed Talosheim and headed for the Heartner Domain.

They flew for three days, with intermittent attacks by Pteranodons and bird-type monsters. Vandal had previously turned the tunnel into a golem, allowing it to be passed through again. They entered the tunnel, and then, after three days of travel and getting golems to clear the blockage at the other end, Vandal finally achieved his long-held desire of reaching the Olbaum Electorate Kingdom.

There wasn't much to be said for it yet. The remains of a path petered out of the tunnel into a sparse wasteland littered with a few trees. Two hundred years ago, when trading with Talosheim, there had been a fine road leading from here, but none of that glory remained.

"The town, our target, should be about three hours east from here," Eleonora said. "If it still stands."

"Supposedly, it has a population of a few thousand, so something should still be there. As far as we know, this is still the Heartner Domain, so there should be a settlement somewhere nearby. Eleonora, you hang out around here. Contact me using the communication undead."

"Okay. But are you sure you want to go alone?"

"I'll be fine," Vandal assured her. "I can manage this." He wondered if he should lighten the mood with a quip but decided not to risk it.

On second thought, maybe he should have—Eleonora still had a worried look on her face as Vandal started down the remains of the road, this time on foot.

Of course, he had a large number of spirits all around him, so strictly speaking, he wasn't alone.

Before departing, he had the golems conceal the exit to the tunnel again, sealing it so that it wouldn't open without a password. The password was "brain repeatedly jumping sideways." He wanted something no one was ever going to say by mistake. Vandal had also created simple lodging facilities on the tunnel-side of the exit. Eleonora and Lefdia would wait there for the ninja unit to catch up.

"I should be close now . . . ."

It had proven to be a pain to navigate the overgrown grass, which was taller than he was. So Vandal was hovering silently above it, moving with Flight. If it wasn't for the pack on his back, he could have been mistaken for an apparition.

He was still attacked, every now and then, by goblins or raven monsters with five-foot-wide wings, but he drove them off easily enough. He could deal with Rank 1 or 2 monsters without much effort. He didn't get any experience thanks to his resident curses, but it would have been so little that it didn't really matter.

"Gegagaga!" More goblins came at him, swinging wooden clubs.

"Geh-gah-gah." Vandal gave a half-hearted reply and then

used his Throw skill, obtained from training with Braga and the ninja unit, to toss some rocks and take them out.

"Seems like about one in five rank 2 Black Ravens cough up magic stones," Vandal commented. "If I can get some of those, they might pay for my passage."

On the Vangaia Continent, it was normal for towns and villages to charge a travel tax for entry. Vandal didn't have any baum, the universal Olbaum currency, so he had some salt in his packs, hoping he could use that instead. He had decided against bringing magic stones or materials from high-ranking monsters, since a kid showing up with stuff that was too good might cause a stir. He chose salt since the Heartner Domain had no coastline or quarries with rock salt, so it would have a high price. *If they've found a decent source of it during the last 200 years and the value has fallen, I'll have to do some hunting.* He could always hunt some rabbits rather than monsters. *That rabbit blood Mom gave me tasted so good*, he recalled, even as he sniped another goblin. Then he pressed on.

Before too much longer, he saw a stone wall in the distance.

Finally, he thought. *But it looks like it's covered in moss and vines. Borkz said this used to be a pretty affluent place.* A trading town connecting Talosheim and the Heartner Domain had grown rapidly after the two regions connected, meaning it had a relatively short history but had been a lively place for all that. With the fall of Talosheim, however, the trade had dried up, and so the town had probably fallen on harder times.

Vandal also felt like there were too many monsters this close to the town. But he hadn't been this close to a settlement since Evbejia, so he couldn't be sure on that part.

"Don't tell me the place is in ruins!"

Vandal was getting concerned, so he used Detect Life to search widely in the vicinity. He was relieved to discover more than one thousand life forms, mostly clustered toward the town center. The settlement had fallen on hard times, indeed, but it wasn't a complete ruin yet.

He noticed some of the life readings were stronger than might be expected from regular civilians. Vandal assumed those were soldiers garrisoned here or adventurers.

"Good news, anyway." Vandal gave a relieved sigh and then dropped to the ground and started walking toward the gates. The guard on watch spotted him coming and started to make *gyah-gyah* noises. Vandal had turned off his Flight so as not to cause alarm, but it didn't seem to have worked.

The impish-looking guard had dark green skin, a long nose, and drooping eyes.

Can't beat around this bush. That's a goblin. It was carrying a spear—a Rank 2 Goblin Soldier, from the look of it. Beyond the gateless opening, he saw a horde of other goblins, chattering, pointing in his direction, grabbing weapons, and rushing toward him.

"Gegiiiiii!" There was one goblin that stood out above the others—literally. Among his child-sized fellows, this big boy was closer to a male human in height and was also shouting the loudest. He had better gear—proper armor and shield—than the crude hides worn by the other goblins. He was also equipped with a halberd.

This was a Goblin King.

"Wow. The last King I met was of the kobolt kind—apart from my own reflection," Vandal quipped. Then he launched off a Death Shot.

The battle between the Ghoul King and Goblin King had begun!

Skill level increased for Brawling Proficiency, Poison Dispersal (Claws, Fangs, Tongue), and Suck Blood!

"I see. So the town had become the base of operations for a Goblin King," Eleonora said.

"You did well, though, to take down a disaster-level threat alone!"

"I wanted to see you in action, King!"

"Oh, it wasn't anything special," Vandal replied. The night after the battle, Vandal regrouped with Eleonora and the ninja unit, including Braga and Zulan, and was sitting, sharing food, and chatting with them.

Vandal had indeed fought the goblins. He had used Astral Projection and Spirit Bodification to divide himself and Substantiation to solidify all the new parts and then fired off Death Shots while raking his foes with his claws, chopping down the scampering goblins in a completely one-sided massacre. He even used Golem Creation to make weaponized Stone Golems from the walls of the town. He had butchered every last goblin in the place.

He hadn't even considered letting Braga and his other ally goblins breed with the female goblins. The black goblins didn't speak the normal goblin language, and they also looked a lot closer to humans. Neither side was going to find the other attractive.

"It was nothing special. A thousand goblins, if that," Vandal said.

"I'd call that special!" Zulan enthused. "A Grade C adventurer would flee from numbers like those."

"Well, I do have my tricks," Vandal said.

"You're amazing, King," Braga replied.

A thousand goblins, led by a Goblin King. A relatively small horde, to say they had a king presiding over them, but regular adventurers wouldn't go near them even if they were in a party, let alone on their own. Even at low levels, the effects of Enhance Brethren would make the enemies stronger than normal. Simply having a king with them turned normally cowardly goblins into vicious warriors. To Vandal, though, they posed no threat.

He was weak against enemies who could launch focused attacks with enough power to break through his Anti-Attack Barrier and Magic Sucking Barrier. But that meant he was close to invincible against enemies who couldn't break those barriers. He protected his real body and soul inside the barriers, while his spirit bodies used Substantiation to fight outside. The Goblin Soldiers and Goblin Generals, equipped with conspicuously rusty weapons, couldn't hope to land anything close to a killing blow.

The Goblin King and Goblin Mages had done a little better, managing to defeat some of his clones, but that barely registered as pain to Vandal. He could also quickly resolve the issue by using Astral Projection again. Once he turned the remaining sections of the town wall into Stone Golems, the goblins couldn't flee even if they wanted to.

In the end, the Goblin King and his minions were

eradicated, at the cost of little more than ten million of Vandal's magical power. That power was itself well on the way to recovery, with his Magical Power Auto Recovery skill and having used Suck Blood on the Goblin King.

"But, Lord Vandal, couldn't you have defeated them even more quickly if you used a sickness?" Eleonora asked.

If he wished, Vandal could have created a viral version of the sickness he had used during the defense of Talosheim against the Milg Shield Kingdom the previous year. Such a disease could have rendered the goblins immobile almost at once. It wouldn't have killed them, but finishing the incapacitated monsters off would have been so easy that it wouldn't have even counted as a battle. There were issues with that approach, however.

"True, but if the goblins had been holding captives, it would have been bad for them. There weren't any in the end, but still."

Goblins, like orcs, captured women to impregnate them. Vandal had considered that possibility, but luckily this particular horde had no captives. There had been some suggestive life signs, but those turned out to be female goblins.

"That's very considerate of you, to worry about women who might not even be there," Eleonora said.

"It was a perfectly reasonable concern. That said—don't stop with the praise." Good food and praise from others were the lubricants of life. Throw in some physical touch, and what else could you need?

"Well done!"

"Great work, King."

Now everyone was giving Vandal gentle pets too. The support of these four finally helped Vandal over the hump of dejection he had been feeling after his first visit to a human settlement had failed so completely. Thanks to his friends, he got the energy to turn the dead goblins into zombies, mainly to tidy up their corpses. Then they started to prepare to sleep rough.

Vandal had no intention of using the dwellings of the goblins, so he gathered suitable wood and stone materials, then used Golem Creation to dig out some rather nostalgic hexagonal sunken homes. It was summer, so they only needed about ten of these.

The Goblin King was actually still alive, clinging on with all his limbs smashed. Vandal had Braga finish him off. He did earn some experience for it, but even the Goblin King was only Rank 4. It wasn't enough to gain a level or anything like that.

"A bit of a waste," Zulan commented. "If you'd defeated this Goblin King after becoming an adventurer, it would have provided a big boost up the grades."

"It's that big a deal? Taking out a Goblin King?"

"Sure," Zulan confirmed. "A newly registered newbie defeating one alone? You'd go from Grade G to E right away, and probably be allowed to take the test for D in short order."

"Wow. A bigger deal than it looks. I suppose a king is a king is a king!"

"Oh boy. That's a huge miss." Vandal groaned, his shoulders slumping. He wasn't taking it so well. Lefdia had to scramble around his head to avoid falling into the cookpot.

A newbie adventurer taking down a Goblin King all alone—that would have been big news, something to catch the attention even of non-adventurers. The subculture content Vandal had enjoyed on Earth often included main characters who quickly achieved something flashy and impressive to make a splashy debut. That would have been possible here, for him—if only he had registered as an adventurer first.

"Don't worry too much. You were planning on leaving town right away," Zulan reminded him. "You wouldn't have had the time for all that."

"That's right," Eleonora assured him. "You defeated this big fish before you even registered. It won't be long until you do the same thing again."

"I guess that's true," Vandal said, quickly snapping out of his funk. "But why was the town overrun with goblins in the first place? The Heartner Domain does still exist, right?"

"Yes. Of that, I'm sure," Eleonora said. "I've never been here to the Olbaum Electorate Kingdom myself, but if an entire ducal domain had been eradicated, word would have reached Amidd. From the look of these ruins, this place hasn't functioned as a town for a while."

"This is only my second time here," Zulan said. "I'm guessing it's because of the end of trade with us in Talosheim? Still, there should be a bigger town to the north and a mine to the south. I would've thought this place could cling on as a waypoint between them."

"Maybe monsters made it too hard to maintain the town," Braga suggested.

"That might be it," Eleonora said. "The same thing has happened on the Milg side as well."

Kachia, a former adventurer from the Milg Shield Kingdom, had told them that Talosheim getting wiped out by the

Milg army had led to a proliferation of monsters that giantling adventurers had previously removed from the equation. These monsters had crossed the Boundary Mountains and started to cause trouble in Milg. The same thing had probably happened here. As Braga had suggested, maybe the duke decided to abandon this place rather than fight to keep it.

"Makes sense. I was wondering why the area is semi-demon barren," Zulan said. "You think they can't thin the monsters out?"

The difference between a demon barren and semi-demon barren was the strength of magical power that polluted the ground. The term "demon barren" required an amount of magical pollution that would corrupt regular plants into monsters by simply growing there, making monsters a naturally occurring phenomena. Another condition was the presence of demon barren produce, such as kobol fruit. A demon barren could be returned to normal land by removing everything that held magical powers—for a forest, chopping down the trees, or for a swamp, draining it—and then having members of the clergy purify the region.

On the other hand, semi-demon barrens were places inhabited by multiple monsters that, for various reasons, moved there from an actual demon barren. For those using the land, this essentially made it the same as a demon barren. But if the monsters were wiped out, no new ones would appear. The land would continue to be a normal forest or swamp.

Based on this description, the city of Talosheim and its surrounding environs, which turned everything growing there into monster plants, legitimately counted as demon barrens. But no one living there cared about that.

"What do you want to do?" Eleonora asked. "Go back to Talosheim?"

"No. We'll try the town to the north."

"That's more promising than the mine," Zulan agreed. "After 200 years, whatever veins ran underground have probably dried up."

"What? Veins of ore in this world can dry up?"

"King, you've been spending too long in dungeons," Braga scolded.

Vandal felt a surge of appreciation for how fortunate of a location Talosheim was.

The following day, Vandal set about turning the remains of the town into a base that Eleonora and the others could use. He turned the water in the wells into Aqua Golems (which looked kinda like slimes) in order to swap it out with fresh stuff and had the black goblins do some cleaning. He smoothly repaired the walls, put up watchtowers, and laid traps, all using Golden Creation. Then he extracted information from the spirits of the goblins he had slain concerning the direction of the town and set out on foot.

He got sick of walking but decided his muscles needed more of a workout than yesterday. He switched to all fours and dashed along by digging into the ground with his claws.

"Once I'm registered with the guild, oh, once I'm an adventurer—!" He was humming a tuneless song to himself, rumbling along for about thirty minutes.

He finally found the road. It was a rough piece of work, likely to rattle some bones if ridden in a carriage, but also definitely the work of human hands.

He looked at it for a while, determining for sure that this was an Olbaum Electorate Kingdom road. Then he raised both arms to celebrate this big step toward another of his goals—before freezing up in place and muttering to himself.

"Traveling alone is no fun." He had tried singing to himself and celebrating his progress, but the feelings didn't last. He couldn't maintain the mood.

Vandal had been lonely in both of his previous lives, but on Ramda he always had people—living or otherwise—around him. His resilience to loneliness had therefore taken a nosedive.

Of course, he had more than a thousand spirits around him in that very moment. However, as soon as a person became a spirit, their personality started to break down. All the spirits around him, including the goblins he had killed the previous day, were closer to tools he made with Golem Creation than allies or friends.

"I need to get to the town quickly or I'm going to start making undead to talk to. North is—that way." Vandal drew his bearings from the position of the sun and started to gallop again.

After a while longer, a smell wafted to his nose that stirred up his hunger. "That's the smell of blood. It's goblin . . . but with human mixed in."

It smelled like goblins and humans were fighting up ahead. *I should help the humans out!* Vandal floated up off the ground using Flight and then zipped off at top speed. He didn't know whether the adventurers or soldiers were winning or losing, but even if they held the upper hand, surely they wouldn't complain about someone else joining on their behalf. That was Vandal's thinking. Still, he certainly didn't feel confident about communicating with people on whom Death Attribute Allure didn't work.

Kasim blocked the club on his shield, then smashed his shield into the enemy.

"Eat this! Shield Bash!"

"Glebah?!" The Goblin Soldier took the shield in the face and went flying away. However, another Goblin Soldier immediately stepped into the gap.

"Hey, Kasim! When did you learn Shield Bash?!" shouted Fester, a hopeful future swordsman.

"I was just saying it!" Kasim, hopeful future shield bearer, shouted back. "I can't actually use the battle tech!"

"That's what I thought!" said Zeno, the scout who rounded out their party of three adventurers. They were out hunting goblins in order to thin down the numbers of the monsters appearing on the road between the village and mine. All three of them were Grade E adventurers who had only recently graduated from the adventurers' academy, but they were confident that they could handle a small force of goblins with maybe a handful of Goblin Soldiers. But they weren't expecting, on a road that wasn't even a demon barren, more than ten Goblin Soldiers at once.

"Gi-gah-gi-gah!" Even worse was the goblin in command. It had featured in their lessons at the academy as a well-known newbie killer: a Rank 3 Goblin Barbarian.

"Why is there a Goblin Barbarian here anyway?! We weren't warned about this!"

"Everyone mistakes it for a normal goblin! That's why it's called a newbie killer!"

Up close, a Goblin Barbarian clearly had a thicker neck and more muscular limbs than other goblins, but from a distance, it just looked like a slightly fatter goblin. In most cases, it also used the same weapon as other goblins—a wooden branch, swung like a club, although maybe a slightly bigger one. Newbies would therefore mistake it for a Rank 1, regular goblin, and close in just to get hammered to mush by its Brute Strength.

"Better than the other type of newbie killer—a Goblin Mage!" yelled Zeno.

The inside of a Goblin Barbarian's head was no different from that of a normal goblin. It might be in command, but the only commands it was going to give were "Don't run away!" and "Keep fighting!"

"Sure, but this is still dangerous! We aren't scaring them off!" Festa chopped down a Goblin Soldier with his sword, but another just stepped up. He had already killed three of them.

Goblin Soldiers would normally get the hint by now and decide to cut their losses and run for it. But a Goblin Barbarian only cared about fighting. The Soldiers were more scared of the Barbarian than they were of Kasim and his party, meaning they weren't going to run anywhere other than into battle.

"Hey, you got any MP left? I can manage a Taunt and then Strone Wall or Stone Body, and I'll be dry," Kasim said.

"I've got three battle techs left," Zeno said. "Festa, what about you?"

". . . Flicker Flash, twice."

Grade E adventurers weren't exactly flush with MP, even if they were Magicians. Kasim knew that it would be hard to make it through this with their remaining MP and overall strength. The only saving grace, arguably, was that they were all men. The worst that could happen was if they all got killed here. That was bad, but being food after death was better than being kept alive for . . . other things.

"Zeno, Fester, I'll use Taunt to draw their attention. Use the opening to make a run for it!"

"Kasim, you can't be serious—"

"If there's a Barbarian on the road, there must be a big settlement of goblins nearby. You need to warn the village!" Kasim lifted his shield as he shouted, preparing to use Shield Proficiency battle tech Taunt on the Goblin Soldiers, who had fallen back a little but definitely weren't running away.

That was the moment when a child with a large backpack floated into view a ways back behind the Barbarian.

"Huh?"

The newcomer then zoomed in, fast as the wind and just as silent.

"Rend Iron." The child swept one hand, from which long claws extended, and popped off the Goblin Barbarian's head.

"Huh?"

"Geh?"

"What in the?!"

The Goblin Soldiers screeched as blood fountained out from Barbarian's headless corpse. It was killed without so much as a sound. Kasim and the Goblin Soldiers were fixated on the silver-haired child, floating like an apparition beyond the spraying blood. It was like a piece of reality had somehow slipped loose.

"Sorry, but if you're planning on attacking those goblins, I would do it now." After a few more seconds of watching them gape, the child—Vandal—gave Kasim and his party this warning.

"Gegah?"

"Huh? Yeah, of course!"

Goblin groans scattered as Kasim and the others quickly used the mace, sword, and knife in their respective hands to slice and smash the stunned goblins into submission. Some of the monsters snapped back to themselves and made a run for it, but Vandal swished his claws around some more, catching all the stragglers.

"Allow me to introduce myself. My name is Vandal."

"Hey, well, thanks. You really saved us."

Kasim and the other Grade E adventurers were still a bit perplexed by the polite death machine in front of them. The child had silver hair and white skin, like wax, with dollish features and a clear, high voice. He looked like an animated toy—or maybe a specter that would vanish when touched. The most vivid parts of him were the delicate, knife-like claws extending from all ten fingers, still dripping with blood, although they were also the hardest part of all of this to believe. Vandal had used those claws to slice clean through the muscular neck of the Goblin Barbarian. A monster that was called a newbie killer at the academy, something far stronger than they were.

Who the hell is this kid? The adventurers could be forgiven for thinking little else but that.

"So, oh mighty Vandal, what exactly—?"

"Please, just Vandal. You're clearly older than me—adults, even." On Ramda, most races treated their youth as adults from age fifteen. From Vandal's perspective, all three of these adventurers looked to be over that age. In fact, they were all exactly fifteen, having graduated from the adventurers' academy this year.

"Okay, then, Vandal—what exactly—are you, exactly?"

"Kasim! What kind of question is that?!"

"What he's trying to say is—are you even human?"

"Festa! Don't be so rude to someone who just saved our lives!" Zeno exclaimed.

Vandal, for his part, wasn't sure what was getting the three of them so riled up, but he decided to answer their question.

"I'm a dhampir," he replied. "I was living with my mom in the forest, away from other people. I don't know where my dad is, or whether he's even alive. My mom fell sick and died recently, and so I'm heading to a town with an adventurers' guild to become an adventurer, which was her final wish for me." He wasn't about to share all the real details of his life, but he had a fake backstory all thought up in advance.

"A dhampir!?"

"Yeah, look. Different-colored eyes and those claws, too. Not that I ever saw one before."

"So, do you have . . . fangs?"

Fortunately, it sounded like Vandal's explanation had worked. Here in the Olbaum Electorate Kingdom, dhampirs had human rights like anyone else, but mixed bloods with vampires were rarely born, and while the state might recognize them, their own kind might be pickier. That meant many people living here had never actually seen a dhampir. Kasim and his party only recognized him from the things they had been taught at the adventurers' academy—the different-colored eyes, the claws, and the fangs. They could therefore easily chalk up anything else weird that Vandal did to his being a dhampir.

I feel a bit like a monkey in the zoo, Vandal thought. "Yes, I have fangs. But shouldn't you be more worried about these goblin ears, first?"

"Ah! Of course!"

Kasim and Festa snapped back to themselves and hurriedly set about their duties of taking the bounty parts from the Goblin Soldiers—their ears—as well as checking their chests for any magic stones. They also collected up the spear hafts from the Goblin Soldiers and even the club from the Barbarian, all wood that could be used as fuel. Vandal was surprised they would go to quite such lengths, but this behavior was normal for newbie Grade E adventurers. Kasim's party might have looked to be fairly well kitted out, but all their gear were hand-me-downs from adventurers ahead of them. Kasim's shield was bronze, but his mace was stone, and his armor was the heavy leather kind made from animal hide. Zeno's knife and Festa's sword were mass-produced items made by pouring molten metal into a mold, and they were wearing cheap light leather armor. If they weren't relatively clean and had guild cards to show for it, they could have easily been mistaken for bandits eking out a living in the mountains. Vandal had seen plenty of those.

Vandal, meanwhile, was dressed not to attract attention. He was wearing a top and bottoms made—with a lot of effort—from soldier's gear stolen from the Milg Shield Kingdom fort built at the entrance to the other tunnel last year. At a glance, anything of any value he might have been carrying was only in the pack, which was bigger than he was.

In reality, the only items of value were the sandals he wore. Talea had made them to allow him to use his claws. The soles were a mixture of ogre and Earth Dragon leather, with strings made of Rock Dragon tendon. Selling his sandals would have afforded a complete makeover for Kasim and his party.

"Here, you can have the bounty part and magic stone from the Goblin Barbarian—"

"No, you take them," Vandal said. "I'm not an adventurer yet."

"We couldn't possibly keep them," Kasim replied. "A Rank 3 magic stone is worth 100 baum, and the bounty part will go for 300!"

". . . So that was a Goblin Barbarian?" Vandal asked. This was the moment when he realized that the first goblin he had killed (that day) hadn't been a regular goblin. The sums of money being discussed didn't really mean much to him, however. "Instead, can you show me to a village or town nearby? If you could tell me a bit about the place and where to find the adventurers' guild, that would be a big help too. I don't know much about things out here," Vandal said.

Kasim and his friends seemed to accept that on face value.

"Okay. We'll take you to the village that we work out of."

And so, Vandal got his first foothold into a human settlement.

Name: Kasim
Race: Human
Age: 15
Alias: None
Job: Apprentice Warrior
Level: 72
Job History: None
——Passive Skills
[None]
——Active Skills
[Agriculture: Level 1] [Club Proficiency: Level 1] [Shield Proficiency: Level 1] [Armor Mastery: Level 1]

Name: Zeno
Race: Human
Age: 15
Alias: None
Job: Apprentice Thief
Level: 65
Job History: None
──Passive Skills
[Detect Presence: Level 1]
──Active Skills
[Short Sword Proficiency: Level 1] [Bow Proficiency: Level 2] [Traps: Level 1]

Name: Festa
Race: Human
Age: 15
Alias: None
Job: Apprentice Warrior
Level: 71
Job History: None
──Passive Skills
[Strength Boost: Level 1]
──Active Skills
[Fishing: Level 1] [Sword Proficiency: Level 2] [Dismantle: Level 1]

The Death Mage

CHAPTER TWO
SAVIOR OF THE PIONEER VILLAGES

Led by Kasim, Vandal headed toward the village that served as their base of operations—the Seventh Pioneer Village.

"A pioneer village, back here?" Vandal asked. "But there's a town and even a mine farther south."

Festa was just as surprised as Vandal. "I don't know about any towns. The only thing south of the village are mountains with a slave mine. Cross those and you'll be in a different domain."

"Hold on," Kasim said. "I do remember talk about there being a town 100, probably 200 years ago. Maybe that's the place Vandal is talking about."

"Ah, right," Zeno said. "You've got a vamp for a parent, haven't you? That time scale would work."

It looked like the Heartner Domain was not flourishing quite as it had 200 years ago.

"What happened to that town?" Vandal asked.

The boys all shook their heads.

"Sorry. We never learned that. Each domain is like its own little nation, run by the duke and his nobles. Kids aren't taught the histories of other domains."

"You aren't from here?"

"Ah, now that's a pretty tale to tell. Tears for the listener, tears for the teller—"

"Festa, let me talk," Zeno interrupted. "I'll tell you everything I know about that town."

According to Zeno's explanation, the direct cause was—as Vandal had guessed—the fall of Talosheim. The town had been created as a waypoint in trade, and so when that dried up, the town quickly lost all productivity. The southern mine started to dry up around the same time. Paying a working wage would no longer cover their costs, and so they had switched to using slaves. That meant the miners were no longer spending money either. The duke at the time, who had only held the post for a few years, decided to evacuate the town.

That's a pretty bold move, Vandal thought. *That wouldn't have been popular in Japan. But in that case, what happened to the first princess?* Zeno's explanation made no mention of the name of Lebia, first princess of Talosheim. He might have skipped over her involvement, if she wasn't directly involved. *I'd love to ask, but it wouldn't be a natural segway.*

Then Zeno made a pretty unnatural break himself, leaping right up to current events.

"In the past five years, though, the Amidd Empire has been on the attack. They've taken over pretty much all of the Saulon Domain, which was north from here. That's where we came from."

"We're refugees," Festa said. "That's the short of it. The empire minds their manners in the towns and large farming villages, but in small places like ours, they do whatever they like. My oldest brother was trying to save his fiancée, and both of them got—"

"Festa. That's not the kind of thing to share with a little kid," Kasim admonished.

So this was the war between the Amidd Empire and Olbaum Electorate Kingdom. It all suddenly felt a lot closer to home.

"Point is, we're refugees, fleeing from the Saulon Domain down here to Heartner. Once the war settled down, Prince Belton—the second son of the current duke—started the pioneer villages to help out refugees, and we ended up living with our folks in the Seventh Pioneer Village. That's where we're heading now."

"Still not an easy life," Zeon added. "Three years after the village was built, we became adventurers."

"I see," Vandal said. "You've definitely had hard lives."

Setting up a pioneer villages seemed like a good move for dealing with refugees. Unlike Earth, Ramda had lots of terrain with no one living on it. The area wasn't a demon barren, the monsters were only Rank 2 even if they showed up, and since the only road led to a slave mine, there weren't bandits, either.

Okay, so I did wipe out a horde of goblins led by a Goblin King just yesterday, but those were more like . . . a natural disaster, let's call it. The appearance on the road of the Goblin Barbarian, which had clearly puzzled Kasim and the others, must've also also had to do with the Goblin King. Probably scouts sent out by it, or a hunting party.

"You could say that. Soldiers brought us here, pointed to the ground, and told us to build. We made fields, dug a well, and made houses . . ."

"They protected us from beasts and monsters and lent us tents and blankets till the village was finished. The food was bad and there wasn't much of it, but they shared that too. We're also exempt from taxes for five years. But it's still been hard."

Listening to Kasim and Festa describe everything, it sounded even harder than Vandal had been expecting. The villagers had done all the work in terms of making houses, wells, and other infrastructure.

"Hey, it's better than being a day laborer in the slums. Don't complain too loudly or that's where you'll end up." Zeno's comment made it clear that things could indeed be a lot worse. "Not to mention, you've clearly seen worse than us, Vandal! Sorry about these two. They can be a bit slow."

"It's no matter," Vandal replied. "I've eaten pretty well, thanks to my mom." He had been so desperate for food that he slurped worm soup once or twice, sure, but he wasn't going to get into that.

They walked on for about three hours, talking about the adventurers' academy and other facts about the Heartner Domain. Then they reached the village.

The Seventh Pioneer Village had a population of 300, putting it somewhere between small and medium sized in the scale of Ramda settlements. Humans were the most prevalent, making up about half the population. The rest included beastmen, dwarves, and giantlings.

The longer-lived races that tended to create their own unique culture, such as elves, dark elves, and dragonlings, also tended to make their own settlements. While they might be seen in human towns, they were rare in villages like this. That held true even in the case of refugees, and members of such races from the Saulon Domain had found homes with their own kind. The giantlings here were also from the Saulon Domain, so they had nothing to do with Talosheim.

The houses in the reclamation village were all low and flat and didn't look especially sturdy. But considering they had been made by the people living here, Vandal thought they did a good job. He was told that, compared to the five other pioneer villages in the vicinity, this one had the largest population.

"Can I ask," Vandal inquired on that topic, "why this is called the Seventh village, when there are only six?"

"The First Pioneer Village couldn't keep going, so they abandoned it," Kasim replied. "They did their best, but the water just dried up. They dug wells, but nothing."

Life was not easy for humans on this world; that much was sure.

"First things first, anyway. Let's collect on these ears."

With that, Kasim led Vandal to the only place of commerce in the village. It was simply called the General Store, but it also served as a tavern, a local branch of the adventurers' guild, and even an inn if anyone was looking for a bed. To survive in this village, it seemed you needed your fingers in as many pies as possible.

No one really paid much attention to Vandal, suggesting people passed through fairly often. He had been curious about the villagers' reactions to him, but then he saw a shrine with a stone marked with the holy seal of Alda, which definitely caught his own attention—

"Ack! Kasim, there's something behind you!" The owner of the General Store was pointing at Vandal, who had become a "something."

". . . Hello."

"Uwah! It spoke?! Someone! Call the priest!"

His humble greeting was met with this. It all felt a little extreme, even for a far-off part of the countryside.

"Hold on, mister! He's no ghost!"

"I know you need the customers. Don't turn one away!"

"There are reasons for this! Just calm down and hear us out!"

The others hurriedly tried to soothe the owner of the General Store, who went briskly back inside. It was at this point that Vandal finally realized people barely realized he was there unless Death Attribute Allure had an effect on them. The reason none of the villagers had commented on Vandal's presence was simply because they hadn't noticed him.

"Sorry about Dad. He can be pretty dumb sometimes." This comment came from Lina, the only daughter of the owner of the General Store and the manager of the adventurers' guild branch located inside it. She was the typical cheerful, folksy—no, rather, she was just a village girl who had taken the adventurers' guild exam and was now running the branch for them.

In small villages, the presence of actual adventurers had a large bearing on whether the village itself was going to last. They had no choice but to open some kind of guild, even if it was only in a small space rented from the only commercial facility around.

"It's fine," Vandal lied through his fangs. "I'm used to it."

The shock of this revelation was still running through Vandal, but his expressionless face couldn't show it. Lina peered into his doll-like features, offered another apology, and then let the matter drop.

"Lina, can you ring these up for us?" Kasim cut in.

"Sure, hold on. Let's have a look 'ear—heh! Hold on, these are from Goblin Soldiers and a Goblin Barbarian! How did you fight these off? You're still Grade E, right?!"

"Actually, it wasn't—"

"Festa, we can get into that later. Cash first."

"Okay, hold on . . ." Lina wrestled with the calculations

in her head and then counted out bronze and silver coins. It seemed like the guild branches in places like this were more part-time affairs, so they didn't ask too much from their staff. If the only adventurers in the village were these three kids, Lina probably only had something to do for the guild every few days.

Vandal, however, was preoccupied with something else. *How does the guild tell goblins apart just from their ears?* The bounty parts from goblins were their ears, which even Vandal could tell belonged to goblins. However, he couldn't pinpoint their previous owners any more precisely than that. Something like a Goblin King was so big, it didn't even look like the same race, and so he could differentiate those. But Goblin Soldiers and Goblin Mages were the same size and shape as normal goblins. The main differences were located far from their earlobes, mainly in things like equipment. Vandal could never have told them apart by their ears.

Maybe they were using Appraisal magic, Vandal considered. There might be special skills taught to guild staff, such as Monster Appraisal or Bounty Parts Appraisal.

"That's bounty parts from ten Goblin Soldiers and one Goblin Barbarian, for 400 baum. Then you've got 380 worth of magic stones, for a total of 780 baum," Lina said, finishing up the exchange just as Vandal had been about to ask about the ear thing.

Seven hundred and eighty baum. If one baum was worth 100 yen, that would be a few weeks' salary on minimum wage. It hardly seemed like an amount worth risking your life for, but he recognized that was just his perception as a former Earthling from Japan.

"That's a split of 260 each! Yes!" Festa was fist-pumping.

"We can coast on this for a while." Zeno simply looked relieved. As it turned out, 260 baum was pretty good.

"How much can you buy with that?" Vandal asked.

"With 260 baum? You could make it working in the slum, if you got a good rate, in . . . what, twenty-six days, maybe?"

Twenty-six days to make twenty-six thousand yen—surely without a safety net in terms of injury or sickness, either. And it was day labor, too, so there were no guarantees of when you would get work. Thinking about it that way, 260 baum might actually be a pretty good reward for a day's work, even with life-risking involved.

"We can only get by on this much because the old man here lets us stay for free," Kasim explained.

"That's right." The old man in question suddenly returned. "Even if they're leering at my daughter, we need adventurers around or we'd be finished." Then he turned to Vandal. "I'm sorry about before, missy. If you wanna stay in the village, that'll be on the house too. Hope you can forgive me." He had a much more pleasant look on his face now—like a totally different person—which was all well and good . . .

"Old man! I'm not leering at Lina, I swear—"

"What's that, Festa? My daughter not good enough for you? And stop calling me old!"

"Please, Dad, cut it out!"

". . . Sorry, but I'm actually a boy," Vandal finally managed to say.

For some reason, this comment was met with five loud exclamations of surprise.

Vandal had heard of culture shock. The shock of coming into contact with a vastly different society and culture. *But the shock I've received from Ramda human society is something else entirely*, Vandal thought. For a start, he hadn't expected to be blatantly ignored. It was also the first time he realized how much he looked like a girl. The ghoul kids often got it wrong, but he always assumed that was because male ghouls had the whole lion thing going on. None of his other friends and allies ever got his gender wrong.

In reality, it had been other clues that gave it away, such as Sam calling him "young master," his title of "king," and his behavior. They certainly hadn't all immediately presumed he was male and especially just by looking at his face.

I'm still only seven years old, he thought. *I'll hit puberty, get a proper manly voice, grow some more hair, get big muscles, and then no one will get it wrong again.* That was how Vandal tried to recover from this shock to his system.

While doing so, he was playing an important role in the village: creating buzz.

"Wow, this is a dhampir? I've never seen one before!"

"Oh my, you look like a doll! Are you sure you're eating enough?"

"I touched a dhampir!"

"Hah! I poked him!"

"You brats! That's rude!"

It felt like he was in a petting zoo. The Reclamation Village didn't have a lot going for it in terms of entertainment, and so getting to see a dhampir for the first time was causing a stir. A steady stream of visitors poured into the General Store's cafeteria.

It was better than being treated like a ghost, perhaps. Vandal was polite and chose to engage with the villagers, meaning they didn't hold anything back.

"You've had tough times too, huh."

"It's not easy, but keep going!"

Luckily, the villagers also all seemed to like Vandal. Vandal assumed they had sympathy for him, as former refugees themselves. But there were actually two additional reasons.

The first was that Vandal's expressionless face and dead eyes made the villagers think he must have been through hell and back. The second was that Vandal was someone they could sympathize with, without it costing them anything. If he had been a helpless orphan, they would have sympathized, but there wouldn't have been much they could do for him. Most of the villagers were young, and while they could work, they weren't well off. They might not be paying taxes, but that was going to change in just two years. No one would be willing to commit to taking in a child.

However, Vandal was planning on becoming an adventurer. If even half of what Kasim and the others said was true, he could handle at least a few goblins with ease. In that case, a little sympathy, some kind words, and maybe a free meal was all the commitment they needed. It was still far more than he would have gotten in an apathetic big city, he was sure.

"It's true! He lopped off the Goblin Barbarian's head from behind with a single attack!"

"I mean, I don't doubt you, but that still seems pretty hard to believe."

"You're definitely doubting me! Please, believe me, Lina!"

"Festa, we saw it happen, and we still don't believe it. You're asking too much of Lina."

Festa and the others were chatting nearby. From Vandal's perspective, killing a Rank 3 monster meant so little to him, it didn't seem worth speaking up to confirm it. After all, only yesterday he had completely destroyed a Rank 4 Goblin King and a thousand goblins. After that, killing a Goblin Barbarian was hardly anything to write home about.

As it turned out, the small guild output run by Lina wasn't able to register new adventurers. They could only buy bounty parts and other materials. Vandal would have to go to a bigger guild branch in the city to register. Borkz had told him that 200 years ago, it had been possible to register even in a small village. That meant the centuries since had not only been hard on the Heartner Domain but also on Olbaum's adventurers' guilds.

"This is the dhampir child you say saved you, Kasim?"

At that moment, two men came in. They were both older, a rarity for this village where most people were thirty or younger, perhaps a few years into the real prime of life. The man in front was dressed like the other villagers, but the one behind him had a dyed cotton robe and a necklace with a design Vandal didn't like.

"Mayor, Father, you finished your discussions?" the general store owner asked.

"Yes, all done. Before that, though, we need to thank this boy."

The mayor turned to Vandal, taking his hands, and giving a bow. "Thank you so much for aiding Kasim and his party. Even though you wish to become an adventurer, it surely took courage for one so young to distract those goblins."

Apparently, the story in the village had become that Vandal caught the attention of the strongest goblin, giving Kasim's party a change to fight back and wipe the monsters out. Vandal was smaller than other children his age, and the villagers didn't know much about what a dhampir could do. This modified version of events was far easier for them to believe than the idea of him so easily slaying the commander of a group of goblins.

"I'm happy I could help." He saw no reason to try to correct the tale.

"You did take a risk, though! Adventurers should think first about coming back alive," the mayor cautioned him.

Strange to think that the people here are nicer to me than anyone ever was on Earth. Vandal was moved for a moment, thinking that there was hope for humans after all. However, he couldn't drop his guard yet. Behind the kind mayor, there was the priest with a smile that looked a little tighter across the lips.

"To meet such a brave young lady as this, when I only happened to be here on my route around our churches. The hand of Alda has guided me, no doubt!" The priest certainly had a gentle tone. He took up the holy symbol around his neck—which looked something like a crucifix—and gave a small prayer of gratitude. He got Vandal's gender wrong again, but that didn't matter.

"Father, actually—"

"Hahaha, my dear mayor, there's clearly nothing to fear. Alda only punishes the wicked. Even a dhampir will face no punishment if it does good deeds! From what I've heard so far, this little one has been living in the forest, far from human habitation. She can't have been baptized yet. I could do that for you if you wish?" There was no murderous intent, no anger or hatred in the man, but the offer sounded awfully flimsy to Vandal. At least he had Detect Danger: Death running all the time, which wasn't throwing out any warnings.

"Oh, it wasn't a full-blown ceremony, but my mom did baptize me in the name of Vida," Vandal replied.

Even if he wasn't dealing with some kind of trap, Vandal certainly didn't want to anything to do with Alda, and so he lied again.

"I see, I see. You had a fine mother, I'm sure." The priest didn't press him any further and left the scene.

The Olbaum Electorate Kingdom had been formed by a number of smaller nations coming together to protect themselves from the threat of the Amidd Empire. As a result, Olbaum did not prohibit the faith of the God of Law and Life Alda. They accepted those who believed in Vida, while also placing no restrictions on faith in Alda. That was because some of the original composite nations had people who followed Alda or his dependent gods.

However, this Alda religion was also not quite the same as the one in the Empire.

The Alda faith had a number of differing sects, for a start. As Olbaum believed in things like human rights for dhampirs, a more peaceful, conciliatory branch of the religion had developed there, which believed in letting even Vida's new races live their lives so long as they obeyed the law and did good deeds. For clergy from the Amidd Empire, such ideas were pure heresy.

While the people in Ramda could be sure that the gods actually existed, such divine beings hadn't actually been boots-on-the-ground for tens of thousands of years. Today, they could only impart their will to the people in limited ways, such as by sending Oracles. That meant that, across nations and regions, people had different interpretations of each god's teachings and different variations in the faiths that they followed.

One perfect example of this was the conciliatory faction.

The conciliators had spread more easily in Olbaum due to there being more of Vida's new races here. There were also political motives at play, as the Alda faithful needed to survive here after the war so badly damaged their reputation.

Earth had a lot of different religions that believed in the same god, Vandal recalled. *I don't know what Alda is thinking, but I doubt he'd be watching over all of his believers at all times and sending messages to correct them about this or that piece of minutia. So long as it works in my favor, I'm fine with it.* Vandal wasn't enamored with the condescending "you are forgiven for existing" tone, perhaps, but he also understood that his chief concern was with getting by—he couldn't kick up a fuss about something quite so minor.

"Father, the medicine you provided . . . I'm sorry, but it doesn't seem to be working."

"In that case, please increase the dose. You should take twice as much in the future."

"Father, can you please come and see our fields?"

"Of course. Alda is the god of all life."

The villagers all wanted a piece of the priest, conversing with him on many topics and asking for all sorts of help. His smile might not have been very convincing, but the people seemed to trust him.

In the pioneer village, the tales of past holy men and great heroes as told by one of the cloth were probably among the only forms of entertainment. With his intellect and skills as a physician, the priest had likely earned their respect.

Then, there came a shout from outside.

"Father, please come! Iwan has fallen from the roof!"

That sounded bad. Vandal used Detect Life and did indeed notice a response that was unnaturally weak.

"How awful. I will come at once."

Even as the priest spoke right behind him, Vandal smoothly slipped out of the General Store. Everyone's attention was focused on the father, meaning no one noticed Vandal leave.

I can probably do something, so long as the poor guy isn't dead. Ah, this must be the place. He flew over to the source of the abnormal reading, to find a man in his thirties lying on the ground, with a slightly younger-looking woman with a big round belly and a child smaller than Vandal.

"My darling! Hold on! The priest is coming!"

"Daddy! Daddy!" The man's wife and child were clinging to him, but all the man could do was moan. His breathing was ragged, too. His face was pallid with the specter of death.

He's badly hurt, Vandal appraised. *It isn't his bones, and it isn't his internal organs.* It was the worst case: something in his brain. That meant medicine on Ramda couldn't do a thing. Magic might be able to save him, but they were on the outskirts of the village. Vandal determined that the man was likely to expire before the priest could even get here—and even when he did, he would need to be damn more skilled than he looked in order to make any kind of difference.

Naturally, Vandal could use Death Attribute magic and probably save this Iwan's life. His wife wouldn't need to lose her husband, and the children—inside and out—wouldn't need to lose their dad. However, his goal for this trip had been to quietly register with the guild and then dash back to Talosheim. A child saving a life that only the highest-level Magicians could save? That sounded like standing out to him.

Do I stick to my guns, or let myself get swept away? Vandal sighed. *I really don't have a choice.*

"A moment, please." With that, he zipped smoothly forward, past Iwan's child, and placed his hands on Iwan's body.

"Eeek!!"

"Ahh! Who—what are you?!" As expected, the wife and child hadn't seen him there until that moment.

"I'm Vandal, the dhampir of rumor visiting the village." Even as he introduced himself, Vandal started Spirit Bodification. He made sure his audience couldn't see what he was doing, extending tendrils from the palm of his hand pressed into Iwan, extending his spirit body inside the man. Vandal found bleeding in his cranium, with the pooling blood putting pressure on his brain.

I can use the tendrils to absorb the excess blood, Vandal thought, setting to work. *Then repair the damaged blood vessel using Enhance Regeneration. Then I can fix the crack in his cranium . . . hmmm, he's got a clot forming close to his heart. I can get that as well. Ah, a polyp in his large intestine. It looks like it might be malignant, so let's fix that. And his athlete's foot? Why not . . .*

"Whatever do you think you're—"

"Mommy! Daddy looks much better!"

"Oh, you're right! Don't tell me, you're healing him?"

"That's right," Vandal assured her. "It won't be much longer."

This Iwan guy wasn't in great shape. The simple life was often touted as being good for one's health, but that certainly didn't apply here.

Vandal had done all he could, anyway. He withdrew the tendrils and turned off the Spirit Bodification.

"That should do it. He will be awake shortly." Vandal provided all of the strength and even nutrition needed for the repairs, so the man didn't need any sleep. The blood pooling in his cranium had been delicious. Vandal decided to consider that the payment for his services.

Iwan stirred. "Ooh, what—happened to me?"

"Darling!"

"Daddy!" His wife and child hugged him at once. It was quite the emotional sight. This was what a family, a household, should be like.

"What's going on? Why are you here?"

"I-Iwan?! You looked like death a moment ago! How are you up and about?"

Just as Vandal was feeling some appreciation for Iwan and the family he had nurtured, the priest and the mayor finally rocked up. Vandal's only hope of getting out of this—apart from fully explaining his presence here—was to spin it as Iwan not actually being that badly hurt, and the man who rushed to the General Store had been jumping the gun.

"This young one—this Vandal—saved my husband! Ah, it was over before she showed up!"

Missus, I have to say—I can't hold your honesty against you.

"I did have some kind of dream," Iwan said. "It was like a terrible reaper had my head in his hands . . . but then I was being cradled by a goddess. I see. It was this girl."

A goddess? Oh boy. With that, Vandal saved the life of Iwan and, in the process, really stood out from the crowd.

Vandal was given a hero's welcome back at the General Store, the only commercial facility in the village.

"Kid, you saved my life," Iwan declared. "I was about to go out like a chump and never be around for my second kid to even see my face. Come on, eat up! My treat!"

"Don't make it sound like you're doing him a favor! This isn't much of much!"

"Not at all. Thank you," Vandal said, replying to Iwan and his wife even though his mouth was full. "I was feeling hungry." He was eating some simple rice porridge. It was made with long grain rice, like indica rice from back on Earth, mixed with some edible wild grasses to hide the powerful smell, plus beans to add some bulk, finished with a little salt. It wasn't anything special. The flavors of the ingredients were all richly represented—but those exact ingredients made up 110% of the flavor.

However, it was summer and also rice harvest time. This was probably what they had at hand. The fact the Seventh Pioneer Village had rice at all for porridge was an indicator of how good they had it—relatively speaking.

Throw in some dried meat or fish from my pack, crank up the salt, and this could be pretty good. However, Vandal chose not to act on his idea. This world didn't have the concept of smoking, and Vandal was hoping to turn dried, smoked meat and fish into one of the specialties of Talosheim in the future. He therefore wanted to keep it a secret.

The bar space of the General Store didn't even have a menu. They served grain-based unrefined booze with sides of fried beans, boiled beans, and some veggies. Those meals were also the exact same thing the family that ran the restaurant ate—in fact, they were just cooking extra to serve in the restaurant.

Vandal had been wondering how they hoped to run a business like that, but the truth was, this was the only way to run any business at all in the village.

The other villagers could easily brew their own alcohol of a similar (low) quality and cooked meals of similar (low) complexity. The only customers willing to pay for such offerings were, therefore, merchants who headed bi-monthly to the slave mine, the guards who protected them, passing soldiers, and the three from Kasim's party. If the operators of the General Store decided to offer multiple dishes, it would do nothing but increase their overhead. Hence, the rice porridge.

"It isn't that great, is it?" The owner sounded resigned.

"Don't say that," Vandal replied, still chewing.

"No need to be polite. Iwan and I would both love to give you a proper treat, after all you've done, but we grow rice here and not much else."

"Dad, you promised not to say things like that. Although I guess the rice in the Saulon Domain was better than the stuff here. It smelled nicer, too."

As it turned out, the refugees had formerly been farmers of a rice known as Saulon rice. This variety was closer to the white rice Vandal knew from Earth. This, of course, had been back when they lived in the Saulon Domain, to the north of Duke Heartner's. After they were forced to flee, they had quickly learned that the weather and soil here in the Heartner Domain did not favor Saulon rice at all. So they had to grow the strain commonly farmed here, called southern rice in the Electorate Kingdom.

"Sounds like the Empire is at fault again," Vandal said. He could've been chowing down on familiar Japanese rice today, if not for the Empire.

"That's right! That muck-mired Empire can suck a donkey's—"

"Yes, yes, the Imperials are the bad guys!"

The pioneer village was comprised of refugees from an Amidd Empire attack. Everyone agreed with Vandal's comment.

"I'm impressed you can use magic, though," Kasim ventured. He was eating the same porridge as Vandal.

"As I am," the priest agreed. "I thought you were a Warrior or Fighter." He placed a hand on his chest with a smile. "The fact you appeared today, to save not only Kasim but also Iwan, is surely by the guiding grace of our lord. We may pray to different gods, Alda and Vida; two who in the time of myth are said to have taken divergent paths. Allow us, however, to join hands toward a common good." Vandal thought his smile still seemed fake, but what he was saying had the ring of conviction. This was definitely a holier man than High Priest Goldan had been. In fact, he might actually be a decent fellow.

"I am not a member of the clergy myself, but thank you for saying that," Vandal replied. He wondered for a moment what the deal was with shrines to Vida in the Heartner Domain. He might see one when he finally reached a city.

"May I ask one thing?" the priest asked. "How are you able to speak so clearly with your mouth full?"

". . . A little trick of mine." He was actually using Astral Projection to make a spirit body face below his clothing and talked using that. "Could I trouble you for some more?"

"More?! Ah, of course, you can—but that's your third bowl."

"I really am hungry. My apologies." Vandal was smaller and more delicate than children his own age, but he ate a lot more than his appearance suggested. He needed more energy than the average grown man, after all.

"You've got strength, magic, and the appetite of an adventurer to boot!" Kasim was not as surprised by this as the owner. Adventurers took combat-related Jobs, which increased physical abilities more than the kind of production-based jobs regular folk took. That meant many of them were thin as rakes, yet packed food away come mealtimes. Kasim and his party would have met such people in their adventures.

"Mayor! Kain from the neighboring Fifth Pioneer Village is here to see the father—urmpf!" The first man to come in was suddenly pushed aside.

"Father! Please, we need you in our village! Our people are falling sick—the pest, Father, it's felling us one by one! We need you!" The second man, doing the pushing, looked battered and worn. He must have collapsed countless times on his way here.

"The pest?!" the mayor exclaimed.

"This is terrible!" said the priest. "But I fear the sun has already set. Venturing to the Fifth at this hour would not end well."

The path between the two villages was little better than a track scraped out by beasts. It took about four hours to traverse, through a region that saw frequent attacks by wolves or monsters at night. It was possible to return to the main road first and then head to the Fifth Pioneer Village, but that route would take an entire day.

"Kain, we will leave first thing in the morning. You should rest until then."

"I can't wait! Everyone at home—my wife and daughter—!"

"Please, you must understand, Kain. It's too dangerous to travel at night. Goblin numbers have been increasing recently as well. Any attempt to provide aid will be pointless if we're dead before we get there."

Kain wailed. "No! There must be . . . something to be done . . ." His shoulders slumped down, shaking with his sobs.

A number of the villagers were already raising their hands in despair. The plight of this regular man who had already risked the crossing once for the sake of his people, wife, and daughter, resounded in the room.

Kasim stood up. "Then we will provide an escort—"

"I can fly him on my back, if you like," Vandal offered.

This proposal kind of shut down the idea of anyone else tagging along.

"Aren't the stars lovely."

"Yeeeeeeees!"

"Look at the moon! Lovely!"

"Nooooooo!"

On Ramda, few had the power of flight. There were certain Magicians, rich folk with expensive magic items, those like Dragoons who tamed flying monsters, and members of Vida's new races who had wings. That was about it. For most regular folk, the idea of flying through the sky was a dream or a hallucination.

Kain was currently having this rare and precious experience.

The man was bound tightly to Vandal's back with rope. Meanwhile, Vandal was carrying his belongings and using Flight magic to proceed toward the Fifth Pioneer Village. Kain was clinging desperately to Vandal and screaming most of the time. He didn't have much time to enjoy the flight.

"Should I be going straight?" Vandal asked.

"Y-yes! There's a small pond . . . look for that!"

"I think we just passed it. I'll keep going!" They were zipping along, 100 feet high. The speed was about what a fast horse might gallop, but for Kain, the terror was so great he could barely open his eyes. Even if he did, he didn't possess the Night Vision skill and couldn't see much.

"We already passed the pond?!"

"Yes. Can you please stop squeezing my neck so hard?"

Vandal's Flight was fast when compared to walking speed, of course, but it also allowed for direct routing to his destination without negotiating the ground terrain. He expected to reach the village in about ten minutes. Of course, all of this drained a lot of magical power.

Thanks to Magical Power Auto Recovery, normally I'd spend as much as I recover if it were just me and the pack. The extra weight of Kain, though . . . I need more training, clearly. I should ask about this pest, anyway.

"About this sickness," Vandal spoke up. "Can you tell me a bit more about it?" Vandal had already heard the basics, but something still sounded out of place.

"I came back from the hunt, and most everyone had collapsed. They were feverish, vomiting, dazed . . . some were coughing blood."

"Was anyone okay, other than you?" Vandal asked.

"Other than me? Yes, I think . . . old man Jozef was doing okay. The young babe wasn't sick yet, either."

"Tell me about Jozef."

"He's an old woodcutter. He had a terrible cold yesterday and was sleeping until I came back. I left him tending to the sick. A strain on his old bones."

"He doesn't have the pest?"

"I don't think so. He had a fever, and his nose was running, but he wasn't vomiting or coughing blood. That's why I asked for his help. He might be mobile, but I couldn't ask him to run all the way to the next village over, and the babe won't last half a day without care."

In other words, all the villagers are sick with the same symptoms, apart from Kain who was out hunting, an old man who was sick in bed, and a baby. Vandal hadn't seen any hint of the specter of death on Kain, either. He certainly wasn't infected with a deadly disease. Just to be sure, Vandal had carefully used Spirit Bodification to check Kain out— with the panicked man clinging to him so tightly, it hadn't been hard to find an opening—and confirmed that Kain was in great health. He would probably live longer than Iwan when all was said and done.

Vandal had already used Death to Bacteria over the Seventh Pioneer Village prior to setting out, in order to get rid of any harmful germs or bacteria. However, he was starting to think this sounded less like a disease and more like poison. That begged the question of how almost all the villagers would have been poisoned at once—and why.

"Did anything else strange happen today?" Vandal asked.

"No, everything was like normal. It was the merchant's first time through in a while, but that's it," Kain replied.

"What merchant?"

"A great man. He lost his store, but rather than give up, he started over as a traveling merchant. He's been a big help, taking the pains to come to our village, so far off the main road. Hmmm, but I didn't see him among the sick. I hope he didn't collapse after he left us . . ."

Sounds more like he's the culprit, Vandal thought. *Still don't know why, though.* In any case, he needed to play doctor before he played detective.

"Is that the village?" With Night Vision, Vandal could see an open space with a few wooden buildings, as clear as if it were day.

"Yes, most likely! Please, the sick—"

"I'll cure them all from up here!"

"Huh?"

"The village looks to run from there to . . . over there. Three million should do it! Detoxify! Detox!"

As Vandal chanted, a wave of something like black fog rolled over the village.

"Husband! You're alive!"

"Daddy!"

"Oh, my darlings! You're all better! Thank goodness!"

Vandal had seen a similar sight earlier that same day. Now it was playing out all over this new village, including with Kain's family.

The villagers' suffering all ended at the same time. Their fevers broke, their vomiting stopped, and their mental fog lifted. The same went for Kain's family. As they celebrated, they had heard a voice from outside. Looking out the window, they saw Kain, illuminated by a pale light. The villagers first thought their recovery was a miracle, caused by none other than Kain's ghost, but that misunderstanding was quickly resolved, and the celebrations began in earnest.

"Phew. They should be safe now," muttered Vandal. Flying over here carrying an adult—or, more accurately, with an adult strapped to him—had definitely done a number on his MP. Flight wasn't the most efficient spell to start with, so it couldn't be helped. As a result, Vandal had spent close to 70 million MP. It was also late, meaning he was tired. A good little boy his age should be tucked up in bed by now. He wondered if he should return to the Seventh first.

It was the least he could do to create some Lemures and search for the merchant who had caused this, even with his head-start of a few hours. Vandal didn't know the surrounding terrain, of course, so it was likely the culprit would give him the slip if he had left the main road.

He might still be jumping the gun by placing blame on the merchant, but the fact that Detoxify had cured the villagers made it clear this wasn't a sickness. The merchant himself wasn't here, either.

"Please, everyone. The poison is gone but your strength is yet to return. Try not to get too excited. Just take it easy for tonight," Vandal advised.

"Husband, who is this child?"

"The savior of our village, that's who! He cured the sickness. Thank you, thank you!" Kain seemed to have completely ignored the word "poison." His face was running with tears and snot as he lifted Vandal up into the air.

"What?!"

"Oh! The savior of us all!"

"A messenger from God! From Ald—"

"Vida, please," Vandal corrected the villager, wanting to avoid any associations with the wrong deity.

"From Vida, from Goddess Vida herself!"

"Like I said, please, try to take it easy—" But the villagers were crowding around, stroking and patting him. *Don't come crying to me if you can't move tomorrow,* Vandal thought, but kept it to himself. It looked like he was staying here for the night.

The Lemures turned up nothing, meaning the merchant in question had made his escape. Vandal might have gotten more clues if someone actually died. Kain's efforts and Vandal's healing had prevented that, but that also prevented any aid from the afterlife in terms of solving this case.

The living villagers could at least explain some of what happened. The merchant had proclaimed the day was a celebration of a god he worshipped (most likely, in retrospect, a fictious name, as none had heard it before), so he had shared tea and confections with the villagers. Kain's wife had saved one of those confections for him, since he was out hunting, and it indeed contained poison. Another strike against this merchant fellow. The merchant had tried to get the villagers to eat them, saying they would soon go bad, not expecting some evidence to survive the night.

Of course, that poison had now been removed by Vandal's magic, so the confection could no longer serve as evidence. Vandal didn't expect that anyone else on Ramda could sense traces of poison that had been removed by death magic. It also seemed unlikely that a merchant going around doing things like this would be properly registered with the merchants' guild. It was also possible that he thought he had killed all the villagers and was just carelessly heading straight to the nearest town.

In any case, Vandal soothed the people, shaken at this betrayal by a man they had trusted, and spent the night in the village. Then he placed a few Lemures around the perimeter to keep watch, before—

"Alllll of them, everyoooone . . . " Singing a simple song, Vandal flew up into the air. He decided to do a circuit around and make sure the merchant from the day before hadn't pulled a similar trick at other reclamation villages. He could have just ignored that question and flown to the town, putting his actual purpose here—registering as an adventurer—ahead of this side quest. But if there was another village out there suffering, it wouldn't sit well with him to ignore it.

We're all in this together, so they say—and a good deed is its own reward, Vandal pondered. In this case, he hadn't wanted to take money from the village folk, and so he had asked them to erect a simple shrine to Vida. It needed to be nothing more than the one he had already seen to Alda: a large stone, with the holy heart mark symbol carved into it, placed under a simple roof. But because it was so simple, it was easy to ask for.

That request also made the villagers start treating him like a messenger from the goddess herself, but he was okay with that.

"It ain't so eeassyy—hold on!" Vandal was flying toward the Sixth Pioneer Village when he spotted a number of people moving below. It was a group of men wearing worn leather armor and carrying dirty weapons, proceeding along the same path toward the village. Vandal took out the map Kain had provided, scratched onto tree bark, to confirm he was in the right place.

Vandal called to one of the spirits clinging to the men and discovered that they were bandits. Vandal asked a few others and got the same reply; they really were bandits.

That seemed like due diligence enough. Vandal decided to wipe them out.

"Listen up, you filthy dogs! Once we reach the village, kill the men, then enjoy the women and kill them too! But any that look like they'll fetch a high price, don't lay a finger on them! Understand?"

"Not really," Vandal said.

"The hell! What's your problem?" The apparent leader turned around to find Vandal hovering in the air. "Huh? Who is this kid?!"

"Boss! Looks like a monster!"

"It just dropped down from the sky! Gotta be a ghost or something!"

"Nothing of the sort," Vandal replied to the ogling bandits. "I'm just a passing seven-year-old with the power of flight."

Of course, that was in no way normal.

"Gah! Cheeky brat! Kain, get up here and crush this nuisance with your Brute Strength!"

At the boss's orders, the biggest of the bandits—a skinhead with a grin plastered across his face—stepped forward.

"Boss, can I have some fun first?"

"You're a sick man, Kain. Whatever you want!"

"Heh heh, I get to have fun!" Kain gave a happy shout, his eyes sparkling as he swung his two-handed war hammer like a kid showing off.

"Boss, we need to get to the village," one of the others said.

"Don't worry. He'll snap a twig like this in seconds."

"Good point."

"Hey, kid! Be nice and I'll only play with you a little after I snap your arms and legs! Fight back and I'll give you the works!"

". . . Yikes, what an idiot," Vandal mumbled.

"What did you say?! I hate being called dumb more than anything! Don't you know that?!"

"Why would I?"

"Still mocking me! Enough!" The bandit Kain was red with anger, looking like a boiled octopus. He proceeded to bash his hammer at Vandal. "One swing is enough to take out a kid like you!"

And if it isn't, you're really done for. You've got nothing but raw strength! You don't even have Club Proficiency, from the the look of you.

Rather than quip back, though, Vandal poked out his tongue. "And my tongue is enough to deal with a small fry like you."

"You little—" Before Kain could finish his shout, Vandal's cheeks puffed up. Even with his expressionless visage, he did look a little cute when doing this. A moment later, though, and he spat something out, his cheeks and mouth returning to normal. Kain froze in place, then crashed backward like a felled tree. His left eye socket no longer contained his rabidly twinkling eye, but a mess of blood.

"Huh?"

"Kain! What's wrong with you?"

The bandits were stunned by this turn of events. Then, something red and snake-like emerged from Kain's eye socket.

"Hyaah!" As the bandits cried out in surprise, the red snake flew through the air, dripping blood as it returned to Vandal's mouth.

"That's an original battle tech I cooked up. I call it Barbed Tongue. Firing it off with some added Virulent Poison seems pretty strong. The downside is that I have to re-affix my old tongue or grow a new one after I use it before I can talk again." This Brawling Proficiency tech made full use of Poison Dispersal (Claws, Fangs, Tongue). First, he used Spirit Bodification to cut his tongue off at the base and then combined it with Remote Control to fire it out.

Of course, Vandal was the only person who could hope to think up, let alone execute such an attack.

"I guess it could be useful as a last resort," Vandal concluded.

"What the hell did you do?!"

"All I did was make sure that the only guy named Kain in these parts is a good-natured hunter," Vandal replied. "I'll just deal with the rest of you more traditionally."

"Run!" the boss shouted. "Run for it! This kid is a freaking monster—what?! My legs can't move!"

"Mine neither! I'm shaking in my boots! Why? What can't we move?!"

Vandal flew up to the struggling bandits, sliding through the air. The claws extending from his small hands were still more than enough to chop through their throats.

"I just spread a little poison. But now, more importantly, I've got just one little question to ask you. I suggest you answer it. Even if I have to kill you first, I'll just ask you again once you're dead."

"I don't know . . . I really don't know . . . anything!" The boss of the bandits had eyes like a dead fish, foam spilling from his lips as he replied.

Vandal gave a small sigh. "I guess you really don't. The timing is odd, though." Just one day after a merchant attempted to poison a whole village, a bunch of bandits were about to attack a different settlement. It was hard to consider this a coincidence. However, neither the bandit boss nor his bandits had any real leads.

The bandits had been on the move, looking for a new base of operations, and purchased info about the pioneer villages on the cheap from a broker in the closest town, a place called Niakki. Learning that only the Seventh had an adventurer presence, they had decided sixth would be a ripe target.

This broker sounded suspicious, offering information on these villages that only a few ever really visited. But none of the bandits knew his name, and his face had been covered below the eyes with cloth. Tracking him down would be almost impossible.

"Maybe I should give you a little more, just to make sure," Vandal mused.

"No . . . please, no . . ."

"Tell me, how many times did you stop, when the people begging you not to kill or rape or sell them asked the same thing? If you stopped even once, I might consider it."

"I . . . never did . . ."

"Exactly." Vandal slid the tip of one of his claws into the open mouth of the boss. It was dripping with poison. This was also a product of his Poison Dispersal (Claws, Fangs, Tongue) and was what might generally be called a truth serum.

He had obtained Poison Dispersal when he took the Poison Master Job. It did exactly what it sounded like—dispersed poison—but, unlike the poison-related skills that ghouls had, this poison wasn't limited to things like their nerve toxins. Before he took the Job, he had thought it would improve his handling of poisons and chemicals. It turned out the poisons he could make were weaker than those made using Death Attribute magic, but that they could have all kinds of effects.

In fact, Vandal practically had turned into a living pharmacy, capable of dispersing truth serum, detox agents, anesthetics, stomach medicine, sunscreen, eye drops, and even vitamins. The cost wasn't MP, but rather nutrition taken from Vandal's body, meaning he couldn't fire them out like magic.

Vandal repeated the same questions to the boss again, but before he could answer, the man started convulsing and dropped dead.

"Tell me now. Answer my question." Vandal treated his death like it was nothing.

"I don't know . . . I really don't . . ."

Vandal also wasn't bothered when the reply was the same as before. He grabbed the boss's still warm body and bit into his neck to use Suck Blood. The blood included the remains of his own truth serum, but his Resist Maladies skill took care of that.

"Phew," Vandal said. "I've been missing out on animal protein since yesterday. That's just what I needed."

He quickly rifled through the pockets of the bandits, finding a reasonable amount of money. He also collected their weapons. Then he used Golem Creation to make a hole for the corpses, used Decay to rot them down to the bones, and buried them.

"That takes care of that." Vandal then used Flight once more, heading toward the Sixth Pioneer Village again.

None of the impending trouble seemed to have reached the village. A crowd of surprised villagers gathered when a white-haired dhampir dropped down from the sky. Vandal asked them if they needed anything, healing a few ailments, and then set off for the next village.

"Please, wait, oh great envoy!" called one of the villagers. "I have to thank you for healing my father's eyes!"

"Oh, no need. I didn't do anything special." After a quick Spirit Bodification surgery, he had created some eye medicine, and then used Golem Creation to make a bottle for it.

"Thank you for healing my son's burns! He has his fingers back!" That had been another simple Spirit Bodification surgery, accompanied by an application of Rapid Healing.

Of course, all of these things meant more in a village that lacked a magician with healing magic. That said, Vandal didn't feel comfortable with being paid for his services. This place looked worse off than both the Seventh and Fifth villages.

"In that case, please erect a shrine to the Goddess Vida. Whenever you have the time, no rush. You need only carve the holy seal into a stone and put a simple roof over it." With that, he flew off to the next pioneer village.

Skill level increased for Surgery!

The Fourth Pioneer Village was a place of poor but hard-working people, giving their all to everything they did.

"Bugaaaaah!"

"Oooooink!"

"Bughhhhhh!"

Until, of course, three orcs smashed through their shoddy wooden walls.

"Run for it! Orcs!"

Screams rose as the villagers fled, each of them trying to be first to get away. Adventurers would rarely have a problem handling orcs like these, but for poor refugees they were a major threat. With just one orc, the hunters and younger men could probably surround it and kill or drive it off, but there wasn't anything they could do about three at once.

If all the men fought together, they might have stood a chance of driving them away, but the village—especially with all its farms—was quite spread out. The orc attack was sudden, so there was no way to coordinate everyone grabbing weapons and getting there in time. The orcs watched the people flee, perhaps choosing targets, and started forward on light and confident steps.

"Nooo!" The first thing they had spotted was a young girl who had fallen over in front of them. She was maybe still a year or two below adulthood, but the orcs and their dark desires didn't care about that.

"Buh-huh!" The three orcs closed in, each one trying to beat away the other two.

"Beth! I'm coming!" That was when a young beastman appeared, sporting wolf ears and a tail. He looked around the same age as the girl and was carrying a hoe in his hands.

"Moris! You can't save her! Run!" shouted another wolf beastman, who looked like the boy's father.

"No! I'm not letting orcs take Beth!" The boy shook off his father's hands and dashed toward his friend—or perhaps more than that.

"Moris! Stay back!" Beth yelled. She knew he wouldn't be able to fight the orcs. Even Moris had to know that. If a kid with farming tools could kill orcs, no one would need adventurers. He might manage to give Beth a few more seconds; a few seconds while they beat him to death with their clubs. Even with that knowledge, Moris was unable to stop himself.

"You pigs! Fight me!" the youth shouted bravely, lifting his weapon.

The orcs grinned at this development. First they found this female, and now a juicy-looking young male was bringing himself to them.

"Buh-hoh!" One of the orcs swung his club at once, looking to make mincemeat of the boy.

"Raaaagh!" Meanwhile, Moris's swing with the hoe bounced right off the orc's blubber. His face paled with despair.

Blood splashed out.

Beth thought it was Moris's blood and closed her eyes tight. Even Moris thought he had just been killed.

"That's one down. Next. Gravifist!"

The other villagers, however, saw what was really happening. A white child had zipped down from the air at high speed, blowing up the head of the first orc.

"Blaaaagh!" The head of the second orc was hit by a powerful Brawling Proficiency battle tech that quickly beat him to death. The technique had a big windup, making it pretty easy to dodge, but it landed with a heck of a punch.

"Buhgoh?!" The third orc snapped to his senses and swung his stick, but Vandal had trained with the likes of Braga. To Vandal, the stick was moving in slow motion. Vandal slipped in his claws, providing a more-than-lethal shot of neurotoxins.

The orc convulsed, dropped to his knees, and then collapsed completely.

"Huh? Hold on?" Moris stood in front of the scene, his mouth hanging open.

Vandal turned to him and spoke. "That was reckless, sure, but humans tend to let their emotions overtake them. I've experienced it myself. What I'm trying to say is—I'm glad I was able to save you."

"Ah, yeah, thank you!" Moris replied purely on reflex, although he was still stunned at the sight of this boy. The child was half covered in blood and had an arm pointed at an odd angle as he floated in the air.

"Er . . . you have nothing to fear from me," Vandal said. As always, he lacked confidence when meeting new people. Just because he had saved this boy from being attacked, it didn't mean the kid wasn't going to cry "another monster!" and charge.

"Hey, your arm . . ."

Vandal had broken it, his limb failing to withstand the speed of his descent and the impact of killing the orc. He promptly used his other arm to straighten it out, then used Spirit Bodification on the insides. He corrected the positioning of the bones and arteries; he'd be all healed up soon.

"I'm healed," Vandal said.

"Already?"

Beth's eyes were open wide as well, but Vandal's next comment snapped them all back to reality.

"Forget me. Do you want to carve up these orcs? Three of them should provide quite a feast for the village."

Vandal had held back from using magic, not only because the kids were so nearby, but also to allow the villagers to collect the meat afterward. It would be a waste not to eat it.

When Vandal asked the spirits of the orcs about why they attacked the village, they told him that their "boss" had given them orders to have some fun in this village.

"Tell me about your boss," Vandal said.

"He unleashed us and went away."

"Is he an orc?"

"No. Human."

"Do you know his face and name?"

"Called himself Boss. Has a human-shaped nose."

"No pointy ears. Darker than you."

"No horns or wings."

The orcs hadn't got any smarter by becoming spirits. That was about all they knew. Vandal estimated that a human Tamer had, for some reason, unleashed orcs on this village. He had some Lemures search the vicinity for suspicious individuals, but they turned up nothing.

He sighed, wondering if there was someone selling a starter pack of local knowledge that he might use. A silly thought he had, while using his claws to slice up the orcs. Most solo adventurers possessed the skill Dismantle, but not Vandal. He did have the skills Cookery and Surgery, and by applying them in liberal doses, he could do the same thing as Dismantle. He stripped down and sliced up the orcs faster than anyone in the village could hope to, and even started to cook the internal organs, knowing that they wouldn't keep.

The villagers told him that they were facing a water shortage, so they didn't have much water for cooking. Vandal could solve this with his death attribute magic, but he didn't want the villagers to see him using it.

Vandal therefore found a moment to sneak away. He slipped behind an empty house and quickly used Golem Creation to dig a well. He used Astral Projection to go underground, locating an underground cavern with water that would be hard to reach digging by hand. Then he used the earth located between the surface and the water source as material to make Earth Golems and Rock Golems, pushing water to the surface. Finally, he used the Rock Golems to harden the walls of the hole, and the well was complete.

Of course, he had also been sure to confirm that the water for fit for drinking.

"Whoaaa, no way! There's a well here!" He called the villagers over, doing his best Conan impression.

"Impossible! There can't be a—there is! A well!"

"What? That's not possible!"

"Water? Is there water?!"

The villagers came crowding around. Vandal took the water he had already drawn from his new well and returned to his cooking. Then he carefully cooked the offal.

"Death to Bacteria and Detox don't physically remove anything from these organs," Vandal muttered. That was why he needed water to wash everything out. Even if it wasn't going to cause any harm, no one wanted to eat the contents of an orc stomach. The same went for Vandal.

"Thank you, great envoy! You not only saved the children but have given us this wonderful well! How can we hope to thank you?"

"The future of our village is assured for years! No, decades to come! Thank you, thank you!"

The villagers easily put two and two together about the

whole well situation. Vandal hadn't expected to be able to deceive them completely—he just didn't want them to know that he was using unknown magic and skills. Now they simply believed he had used earth or water magic to make the well.

"Sorry, I really am in the middle of cooking," Vandal said. "If you want to show your gratitude, please, just make a shrine to Vida."

"Very well! Once our village flourishes, we shall build a mighty temple!"

"No, just a small one will do," Vandal replied.

The water shortage had been far worse than Vandal had thought. He heard later that if things hadn't changed within a few years, the villagers would have been forced to abandon their home.

"Where are you heading to next, Lord Vandal?"

"The Second Pioneer Village," Vandal replied.

He was flying again, using his communication magic item—the shrunken goblin head—to talk to Eleonora and the others.

"Might I ask, why are you visiting all the villages, Lord Vandal?" Eleonora asked. "The purpose of this trip is to register with the adventurers' guild, correct?"

"Don't be like that. Helping people is good."

"You're doing good, King! By the way, I met a—"

"If you stand out too much, you might catch the attention of more vampires who worship Hihiryu-Shukaka," Eleonora cut in. "I don't think you should stir things up too much."

Zulan seemed keen on the people of the Heartner Domain, a region he had traded with back when he was alive. Eleonora, however, maintained her stance that Vandal needed to register with the adventurers' guild as quickly as possible. Her concern was a practical one: taking risks for these people, who weren't even residents of Talosheim, without much hope of reward was simply reckless.

A normal passerby would probably think, "That's pretty rough," but then carry on. A Magician with healing magic might have helped out Iwan at the Seventh Pioneer Village. But would he have then also gone to the fifth village as well? And then to the others? Someone with no obligation, who wasn't even an adventurer?

True, Vandal hadn't really gained anything from his efforts. He had earned gratitude and respect from poor folk, rough lodgings and crude meals, and promises of building shrines to Vida. None of these things would help him to achieve his goals. He could register as an adventurer regardless. Even his desire to eventually become a noble didn't rely on the support or opinions of those at the bottom of society's barrel. His charity wouldn't help him being back Dalshia or kill Heinz and the others left on his shit list. Rather, he was only increasing the risk of the enemy vampires finding them—that was how Eleonora saw it.

"I do see your point, but if I can help them, surely I should," Vandal replied. "There's no harm in a good deed, as they say. Karma comes back around."

"They do? It does?" Based on Eleonora's life experience, Vandal's reply sounded like the argument of a naïve child.

"That's right," Vandal assured her. Vandal was confident precisely because he believed in the ugly, stupid, vindictive, evil nature of people—he couldn't deny the presence of those qualities even in himself.

However, that truth had led him to a deeper understanding: there could be no ugliness without beauty, stupidity without intellect, vindictiveness without mercy, and evil without good. If the entire world were filled with nothing but ugly, stupid, vindictive, evil people, such words wouldn't exist in the first place. All things now considered negative would simply be thought of as being normal. That was why he felt sure that people could also possess beauty, intellect, mercy, and goodness.

"I'm not about to say 'with great power comes great responsibility' or anything. I just want to be happy myself, so I'm trying to make other people happier," Vandal explained.

"But what about the vampires?" Hearing everything he had said so far, Eleonora figured that Vandal was implementing a message often taught to young children: "If everyone is smiling, you'll be smiling too." It did seem to be the way he generally operated, with the exception of his enemies. She could accept that. Sure, he was a soft touch, but that softness of touch was the reason why she—an assassin originally sent to kill Vandal—was still around to tell that and other tales.

Nonetheless, Eleonora was still concerned about attracting unwanted vampiric attention. But Vandal's reply was yet again nonchalant.

"It shouldn't be a problem yet. Even if Gubamon and the others who worship Hihiryu-Shukaka are the most powerful vampiric group on the continent, they still don't have the clout to have agents implanted in new refugee villages. It should be a while before merchants are around this way, so no one will find out about me anytime soon."

"If you say so . . ."

"Do you want us to join you closer to the reclamation villages?" Zulan asked.

"Well, just make sure none of the villagers see you."

"King, about my—"

"Also, if you could ask about our descendants and Princess Lebia, that would be great."

"Sure thing. But I doubt these people know anything about that."

The last of the pioneer villages Vandal visited, the second one, didn't have any immediate issues. No murderous merchants, creeping bandits, or unleashed orcs.

However, they did have a chronic problem they had been suffering with for a while.

"It was fine the first year, but the rice harvest has been decreasing ever since. We've been trying to improve the soil, whatever we can do. Forget paying taxes in three years' time, we're going to starve this winter if things don't improve. Envoy of Alda, please, save our village." The chief, a dwarf, and all the other villagers bowed their heads low to Vandal.

The whole village had been gathered to pray for a bountiful harvest just as Vandal descended from the sky, meaning they had been even quicker than the other locations to decide he was heaven-sent.

"I can take a look," Vandal said. "But I'm a dhampir who worships Vida. I've got nothing to do with Alda." Just like the other villages, this one only had a shrine to Alda. The priest he met in the Seventh must be really good at converting folks.

In any case, Vandal wasn't sure what he could do to help them improve their crops, but he decided to go to the fields and check the soil. The rice fields here were dry, not flooded with water like the ones Vandal knew back in Japan. Using the knowledge from his Agriculture skill, he did observe that the rice seemed to be weakened by something. There was plenty of irrigation and the crops didn't seem to be sick. He licked a little of the soil to check its components, and that was when he got a slight hit on Detect Danger: Death.

"Is that some kind of poison? Detox."

The spell removed the problem from the soil at once. Something intended to harm human physiology was mixed in with the soil. All he had to do was use Detox to resolve the problem. Maybe that was what caused the lower yields?

"Why would the soil be poisoned, though?" Vandal asked. The soil here looked the same as in the other villages. If there was poison in the water they were using for the agriculture, the irrigation system would have responded to Detect Danger: Death. Maybe they were using a special kind of fertilizer. Vandal asked questions along those lines, but everyone shook their heads.

"We make our fertilizer from ashes and human waste," the chief told him. "The same as all of the other villagers around here."

"Father, remember when those knights came around on training, and they brought that pesticide for us?"

"That's right. It was the knights led by the eldest son of the Duke, Prince Lucas. But I believe he took the same pesticides to the other villages."

The conversation between dwarf father and son—who Vandal could only tell apart by the respective colors of their beards, gray or black—did not provide any further edification. This pesticide sounded suspicious, but there seemed no reason for knights to be poisoning the fields of a village of refugees.

Not unless there was something unpleasant brewing back in the ducal keep.

I already know this reclamation work is being led by the duke's second son, Belton, Vandal thought. *Now we have his eldest son, Lucas, a knight captain. Throw in merchants, bandits, orc Tamers, and the fields in this village—there's something up.*

Even if the family was feuding, Vandal saw no reason for them to embroil these poor villages. They could brutalize each other in their castles or fine houses, surely, and leave the common folk out of it.

"In any case, I've cleaned the poison from the fields." Vandal did consider for a moment that maybe he was destroying evidence, but if the perpetrator had any kind of powerful backing, it probably wouldn't matter even if he had a sample.

The villagers all gave a cheer, but for Vandal, it didn't feel like a big win. Even with the poison gone, frost or bugs or disease could still harm the crop. Winter could still see this village starve.

He wondered if there was another way to improve the yield here. He could pump some MP into the fields, which would help things grow—into crazy rice monsters or something. He needed another method.

Then he had a flash of inspiration. Maybe it was due to the former presence of the Goblin King, but there were still more goblins around the villages than normal. That meant he could probably find some gobgrass.

"Okay, everyone. I'm going to teach you a way to eat goblins that you'll find quite palatable, and that you can use in an emergency."

Time to make ghoul emergency rations—time for gobgob.

The Death Mage

CHAPTER THREE
THE GUY WHO WANTS A FOURTH LIFE

Kanata Kaito was half-American and half-Japanese. Both his parents were Asian, however, so he looked Japanese, and few people believed he was anything else. That meant he had never been picked on—but also never attracted attention from other students or been especially popular. His academic performance was average and slightly above average in sports and PE. Native English speaking didn't help him with the nitty-gritty English grammar taught in Japanese schools, so his performance there was actually poor.

Then he had got blown up and killed during their school trip.

"Kanata, we're close to the drop point."

The pilot's voice snapped Kanata back from his recollections of the past. "No problem." He checked over his parachute and gear one last time. Once before he had got too cocky and almost died during a practice drop, so now he always checked his parachute carefully.

He had his magic and his cheat all loaded—here on Origin, what they called his "Gift." But still, from his 28 years of life here, Kanata knew that even those who had been reborn here could still very much end up dead.

"Okay. Let's wipe out these terrorist scum."

"Hey, Kanata. Don't forgot, your mission is to rescue the president's kidnapped daughter."

"I know. Hey, do you think the pres will get mad if I ask his daughter for her number?"

"No comment. I will say—Hanna is only fifteen. She's half your age, old man."

"I'm still in my twenties, okay! I'm not old yet!" If his past life was added in, he was over forty.

"Whatever. You are cleared to jump, Gungnir."

"I really hate that codename." Kanata gave a sigh, and then leapt out of the helicopter, which was protected by optical camouflage created using light attribute magic.

When Kanata Kaito had been reborn on Origin, with his memories of Earth and incredible powers, he had been Kanata Smith. He certainly hadn't needed the god to leave him with the same first name, but it didn't take him long to adjust to everything.

Apart from the fusion of science and magic, Origin was a lot like Earth. It had the same number of continents, in similar shapes, and the international situation was similar too. All of this helped him quickly adapt.

While Kanata concealed his cheat power, trying to use it as little as possible, he couldn't hide the affinity for magic he had been gifted. So he had a bright and fun childhood as a magical prodigy. His parents were richer than his folks had been back on Earth, and they spoiled their little genius, buying him whatever he wanted. He was constantly the center of attention at school, and always had a girl on his arm through his teens.

It was like a dream come true. He couldn't have asked for a better second life. He might have had more difficulty with his studies at college, but he had expected to become pretty famous simply by working on his magical talents.

That had been the plan, anyway.

However, before he even hit twenty, he met *them*—the others who had been reborn here.

I know exactly who to blame for the fact I'm skydiving out a helicopter to attack a bunch of terrorists with an assault rifle and combat knife, Kanata thought.

That would be Hiroto Amemiya. He was a hero on this world, and the leader of the 100 reincarnated. Kanata only had one cheat, but Hiroto had multiple such abilities, so he was overwhelmingly powerful. He had been searching for others like himself, seeking to use his power for world peace or some crap like that. That guy definitely read too many comic books. *With great power comes great responsibility? Who says that outside of a movie?*

He wondered for a moment what was going on with that series back on Earth. The hero in question didn't even have his own movie here, as the big green guy was much more popular on Origin. Maybe because he defeated his magical enemies with nothing but raw strength? He heard one critic theorize it was some kind of pushback against the magic-dominated society.

As he mulled these things over, Kanata opened his parachute and cast the magic he had been preparing. He controlled heat and air, bending the light around himself to hide from the terrorists below, as in a heat haze.

"I hope that keeps them off my back—nope?!"

A few holes were instantly punched into his parachute. He was being fired on from the ground. Kanata promptly cut his parachute loose and dropped down into the ruins on the outskirts of the terrorists' base.

Kanata had a very low estimation of how things had gone, ever since he met up with Hiroto Amemiya and the others. Hiroto called their cheats "Gifts" from God and formed up a special ops team capable of operating internationally—a team of heroes.

They fought natural disasters, monsters, and undead, attended charity gatherings and signed photos for kids, and appeared on TV to give interviews.

Hiroto had skills, of course. Kanata admitted that. On Earth, Hiroto had been an unemployed slacker living at his parent's place; they eventually kicked him out, and he had been taking the ferry to a relative's factory for a live-in position when tragedy struck. But the way he acted here was nothing like a freeloader.

Kanata also didn't appreciate getting dragged into all this.

He had never wanted to go on an adventure or be in an action movie. And he wasn't one for sweating his ass off for the sake of folks he didn't know and would never meet. He just wanted everyone around him to sing his praises while he enjoyed the easy life.

What he found hard to believe was how many of his old school friends supported Hiroto Amemiya. All of them were overjoyed to become superheroes. They happily went west to help out with the next calamity, then east to cooperate on investigating criminal activity, and loved their lives in the limelight with all the media attention.

Most of them did, anyway. Some of them shied away from the media exposure. But they still supported Hiroto overall. They believed that it was safest for them to be in a single organization in order to prevent them from being misused by the nations of this new world. Having formed such an organization, it was then necessary to make their existence as widely known as possible, especially among the common people, in order to earn the trust of the people. With most of the reincarnated supporting Amemiya, it would take a lot of courage to speak out against him.

It also seemed that the governments of the world had known about Kanata's special ability even prior to his reunion with his old friends. They knew his face and name using the MP imprint that was the Origin version of fingerprints or retina scans on Earth. If he hadn't been reunited with Amemiya and the others, the government would have found him eventually, and he'd simply be working for them instead.

Amemiya's plan to gather in a single organization with a lot of media exposure would keep all information open, preventing the reborn from being used by clandestine or criminal organizations. The thing was, Kanata didn't care about any of that.

Once he was placed with 99 other reborn, his excellent magic proficiency, superlative talents, and high MP were quickly buried by the excellence of everyone else. He became something he had never been on this world: a regular person. In terms of magic, he only had a high level of fire attribute plus average wind magic. His cheat ability was also highly suited to work in the field. That was where his silly Gungnir codename came from . . .

"And why I'm out here, risking my life on secret missions for almost no pay!"

He opened his backup chute just before crashing into the

ground, using some wind magic to make sure it opened completely, lessening the impact. He tumbled and rolled, managing to pull off a safe landing. He recalled the map that he had memorized, and then muttered, "Light, heat, MP." With that, Kanata vanished.

Well, I just became see-through. With his field of vision enveloped in darkness, Kanata proceeded based on the map in his head.

Kanata realized that he had been detected during his parachute drop because the magic he had used had been caught by a sensor. *Terrorist scum! Where did they get the latest MP sensor technology from?* For that reason, he decided to turn invisible to the naked eye, heat sensors, and MP sensors. Now he was quietly closing in with his target.

That was Kanata's cheat ability.

The reason he hadn't used this on his descent was because the cheat abilities still took MP to use, and he wanted to conserve it for later. Using the ability in this way also blocked his own vision, meaning he could have easily crashed into something if he tried to land blind.

He finally reached the building where the terrorists were holding the president's daughter.

"Detect Biological Heat." Kanata turned off his cheat ability, getting back his eyesight, and then checked out the building with magic that detected the heat from living organisms. It also detected small wild animals in the vicinity, but he ignored those.

There were seven heat sources of adult proportions. Four of them were scrambling around. They had to be the ones who noticed Kanata's descent and fired at him. The remaining three were all close together. Two of them were low, suggesting they were sitting down. The third was high, standing up.

"There's no way two terrorist lookouts are sitting down on the job in front of a president's daughter who's bigger and heavier than me." Kanata had seen pictures of the girl—she was small and only 15 years old. Even if she were big for her age, the standing figure couldn't possibly be her.

"I'll start with the other four." He couldn't tell which of the sitting ones was Hanna, and so he decided to take out the moving targets first.

"Structures." With that murmur, he pointed his assault rifle at one of the heat sources and pulled the trigger. A gunshot rang out, but the shot that he fired passed through the walls of the building without leaving a sound or trace behind. He quickly followed up with the other three targets. The terrorists had realized that Kanata was using magic again and were hurrying to locate him—when all four of them suddenly stopped moving.

They had been shot, without any warning, by bullets that had suddenly appeared from the walls and floor. This was how Gungnir did business. Impediments meant nothing to him, allowing him to easily shoot the weak points on any target at any time.

"It's a little over-the-top. And what's the point of a codename if it connects to my ability?" Kanata sighed. "Structures, metal."

With that, Kanata started to move through the building, passing through the walls and floor. He gripped the enhanced resin hilt of his knife and rushed for the room with the three remaining people.

"Gungnir?!"

The big terrorist gave a shout, but Kanata quickly replied with his knife. Then he checked out the remaining two. One of them was a female terrorist, firing haphazardly at Kanata's back. Even here in Origin, where magic actually existed, a gun or knife was best for quick counterattacks, since magic took time to cast. Of course, the metal bullets just passed through Kanata and hit the large man's body.

"You're hot. What a shame," Kanata said. The white woman's face paled at the sight of her bullets having no effect, and then he killed her with his knife.

If the president's daughter weren't here, he thought bitterly, *I would have disarmed this sexy piece of terrorist ass in invincible mode and then fired off one . . . or two.* She was too hot to waste. The chance for stuff like that was one of the few good things about being sent to kill people.

"Wh-who are you?"

"Are you okay? I'm Gungnir, from Bravers. I'm here to rescue you." Hiding his inner thoughts, Kanata introduced himself like a gentleman.

Bravers was the name that had been given to the team of reborn that he belonged to after a certain incident. The full name was Hundred Bravers. A little too on the nose for Kanata's taste. *Thinking about it, that was also the time when we moved from only taking rescue and support missions to ones involving killing targets,* he thought. The incident in question had been the rampage of an experimental undead in a secret lab belonging to a European military state. Undead popped up frequently here on Origin, as animals and monsters were sometimes transformed by Magical Power; the team had dealt with such incidents before. But this particular case was something else.

First, there was the prophecy by Koya Endo. He was the Oracle who provided prophesies about the approach they should take. He made his prophecy as always, but it was a strange one. They were to stand, exposed and undefended, when the undead emerged from the lab. They were not to let on about their hostile intent. Then, once the undead dropped its guard, they were to all attack together and destroy it at once.

Kanata had thought it odd that they were expected to give a dangerous enemy such an opening. But when the events unfolded, the undead did indeed drop its guard, allowing them to eradicate it without any trouble. Kanata had really been confused about what was going on.

That's when things started to rapidly change.

It turned out that the Magical Power from that undead—or, more precisely, the human it had formerly been—was the source of all the latest medical products and treatments exported by that military. It was death attribute magic, something previously completely undiscovered. And Kanata and the Bravers had utterly obliterated the only known source of it, eradicating the undead down to the smallest scrap of flesh.

Of course, all such exports stopped. The new pharmaceuticals and magic items couldn't be produced anymore, and fighting erupted around the world. Every nation started to try to find—or even create—the second Death Mage, based on the data scavenged from the laboratory and the testimony collected from the handful of survivors.

Kanata and the others were repeatedly asked if they could use their Gifts to replicate death attribute magic. Koya, who should have been able to provide an answer in his position as Oracle, only said, "He was something that should never have existed in this world. What we did was the only way to save him," and then stoically held his peace on the matter.

Kanata figured Koya was soft, getting all emotionally attached to one experimental guinea pig. But then they investigated the illegal lab, as well as death magic, for themselves and realized just how completely broken that undead had been. If the undead hadn't simply let them kill it, they would've ended up dead themselves. At the very least, more than half of the reincarnated onsite would have been killed. After that, Kanata almost felt the same sympathy that Koya did, although he wasn't going to start attending church mass every week.

Achieving mastery of death attribute magic was close to achieving immortality. There were those in power who wished to obtain that for themselves, and those in the church who did not want to acknowledge such a possibility. The other test subjects saved by the single undead were placed under government protection for a while, but they eventually escaped and formed a violent terrorist organization called the Eight Guidance. Now they were a major thorn in the side of nations across the world. That had led to these terrorists kidnapping the president's daughter and Kanata being sent in to save her.

Huh? What's this walk down memory lane in aid of? In fact—
"Gwaah!" When Kanata snapped back to himself, he found himself spitting blood from his mouth.

He could barely speak. "How did . . . you know my weakness? You aren't . . . the pres's daughter, are you . . . "

One moment the president's daughter had been coming in for a hug, and the next her pointed hand was rammed deep into Kanata's solar plexus. That wasn't something the president's daughter should be able to do.

"It's me, Kanata." The girl replied as her appearance started to silently change. The white girl turned into an Asian woman in her later twenties.

"It's you, Metamor . . . but why?"

Kanata recognized her at once. It was Mari Shihoin, another of one the reborn and—he had thought—a member of Bravers. She had the cheat ability to transform into pretty much whatever she wanted. Mari's face was as placid as a mask, but her eyes were burning with hatred.

"I used these terrorists to kill you. The real president's daughter is currently being rescued, right now, somewhere else."

"To kill me? What did I ever do to you?!"

"This is revenge for my mother."

"Hey! Wait! You've got the wrong idea!" Kanata staggered backward, trying to put some distance between the two of them, but his body was shockingly unresponsive.

He burnt the wound she left, stopping the bleeding while he tried to find some path to survival. "I didn't kill her! Yes, okay, I couldn't save her, and in the end I'm the one who stopped her heart. But she was already missing everything from the neck up! Thanks to me, your mom lives on somewh—"

"If she was missing everything from the next up, tell me why her corneas currently reside in the head of a mafia boss?" she screamed. "You scum-sucking monster!" Mari reached for his head even as Kanata scrambled back across the floor on his butt.

This was bad news. Mari's Metamor was the perfect answer to Kanata's Gungnir. If he had been uninjured, he might have had a chance to escape, but that wasn't going to happen after all the damage he had taken.

"H-hold on! You think you can get away with this? You won't be able to hide it! Hiroto and his damn sense of justice won't allow it! Please, stop! I don't want to die yet! She was only the woman who gave birth to you on this world, anyway! Not even your real mom! Aren't we friends?!"

"No. We're not. You chopped up my mom and sold her for parts. I would never be your friend."

Kanata barely heard her say those words, and passed out before he could reply.

Kanata Smith, a member of the Hundred Bravers. On Earth, he had been called Kanata Kaito. He was discovered close to death, transported to a medical facility, and given every possible treatment to no avail. Three days later, he passed away. He had been taking part in a mission to rescue the daughter of a certain nation's president. It was presumed that a weakness of his Gift was somehow exploited to kill him. Kanata Smith was remembered as the first of the hundred heroes to fall, and his passing had a profound impact on at least ninety-eight of the remaining ninety-nine of Hiroto Amemiya's heroes.

Watching events on Origin unfold, Rodocolte gave a short sigh.

"That's the first one." Kanata Kaito was dead. His death would shake the reborn, who Hiroto Amemiya had done such an excellent job of bringing together. Some of them were now sure to leave his organization. It wouldn't be long before more of them started dying. Dozens, perhaps, if not more than half.

Rodocolte had done much to ensure that they wouldn't die easily, but he also hadn't made them invincible or immortal. The reborn could die, just like Kanata had. It certainly wasn't going to be only Hiroto Amamiya and Kanata Kaito who failed to live out their natural lifespans on Origin.

"Huh? Where am I . . . gah! Mari! That bitch! She really did kill me!" Kanata appeared in front of Rodocolte, shouting as soon as he awoke.

The other Hiroto had shared a few choice words—and screams—of his own when he showed up here from Origin, Rodocolte remembered.

"Hey! You're a god, right? Give me another chance! I wasn't even thirty! That's not much of a life!" Kanata Kaito was more practical than Hiroto, however. He immediately started to beg Rodocolte for another life.

Rodocolte didn't consider it all that short to say that over two lives he had lived for a total of more than forty years. Many died almost as soon as they were born, and others before they even got that far. Kanata had also killed people on Origin who were younger than thirty themselves, included the terrorists he killed right before his own death.

"Please! I'll do anything!"

"That isn't going to happen," Rodocolte responded. "Your third life has already been laid out for you." Just as Rodocolte had done with Hiroto, he told Kanata about Ramda and how he would be reborn there.

Kanata froze up in surprise for a moment, but then he looked sullen. "God, I know I asked for another chance, but can't you find a better world for it than that?"

"You don't like Ramda? It's a world of swords and magic.

I thought you all loved those. They have dragons and giants and dungeons with treasure. Princesses, beautiful elves, and dwarves. Unknown islands and continents. There's a demon king sealed away there, sure, but don't you find it tickles your desire for adventure?"

Rodocolte assumed that a (former) Japanese boy would jump all over this. Kanata Kaito did not look happy, however. In fact, the exact opposite expression was plastered all over his face, and Kanata was shaking his head.

"Hold on, hold on," Kanata said. "You're just twisting everything to make it sound good for you. What you're actually saying is this is a dangerous world filled with monsters that don't exist on Origin! I'm also not crazy enough to want to go on an adventure in real life." Yes, if he could get a look at some dragons or giants, Kanata might be interested. If asked if he wanted a bucket for treasure for free, he wouldn't have to think twice. However, if asked about actually fighting monsters, then he would say no. If asked to risk his life for the bucket, treasure or otherwise, the answer would, again, simply be no.

Those kinds of things were fun in a video game. Fun because you weren't actually having to struggle to do them, as far as Kanata was concerned. After all, he hadn't been pleased about risking his life fighting terrorists and criminals on Origin. Why would risking his life on some big, silly adventure be any more appealing?

"I don't need gods and demons. I've had my fill of the crazy stuff on Origin. I'm not interested in helping the world grow or any of that bull either. Boring! You should be asking Amemiya if you want help with stuff like that."

"Hmmm. You will get to take your experience and abilities over with you, though. With a little training, you'll quickly get stronger. You'll be pummeling dragons before you know it. Clearing dungeons will be a breeze."

"Still not interested," Kanata replied. "I had enough training montages on Origin, thanks." What he wanted was to live a laidback life of leisure, a golden spoon in his mouth, all the while everyone around him praising everything he did. A certain amount of hard work and study would still be required, sure, but he didn't want to have to work his butt off.

Rodocolte paused. "You could live like a king. Have a harem of women. How about that?"

"A king who doesn't have lightbulbs or the internet, right?" Kanata snapped back. "How much fun can one really have in a middle-ages fantasy world?"

Rodocolte thought some more. "They have magic items. You can replicate certain things to the same level as on Earth and Origin, I'm sure."

"Certain things. Not enough to heat or cool a room and have a hot shower every day. I'm not interested in a harem, either. I only need to ride each woman a few times and then I can move on. I get plenty of elves and cat girls and whatnot from games, too. Don't need real ones."

Kanata Kaito was far less interested in going to Ramda than Rodocolte had expected. Of course, Kanata had no say in the matter. There was no way for him to avoid being reborn there.

"Oh. Hold on. Mari will be reborn in Ramda too, right?" Kanata suddenly sounded a lot more interested—and that worried Rodocolte.

". . . Yes, that's right," the god confirmed.

"Perfect! This time, I'll be the one to kill her! I'm not going to drop my guard a second time. I'll avenge myself!"

Rodocolte shook his head. Letting them take their memories and personalities from their previous lives carried over their pain and hankering for revenge. That said, reincarnating them without either their memories or personality would screw them up mentally. And if he wiped them both, then there was hardly any point in doing all this in the first place.

It would have been hard for Rodocolte to pull a trick like removing the memories relating to Kanata's desire for revenge, too. He specialized in souls, not the mind. The two areas were related, but different in many ways. But the biggest problem was that this whole process had been set up when they all died on Earth: Rodocolte couldn't take the time now to start changing and erasing memories.

However, it still felt like things might work out. He was only dealing with one person, and he had an urgent problem to solve. A solution that would be easy to ask of someone brimming with violence like Kanata.

"Before you do that, I have something to ask of you."

"What is it, God? You can ask anything of me, the great Kanata, first of the Bravers to die! Anything that won't be a pain in my ass!"

"Actually, you weren't the first to die. That was Hiroto Amamiya," Rodocolte corrected him.

"Hiroto Amemiya? He's dead too?!"

"No, not him. Ama, not Ame. An easy mistake to make, trust me."

Kanata shook his head. "Not following you." He didn't have much recollection of Hiroto Amamiya. They had been in different classes at high school, and Hiroto was a wallflower who tucked himself away. "Hmmm, hold on. I did hear something about two people who turned down your offer for resurrection. And one of them had a name like Hiroto Amemiya. The guy's girl was pretty cut up about it."

Narumi Naruse. She had been popular, meaning Kanata remembered her even though they had been in different classes. On Origin, she had gotten close to Amemiya because she thought he was this Amamiya guy. Things had cooled off between them when she found out her mistake, but in the end, they dated and got married. Thinking over that now, he realized that this "guy with a similar name" from the rumors must be the Hiroto Amamiya Rodocolte was now talking about.

"Allow me to provide you with everything you need to know," Rodocolte continued.

"No, I don't need any more clutter—uwaaah! He was that undead we killed?! God!"

"You need something?"

"I'm not talking to you!"

Kanata got another infodump from Rodocolte, discovering in the process that the user of death attribute magic on Origin had been Hiroto Amamiya. When he also learned that the guy was already down on Ramda, he let out a shriek. Forget taking revenge for his own murder—he was going to be the one getting revenged on if he went down there!

"I knew it! Cancel this bullshit! I can't beat that monster alone! At least wait for some of the others to die and get here!"

That undead was so powerful that Kanata paled at the thought of having to fight him. First, he could throw up barriers that cancelled magic and physical attacks while still being able to launch his own attacks. There was none of the comic book crap about having to open the barrier when he attacked. He also surrounded himself with poison, bacteria, and mold at all times, a single touch of which meant death. The only way to get close to the guy would be to put on a freaking spacesuit.

If that was all, then Kanata could use his cheat ability to pass through the barrier. But it wasn't the least of it. The security guards trying to flee had suddenly gone crazy, gouging their own eyes out while they laughed their heads off. One of the research assistants had turned into a mummy on the spot, and a female researcher had gotten eaten inside out by bugs as she begged for her life. The monsters had all sorts of bizarre ways to attack. Kanata's strength was useless if he couldn't even name what he needed to pass through. The guy was basically the ultimate enemy of life itself.

However, there were also records that indicated that he helped the other test subjects in the facility escape. He had kicked down the door to where they were being held, destroyed the control devices embedded into them, and led them out. Considering the way it looked like he wanted Bravers to kill him, you could make an argument that the undead had retained some measure of rationality.

Rodocolte spoke. "I want you to find this Hiroto Amamiya—on Ramda, he is called Vandal—and kill him."

"I'm telling you, I can't!"

"He's much weaker now than he was in that undead form. You should be able to take him alone."

". . . Seriously?"

Rodocolte nodded, and proceeded to share the rest of the information he had on Vandal. However, he couldn't reveal the existence of the reincarnation system to a mortal being, meaning he also held his tongue concerning Vandal's ability to crush souls. Rodocolte simply said he needed Vandal dead because he didn't want Kanata and the other resurrected getting wiped out by him. *And if he hears about maybe getting soul-crushed, he'll probably get all scared again,* Rodocolte thought.

On the other hand, Kanata—who still didn't have the full picture but did have plenty of it—was starting to think that Rodocolte was exceptionally dumb for a divine being.

Why, for example, did the god try to curse Vandal or force him to commit suicide? How convoluted and pointless. After Amamiya died on Origin, the god should have tried to win him over to his side. That's what Kanata would have done. He could have promised to let him be reborn in a rich family, or given him cheat abilities, or promised him the harem that he had proposed to Kanata. There had to be all sorts of better ways to do it.

Putting that aside, though, *fine,* Kanata thought. At least he understood the assignment. He still wasn't keen on it, and he felt a little sorry for Vandal. At the same time, however, he considered this an opportunity.

"Hey. I'm happy to kill this Vandal guy, but I have two conditions."

"Conditions?"

"You bet I've got conditions. For wiping the butt of a god? You bet!"

"This is also about protecting yourself, is it not?"

"Hey, I could easily beg him for my life," Kanata chirped back. "I'd lick his boots if I had to. Tell him I didn't know what was going on. That I was only doing what Hiroto Amemiya and Koya Endo told me to do. Given him all the information I know and beg him to save my life. If I pushed it hard enough, he'd probably forgive me. He seems pretty kind." Even as an undead, he had tried to save the others from being experimented on, after all.

Rodocolte stayed quiet for a while and then prompted Kanata to continue. "What conditions?"

"First, a reward. If I lop off this Vandal's head, I want you to put me into a world, either Earth or one like it, without any magic or monsters or fantasy bullshit. Just memories and personality intact. Not Origin, either. I want to belong to a rich family, with all the good stuff in life. You can make me handsome too."

"You want a fourth life? But you will have to die on Ramda for that to happen."

"So I have to die, so what? I'll kill myself the moment Vandal is dead." *I'm not interested in another backwater world. As soon as I've done this task, I'll off myself, and head on over to an Earth-like world to live it up in fun and games until I die. Let the others crawl through the muck in a world of crap.*

Rodocolte knew exactly what Kanata was thinking, of course. Among the 100, Rodocolte knew that Kanata hadn't done much to improve things on Origin, meaning he probably wouldn't have much effect on Ramda either. All he had going for him was his combat abilities, making him the perfect card to spend and discard on resolving this particular issue. Furthermore, the reward that Kanata was asking for was something Rodocolte could easily realize.

"Very well. I can promise such a reward. What is your second condition?"

"I need proper backup, of course. First, that means putting me in Ramda in an adult body."

"Rather than being reborn normally?"

"Of course, rather than that. How many years were you planning to wait for me to get this job done?"

Kanata was skilled at man-on-man combat, but that wouldn't matter in the body of a baby or child. It could take a decade, fifteen, even twenty years before he could move around and get away from his parents enough to go off on a murder mission. If he started out as an adult, he would also have an advantage over Vandal, who was still a child. He wouldn't have any parents looking over his shoulder, either. But most of all, Kanata wanted to avoid having to live for two decades on some crappy fantasy mudball.

"Very well. It will take a little of my strength, but it isn't impossible." Rodocolte wasn't a fan of this idea, but there also didn't seem to be much choice.

"I'm also going to need resistance to poison, sickness, and this death attribute magic. And if I do get killed, I need you to collect my soul at once, so I don't get turned into undead."

"The souls of all of you resurrected are set up to return to me upon death," Rodocolte replied. "Hiroto Amamiya turning into that undead was an exception due to his own magic. I'll also make it so that you receive skills relating to poison, sickness, and death attribute magic, as you asked. But resistance to death magic isn't normally a skill humans can learn, so the highest you'll be able to get is Level 5."

"What do you mean, skills?"

"They have skills and Jobs on Ramda and stats you can check to see them."

"What? That sounds like a video game! Maybe they aren't making any progress because they're too busy playing around with stats?"

"Anything else you require?"

"Combat gear, for sure. A gun and a knife—"

"Hold on. It isn't possible for you to bring anything that doesn't exist on Ramda."

"Seriously? Not even, you know, a sniper rifle?"

"Why would you think that might be okay, of all things?"

"Bah!" Kanata had been hoping to play this mission on easy mode with a long-range kill. He clicked his tongue.

But Rodocolte could not bend on this matter. If such a thing were possible, he would have been sending all sorts of things from other worlds into Ramda already. The power he commanded simply didn't allow for it.

In the end, Rodocolte was the Reincarnation God. Nothing more.

"You can at least give me some clothing? You aren't asking me to be reborn naked, are you?"

". . . Everyone is normally born naked. But fine, I should be able to make some adjustments. I'll also tweak your destiny so that you'll encounter Vandal—"

"Hold it! You'll need to adjust that too. Can't you make it like, a radar or something? I don't want to bump into him when I'm not ready or not expecting it!"

"Okay." Rodocolte agreed to this too, although the growing list of demands was starting to anger him. At least that last adjustment was easy to make. "I'll give you a radar that can search out powerful death attribute magic and a fate that will lead you to encounter him. That should do it."

"Great. That's all I needed."

So that was finally the end of the laundry list.

"In that case, I will send you to Ramda at once. Once you are alive, you should register at the adventurers' guild and the other guilds, take a Job, level it up to improve your stats, and learn how to use your skills."

"Like I said, I'm not going down there to play games. I'm

gonna kill him quickly, without any of that stuff."

And with that, Kanata was off into his next life.

Standing before the villagers of the Second Pioneer Village, Vandal started to cook the ingredients he had gathered. He felt like he was making a cooking video to post online.

"First, you need some goblin meat and some gobgrass. For the meat, you can use breast, thigh, or even heart. You'll need at least one goblin's worth. Ah, the liver works too. For the gobgrass, you'll want about half the weight of the goblin meat." Vandal pointed at the piles of goblin meat and gobgrass that he had prepared.

Some of the villagers responded with unpleasant groans. That response was to be expected. While the meat of humanoid monsters like orcs was regularly consumed here on Ramda, goblins and gobgrass were treated as lower than wild beasts or even waste matter.

"Next," Vandal continued, "you need to crush the gobgrass. The juices that will spurt out smell bad and will stain your clothing, so try to keep them under control. I've prepared a special pestle to use exclusively with gobgrass." He had made the pestle in the night, using Golem Creation. He carried out from where it had been lurking in the shadows, causing gaps of surprise.

The reaction was actually to the fact that this massive pestle, which even an adult would have trouble carrying alone, had been picked up and carried so easily by a child. Vandal thought it was that his pestle craftsmanship was just so good.

He proceeded to crush the gobgrass down, with the stinking juices collecting in a trough at the bottom.

"Then we cut the goblin meat into suitable pieces. I don't have a knife with me, so I'll be using my claws, but they are very clean. You have nothing to worry about." With that, he briskly chopped up the meat. More sounds of surprise. "Once the meat is all chopped, we put the meat and juice into a barrel. At this point, make sure all the meat is submerged in the juices. Once that's done, put on the lid, leave it for three days, and it's ready. I have one here that I made earlier."

"Huh? Earlier—when?" One of the villagers was a little too quick on the mark.

"It must have been a divine messenger," Vandal replied. He didn't want to reveal that he had used Elapse Time, so he just made something up. "Here is some finished gobgob. Please, give it a try."

Vandal opened the second barrel, taking out some of the now purple meaty substance and serving it on plates.

The villagers didn't look especially excited by it. Again, a very normal reaction to purple meat.

"This is . . . really edible, is it?" The village chief stared at his plate.

"I promise you it is," Vandal responded. "Shall I eat it with you?"

"No, that's fine! I'll try it!" The chief firmed up his resolve and grabbed some gobgob, closing his eyes tight and taking a bite. After he started chewing, however, his screwed-up face gradually started to relax. "This . . . isn't delicious, by any means, but it's also not disgusting. It doesn't smell bad, either." This three-star review by the chief was enough to get more of the villagers to timidly reach out and put some gobgob in their own mouths.

"Oh, he's right! This is at least edible!"

"Much better than the tree bark dumplings and grass soup we had last winter!"

"Yeah, much better!"

They've had quite the diet, Vandal mused. He felt a rush of sympathy at them for actually finding gobgob more than palatable. During the harsh winter months, they had been eating disgusting food with no nutritional value, purely to stave off their hunger.

"It's much better than eating regular goblin!" It sounded like some of them had tried that as well, probably out of sheer desperation. If a slave merchant had come along, they may have sold off their children rather than let them starve. But now, they had found a way to use goblin meat, which they would otherwise throw away, and gobgrass to make rations that last. Nutritionally speaking, it was still meat, so loads better than tree bark. Of course, they were going to be overjoyed.

"Okay! If you're willing to make a shrine to Vida, I will provide the pestle and twenty wooden barrels. I'll also throw in some salt. If you apply it to the meat before putting it into the juice, you'll find it tastes a lot better. What do you say?"

"Wonderful! I'll convert to the Goddess Vida at once!"

"No," Vandal quickly said. "No need to convert—"

"You're even giving us precious salt! Thank you so much!"

"We didn't build a shrine out of respect to the duke and the priest who does the rounds here, but we have been praying to Vida. It seems our prayers were heard!"

Vandal felt so bad for these people that he decided to give

them the Talosheim sea salt he had brought along in case he needed to pay an entry toll. He still had the rock salt, plus some coin from the bandits, so it should work out.

He decided to ask the villagers what they meant about praying to Vida. As it turned out, back in the Saulon Domain, most worshipped Vida rather than Alda. Looking at the residents of the reclamation villages, while most were humans and there were no dark elves, there was a fair number of beastmen and giantlings. But in the Duke Heartner domain that welcomed them in, most of the nobles including the duke worshipped Alda and his dependent gods, meaning it was those temples that flourished. When setting up the pioneer villages, the soldiers had erected shrines to Alda, not to mention the priest who did the rounds belonged to the Alda faith. Worship of Vida wasn't forbidden, but there was pressure not to put up shrines to Vida and the other gods like they had back home.

I don't like to hear that. It weighed Vandal down a little, but he was most concerned about Princess Lebia and the other refugees from Talosheim, including Borkz's daughter. If Alda held strong in this domain, it might have been difficult for them to carve out lives for themselves. *I'm still concerned about these villages. I guess I'll leave Lemures around them and bury some Stone Golems at strategic points. If I carve a holy Vida symbol into their chests, the villagers should hopefully see them as allies.* He was sure everything would be fine.

"We finally caught up with you!"

Vandal turned to see Kasim, his party, and the priest all rushing over as he finished placing the horde of Lemures he had been making the past few days. For some reason, they had come all the way from the Seventh to find him here.

"I didn't expect you to actually visit all of the villages!"

"Come back to the Seventh, will you? Everyone is worried!" Fester exclaimed.

"We set out for the Fifth the day after you flew off with Kain," Kasim explained. They wanted to make sure their fellow refugees from the Saulon Domain and the one who had saved their lives were okay. Joined by the Alda priest, the four of them rushed to the Fifth. They found Kain and the other villagers there, planning to erect the shrine to Vida. "They told us how you flew off, so we've been chasing after you ever since! Really, what are you?! I can't believe all the stuff you can do!"

"The villagers were worried you and Kain might have fallen out the sky, so we ended up going around every other village to find you," Fester continued.

"And you've been working all sorts of miracles everywhere you go, by the sound of it! It sounds like we've been chasing a saint rather than a flying child! Right, Father?"

"Exactly right." The priest of Divina Alda, mopping the sweat from his brow with a sleeve, had a strange look on his face. It felt more . . . human than his fake smile, at least. "Before, I suggested we might work together. But it seems more prudent to suggest that you give me instruction in your arts. How have you cured entire villages? Healed the scars from burns? Dug a well in mere moments? Some speak of receiving holy waters from your hands, freeing them from a multitude of ailments. Please, share your knowledge with us!"

Hearing all of this, Vandal was faced with exactly how impressive his deeds were, at least to these people. Turning the eyedrops from his claws into holy water was gilding the lily a little, but still.

Vandal also wasn't sure how to respond. He couldn't fob off a real priest with a line about a divine messenger, but then he also didn't feel like telling the truth. He decided to share a partial truth.

"I've got a few unique skills, that's all."

"Unique skills?" the priest exclaimed. "So that's it!"

In this world, there were unique skills, such as Vandal's own God Smiter. These superpowers and special talents were incredibly rare. Around one in ten thousand people might have one.

The priest and Kasim were quick to accept that everything Vandal had done was thanks to these unique skills. "What kind of skills do you have?!" the priest asked, eyes agog, body leaning forward.

Vandal shook his head. "I'm planning on making my living as an adventurer. I can't afford to share that information."

"Please, don't be like that! It will be between me, you, and God!"

"No, Father!" Kasim and the others stepped in. "Adventurers live and die by what they can do. It's not polite to pry too much about skills."

"That's right! I'd like to know too, but Vandal has done so much for us. We can't repay that by twisting his arm for personal information."

As adventurers themselves, Kasim and his party understood that the information displayed on a person's status showed both their strengths and weaknesses. It was one thing if someone decided to share that information themselves, quite another to force them to reveal it. It was akin to asking someone to expose their greatest weaknesses. Vandal had shared his plans to become an adventurer in the future, meaning the same thing applied to him.

"Yes, of course. My apologies." The priest snapped out of it, thanks to Kasim, and backed down.

"No need. Your understanding is all I ask."

"If you are capable of such feats, though, why limit yourself to just being an adventurer?" the priest asked. "Surely you could become a great man of the cloth yourself!"

Vandal wasn't sure what to make of this suggestion. He couldn't imagine that a backwater priest like this guy had connections that could help him.

"Maybe, but I'm still young. I want to expand my horizons as an adventurer and build up some experience before I decide to do something like that." If he started serving a noble or merchant, it would make it harder for him to achieve his goal of acquiring his own noble rank. It would also make it hard to quit even if he no longer needed the position. Vandal wanted to avoid such complexities.

"I see. Expanding your horizons is important. You've got a good head on those shoulders, for one so young."

"Yeah, he's certainly thinking more about his future than Fester," Kasim said.

"Hey! Why are you dragging me into this?!"

With that, they headed back to the Seventh Reclamation Village. There was a spring in Vandal's step because he hadn't told a single lie. Death attribute magic was, after all, also a skill.

Kanata Kaito, reborn into Ramda, took a moment to enjoy the sudden resurgence of his corporeal form and the sense of satisfaction it elicited. His limbs had felt worthless in that dream-like dead state, but now they surged with strength, while a vital heart beat healthily in his chest. He let out a whoop of joy as soon as he opened his eyes, quickly followed by a less jolly whoop.

"God damn it, I knew it! Naked!"

He quickly composed himself, however. He might not have desired it, but he had received military training. He knew how important it was to stay composed in unfamiliar territory.

Of course, a better man would have been composed from the start.

In any case, Kanata checked his surroundings. From the height of the sun, it looked to be just before noon. There was low scrub and grass growing around him. It looked like some sort of empty plain, with no dangerous living creatures—human or otherwise—anywhere to be seen.

"They call us 'mankind' here," Kanata recalled from the brain download he had been subjected to. "And there are intelligent races other than humans. Seriously, this place is a freaking video game!"

With that, he looked himself over. He didn't exactly have a mirror handy, so there he had to forgo a close inspection. Apart from the absence of the gaping chest wound, however, everything looked as tucked and toned as his body had been on Origin right before his death. Even his moles were where he left them.

And as he had previously shouted about so enthusiastically, he was also standing there with a body but nothing else.

When he looked around, however, he did spot something.

A scattering of white bones, and some scattered packs of belongings.

"I guess this is what His Holiness meant when he said he'd make it work." It didn't seem very hygienic, but Kanata also wasn't planning on fashioning clothing from plants, grabbing a big stick, and trying to kill Vandal like some primitive.

He searched through the belongings. He found some old but serviceable clothing and one rusty knife. There were also some silver and copper coins. Their original owner had clearly been killed by a beast or some other mindless creature.

"Wow, this stuff chafes. They don't have cotton here? Hopefully it's not covered in germs. Anyway, time to start hunting down this Vandal character—"

"This message has been set up to play automatically once you arrive on Ramda," Rodocolte's voice suddenly rang out.

"Ack! What the hell?!" Kanata leapt in surprise, grabbing the knife and darting around, but there was no sign of the god. Then he grinned sheepishly when he realized the voice was coming from inside his own head. "Some kind of game tutorial, is it?"

"First, collect the clothing and some money to get you started from the corpse on the ground nearby—"

"Yep, done that."

The message from Rodocolte sounded pre-recorded. It didn't answer his questions and didn't change what it said based on his actions.

"Next, you need to check your status. Just think about it and it will appear for you."

"Status, huh." He still didn't like the feeling of having been turned into a video game character, but he did as he was told and opened his status.

Name: Kanata Kaito
Race: Mankind
Age: 29
Alias: None
Job: None
Level: 0
Job History: None
Status
Vitality: 650
Magical Power: 42000
Strength: 95
Agility: 157
Muscle: 204
Intellect: 270
——Passive Skills

[Resist Poison: Level 10] [Resist Death Attribute: Level 5] [Resist Fire Attribute: Level 4]

[Muscle Enhancement: Level 5] [Magical Power Enhancement: Level 5] [Spiritual Pollution: Level 5]

——Active Skills

[Fire Attribute Magic: Level 8] [Wind Attribute Magic: Level 4] [Magic Control: Level 5]

[Bow Proficiency: Level 5] [Dagger Proficiency: Level 5] [Thrown Projectile Proficiency: Level 5] [Brawling Proficiency: Level 5]

[Cooperation: Level 5] [Survival: Level 3] [Sneaking Steps:

Level 4] [Horse Riding: Level 6]

[Lifesaving: Level 4] [Discretionary Active Skills: Level 5]

——Unique Skill

[Gungnir: Level 10] [Target Radar: Holder of Death Attribute MP Over One Hundred Million] [Blessing of the Reincarnation God]

". . . Okay. So, this is me." He hadn't had his own strengths, skills, and experiences written out like this since his last school report card.

He looked over his status, appraising his situation. His Job and Job History both showed "None," painting him as a bit of a freeloader, but he liked that the Alias space was also blank. Regarding his stats, he didn't really have context for them. His Magical Power looked pretty good, but he had no idea about anything else. Things like Strength and Agility had never been turned into numbers on Origin. It had been the same as on Earth; strength was measured by how fast you could run 100 meters, how many pushups you could do, and the weight of the dumbbells you could lift. His MP was the same as when he had got that tested on Origin, though, so he presumed the other numbers were in the same ballpark as his previous body.

In terms of skills, the Resist Poison and Resist Death Attribute were clearly the things he had specifically asked for. But he wasn't sure about the "Active Skills."

"The magical ones, I think I get it. But Bow Proficiency? Horse Riding? I've never used a bow or ridden a horse! The Dagger Proficiency and Brawling Proficiency must come from all my knife work and military combat training. No idea what Discretionary Active Skills could be, though."

Another message from Rodocolte sounded. "Your proficiency with things that don't exist on Ramda, such as guns and motorized vehicles, have been turned into equivalent skills: Bow Proficiency and Horse Riding. The remainder fit into Discretionary Active Skills. You can assign them as and when you need them."

"Suppose that's better than a bunch of useless skills," Kanata mused. But he had trained a lot to gain his skills with guns, vehicles, helicopters, and boats. He wasn't all that pleased about those abilities getting swapped out. "I need to kill Vandal ASAP and get back to a comfortable world like Earth."

He only needed this junk until he finished what he came here to do. He had his unique skills, Gungnir and Target Radar. Surely the task wouldn't take long if he used them. He wasn't sure if it would do him any good, but he had the Blessing of the Reincarnation God as well.

"Okay, let's get this radar party started! Concentrate on what I want to use, right?"

It worked at once. Kanata saw inside his head both which direction Vandal was in relation to him and the distance to get there. It wasn't even that far away. If he had a helicopter, maybe a day. Same with a car if he went fast—

". . . No helicopters or cars here, huh. I don't fancy that on foot. Maybe I can steal a horse? I know, I said I wanted to be careful, but you didn't have to drop me in quite so far away, did you?"

Kanata frowned as he faced his limited prospects for getting around. Wind magic might allow him to fly, but his MP wouldn't allow him to cover that much distance. If he encountered any hostiles while flying around, he would also have limited means of attack. He was missing his firearms already.

"Although you have skills," Rodocolte's voice continued, "your combat abilities will not be all that high compared to those on Ramda who make a living from battle. You should start by going to a town, registering at an adventurers' guild, getting a Job, gathering equipment, and learning about battle techs."

"Like I said," Kanata replied pointlessly, shaking his head in annoyance, "I didn't come here to play a video game." There was one part of the message he agreed with, though—gathering equipment. This job was clearly going to take more than just a few days, so he needed food and supplies.

"If you walk directly east from the location of your resurrection, you will find a road. That will lead you to anything else you need."

"Now that's a direction I'll happily follow."

He wasn't planning on eating grass while hunting for game out here, either. Kanata did as he was told—for once—and started east.

Before long, he heard screams on the air.

He dashed forward to find the road. He saw a bunch of ruffians attacking a carriage.

"Hanna! Hanna!"

"Father, run!"

"You there! If you value the life of your master's daughter, throw down all your weapons!"

It looked like the bandits had taken a merchant's daughter hostage and were trying to get his guards to drop their weapons.

"Isn't this all delightfully clichéd."

Kanata could tell that Rodocolte was spoon-feeding him directions to the town, a means to travel there, and some food to eat along the way. Reading the situation in an instant, he started to chant some magic.

"The girl and everything the humans are wearing. Great Conflagration!"

Raging flames erupted from a five-pointed star in front of Kanata, swallowing up the bandits and their hostage.

"Gyaaaaaaaah!"

"Eeeeeep!"

"H-Hanna!"

There were the screams of the burning bandits, and then the girl and the merchant.

"Huh? It isn't hot?"

Even though she was surrounded by flames, the girl wasn't taking any damage. Neither her clothes nor the clothes of the bandits were even singed. The only things burning were the bandits' bodies.

"Using Gungnir, feels just as good as it did on Origin," Kanata said brightly. This was the cheat ability that Rodocolte had given him: the ability to make anything selectively transparent. For anything he selected, physical matter, magic, and all forms of energy would pass right through. Using it was simple. He just had to speak the names of whatever it was he wanted to affect.

On Origin, before he died, he had used it to pass his shots through the walls to snipe terrorists and let enemy bullets and weapons pass through his body, making him close to invincible. In this instance, he had selected the girl and the clothes everyone was wearing, leaving them unaffected by the flames of Great Conflagration, while the bandits' bodies swiftly burned away.

The wider the range he used Gungnir across, the more MP it cost him. With his 42 thousand MP, he could still use it effectively so long as he didn't go completely off the chain.

It had its weak points, too. Gungnir allowed him to attack while ignoring enemy defenses and avoid enemy attacks. However, by watching what Kanata did, it was possible to work out how to attack him. If he set bullets or knives to transparent, then he couldn't use guns or knives himself. If he set light, he could become invisible, but that also meant his eyes couldn't see light, blinding him. If he set heat, his body would rapidly cool. And if he set human bodies, then he wouldn't be able to touch those bodies.

As a result, in moments like the one when he saved the "captured" president's daughter, it would always be possible to attack and hit him hand-to-hand. *That's what Metamor used to attack me, after all. Her own hand.*

She had exploited his weakness. He would have to be more careful when he stepped into close combat in the future.

"Ah! It's like a miracle! Hanna, Hanna!"

"Father!"

"Thank you so much for saving my daughter!"

The happy calls from the merchant snapped Kanata back from unpleasant memories of his former life.

"Can you tell me," Kanata asked casually. "Which way to the nearest town?"

He also realized they were speaking Japanese. The merchant seemed a little puzzled by his attitude and perhaps by his not sharing his name, but he still answered.

"A town? The closest is Tearcity, in that direction down this road."

"That way? Just keep going? No turns or anything?"

"A few small ones, along the way, but just keep to the main road. I'm sorry, are you lost?"

"Nope. Not anymore. I've got transport, funds, food, and equipment now."

"What do you mean—"

"I guess we start here. Man." A dull impact hit the merchant.

"Urk . . . nggh!"

Before either of them understood what was happening, his beloved daughter opened her eyes wide, blood exploding from her mouth.

"Ha . . . Hanna!" His daughter, whom he had been holding in his arms, suddenly had a rusty knife buried deep in her chest.

"Wow, that just slid right in there. Thanks to these so-called skills, I take it?" Kanata just watched nonchalantly as the girl twitched, eyes wide in disbelief, while her father cried out in agony.

"Hannaaaa!"

"What are you doing?!"

This shout came from two adventurers who were farther down the road. They pointed their weapons in his direction, shocked at the turn of events.

"What am I . . . ?" Kanata sighed. "Well, I guess it's because her name is Hanna. Hah. The same name as the president's daughter Mari disguised herself as. Not a name I like anymore. I guess that dumb god set this up, too? A way for me to blow off some steam. Wrong place, wrong time! Hahaha, sorry!" His voice was almost sing-song.

"What are you talking about?!" One of the adventurers seemed terrified by this string of babble from Kanata.

The other seemed to have decided to simply treat him as a hostile. "Die, you crazy bastard!"

The adventurer thrust forward with his spear, but Kanata dodged it as economically as possible and easily zipped in close to his target.

"Do I even need to bother? But just in case, weapons and armor."

"Wha—gaaah?!"

The biggest piece of bad luck faced by these two poor adventurers was that Kanata's military-trained Brawling Proficiency skill level was about the same as a Grade C adventurer. These two were Grade D and Grade E, meaning they couldn't overcome such a gap.

To add insult to injury, Kanata was still making full use of Gungnir even in this one-sided encounter. This allowed him to slip through the weapons the adventurers attempted to attack him with. Meanwhile, his own attacks went straight through their armor and directly into their bodies once his fists and feet got within range. They didn't stand a chance.

Mere moments later, both adventurers were on the ground, eyes rolled back in their heads.

"Even if her name hadn't been Hanna, the only difference is I would have raped her before killing her," Kanata said to the merchant. "Don't blame yourself, thinking you caused all this by choosing that name."

The man was completely out of it, clutching his dead daughter with the knife still lodged in her lungs. Of course, the merchant wasn't thinking anything of the sort.

"D-do you think you can get away with this?!" the merchant howled. "One day, one day, you will face judgement!"

"Seriously, my dude, what are you getting so worked up for?" Kanata sighed. "You're an NPC in a video game world. It'll be fine. His Holiness Rodocolte will pump you back out before you even know it. That's what's going to happen to me, long before anyone gets a chance to judge me for anything I do here."

Kanata laughed off the sadness and anger the man felt at losing his daughter and then repeated the same thing he did to the bandits, burning away their bodies.

"I've never handled a horse before, but I do have the skill. Should be fine." Kanata loaded up the wagon with the items and equipment from the merchant and the adventurers. Then he climbed onto the driver's seat and set off for the town. In his belt, he tucked the knife he had taken from the merchant, which was decorated with some kind of lightning design on the handle, maybe for good luck.

This was the greatest mistake that Rodocolte had made: he hadn't vetted the souls of the resurrected.

Yes, Rodocolte had removed the terrorists themselves from the pool souls killed in the ferry explosion. But he had only asked the remaining passengers and crew if they wanted to take part. He hadn't examined them and actively made selections. Personality, proclivities, mental fortitude, and world view—he hadn't considered any of these things whatsoever. Any attempt to determine if the individual had been a bad person at the time of their death on Earth had been perfunctory at best.

Despite all that, he proceeded to subject them to serious mental trauma, with plans of having them die and be reborn multiple times in completely different worlds. As a result, there were some like Hiroto Amemiya, who had achieved great things on Origin. But there were also those like Kanata. Rodocolte hadn't expected Kanata to be quite so extreme in his methods, but he was already on Ramda. The god could no longer do anything to restrict or control him; his only way to even get in touch was with unreliable Oracles.

"This wasn't exactly my intention when I sent him down there," Rodocolte murmured. "But . . . I suppose it's only a minor issue."

Considering the abilities Kanata Kaito had at his disposal, he wasn't close to the scale of disaster that Vandal could wreak. Even counting innocent bystanders and miscellaneous crimes he might commit along the way, Kanata's death count likely wouldn't exceed one thousand. That wasn't a number that was going to affect the fabric of the world itself.

"Still, he really doesn't plan to get a Job, or raise his level, or learn any battle techs? Ramda might be backward in terms of culture and civilization, but the average fighting strength of each individual is much higher than on Earth or Origin . . ."

Flot had never been lucky, but he always thought he had something to offer. Concerning his latest plan, he had been hoping to finally get a little of that luck he always missed out on. He had been convinced that, with a sprinkling of luck, everything would go smoothly, and he would obtain his reward—a position as a Magician serving the new Duke Heartner.

So much for that dream! Who the hell is this brat?! Flot was walking with Kasim, his party, and Vandal, back toward the Seventh Pioneer Village, but Vandal was the one he was constantly looking at.

The house of Duke Heartner was currently embroiled in a fairly common occurrence: family feuding. The current duke was still clinging to power, but he was sick, laid up in bed, and unable to conduct his duties. He had two sons, both with an eye to succeed him.

The first was Lucas, the duke's oldest son but the product of union with a concubine. He was brave and skilled in military matters, the current captain of the knights, and had unshakable support from the duke's army.

The second son was Belton, mothered by the duke's actual wife. He was skilled in politics, with supporters among the ministers and his connections in the capital, meaning he could likely bring great wealth to the Duke Heartner domain in the future.

Normally, the post of duke would fall to Belton, as he was the son of the duke's wife. Meanwhile, Lucas would use his military chops for the sake of the duke's army, which held a great importance now that their territory was on the frontlines of the war with the Amidd Empire.

However, the two brothers did not see things that way.

Belton believed that they needed to shore up their defenses against the Amidd Empire, then focus on internal politics. First and foremost, that meant protecting their lands from the threat of invasion. One way he sought to achieve this was with his refugee policies. These interlopers were a significant reason for unrest, and so he had created the "pioneer" project as a plan to simply abandon the refugees, packing them off to the boonies and greatly reducing their numbers in the cities. He would then send residents who failed in their development efforts to the slave mines to produce metallic resources or transfer them to bolster security personnel.

On the other hand, there was Lucas, the eldest. He wanted to apply military might to the noble goal of taking back the Saulon Domain, piercing the shield of the Amidd Empire, and bringing glory to the Heartner Domain. The refugees were certainly a cause of unrest, but he planned to conscript them as low-ranking cannon fodder. He would pour money into the armed forces, increasing their size. Soldiers and adventurers would handle keeping the peace domestically.

The two ideas were directly opposed, but both brothers had also given them a lot of thought and believed them to be the best for their domain. Thus, they fought. Supporters flocked to one brother or the other, in pursuit of the wealth they hoped to receive if their chosen side won out.

Flot was at the bottom of the barrel of the Lucas faction. He had failed to secure any kind of position for himself in the magicians' guild and was on the brink of spending his days forgotten in petty bureaucracy when a knight from the Lucas faction had taken notice. The man had been looking for someone to infiltrate the reclamation villages by pretending to be a priest of Alda.

The reclamation project had originally been a way to get rid of the refugees. Unexpectedly, however, it was going pretty well. One of the villages had failed, but the remaining six—with a little variance in overall wealth—looked to last longer than five years.

However, the plan had been predicated on its failure. If it were to succeed, the Belton faction would get more ammunition, fostering further talk of how only the trueborn son was suitable to rule, especially compared to his roughrider brother. It wasn't going to decide the fate of the feud, but the Lucas faction wanted Belton to have as few successes as possible under his belt and as many failures.

That was where Flot and some others came in. He had become a traveling priest of Divine Alda a few years previously, and now he moved between the villages—working separately from other Lucas faction spies, which included a merchant—to obtain information and pass it back to his masters.

It hadn't been hard to earn the trust of the villagers. Priests didn't have a system like the adventurers' guild cards, and there were plenty of wandering priests in the world. Even large-scale shrines didn't keep track of them. High priests might have ranks and titles, but there was nothing like that lower down the ladder, and if a priest didn't work at a shrine, there would be no record of them at all.

At its most extreme, anyone could call themselves a priest if they dressed the part, carried some scriptures, and memorized a few lines to interject at opportune times. Proper manners and a dose of magic, not even necessarily light or life magic, and the ruse was set.

There was such a thing as a Clergy skill on Ramda, but that was mainly held by individuals with certain abilities like performing ritual purifications or giving sermons. It was easier than Flot had imagined to work around that stuff. Clergy who visited small villages like these were expected to share their knowledge of medicine and reading and writing and provide entertainment with bible readings and tales of the great heroes and saints.

Based on the information Flot and other such spies had collected, a plan had finally been put into motion to eradicate the villages. It would reduce the potential for conscripted cannon fodder, but making Prince Belton look as bad as possible was well worth it.

That's all in the crapper now! Thanks to this flying waif!

Each plan had been haphazard. Flot and the others might be acting as spies, but they didn't have training as agents of clandestine mayhem. But sending in elites only gave the Belton faction a better chance of realizing something was going on. The only ones with a chance of pulling this off, ironically, were those without proper training, like Flot. These were small villages, teetering on the cusp already. Just a little push should've done the job.

Vandal had saved Kasim's party and then Iwan, but that shouldn't have caused any problems. The Seventh was located close to the road, meaning they had planned to come for it last. However, the merchant-spy's failure to wipe out the Fifth with poison was a huge hindrance. All because the man hadn't poisoned Kain, the hunter. Flot was sure he had selected a day when Kain was supposed to be at home, but either Kain had changed his plans, or the spy had screwed things up. In any case, Kain had shown up at the Seventh, seeking help.

Of course, Flot would never have saved the villagers, and there hadn't been time to reach them anyway. They would have arrived the following day to find everyone dead, and Flot would proclaim it to be the pest, burying this mass-murder along with its victims.

That, of course, had been the plan—before Vandal flew off to the rescue with Kain on his back. Kain had shown some trepidation, but Vandal had already cured Iwan. Everyone in the Seventh spoke up for him, and Flot couldn't say otherwise. He couldn't stop the situation from spiraling. Still, at the time,

Flot believed that it would be a wasted trip. Vandal might save a few individuals, if that. Indeed, commonsense suggested that he would fall from the sky due to lack of MP before they even reached the village.

That's what Flot continued to believe the next day, as he feigned concern and headed to the Fifth. To his great surprise, every villager was alive and well.

It was a nightmare. He had barely managed to keep a smile on his face, muttering what a miracle it was, and set off after Vandal, who had already departed for the other villages. Before long, he heard all about the other "miracles" Vandal caused. If this was a nightmare, he certainly hadn't woken up yet.

The child cured the villagers' sicknesses without even casting magic, cured burn scars, made medicine from his fingers (rather, his claws). A Tamer, who was also one of Flot's fellow conspirators, had unleased some orcs toward one of the villages; Vandal had dropped down from the sky and wiped the monsters out. At that point, Vandal vanished for a few moments and created a new well, complete with a bucket and pulley.

Some of the villages had also been slated for destruction by bandits, but nothing had happened yet. Flot could only assume Vandal's involvement.

In addition, in the Second Pioneer Village, Flot's carefully laid, laborious scheme involving the poisonous pesticide had come to naught. Vandal not only removed the toxins but also taught the villagers how to make edible food from goblin meat.

It was like actual divine intervention.

Who the hell is this dhampir? Flot thought, trying to keep his smile tight. *An agent from the Belton faction? But no, they wouldn't waste exposing someone so powerful for these tasks. They wouldn't send their trump card in to save these villages. Which means—he really is just a passerby?* Flot risked another glance at Vandal and found him looking right back. *Oh no! He suspects me! I knew it!*

". . . Is something the matter?" Flot felt a cold sweat break out on his brow. His own face, eyes wide in surprise, was reflected back at him in those all-seeing eyes.

"No, it's nothing," he managed to reply, somehow keeping a tremble out of his voice.

"Okay," Vandal replied and looked away.

This brat is too dangerous! I need to report to Master Carlkan at once! The Carlkan in question was a member of the knights, Flot's superior and the commander of this operation. The merchant would have moved on without seeing the outcome, so he might still be in the dark, but Tamer at least should have already headed in to report what happened. That wasn't going to be enough, though. Once they got back to the Seventh, Flot would himself need to go into town to report everything he had seen.

Vandal himself, however, was not suspicious of Flot on any real level, even as Flot fretted his skin off. Vandal's Detect Danger: Death would not pick up on any intent that didn't involve direct death or harm to himself, and he wasn't sharp enough to work out what others were thinking simply by deduction. Flot thought his eyes had met due to Vandal's suspicions. In fact, the dhampir had simply been looking up into the sky and happened to meet the fake priest's gaze.

Vandal's generally blank expression meant people often thought he looked angry, but that was simply a product of his doll-like features. His face was a canvas onto which the observer could paint whatever emotion they desired—or feared—to find there. The people of the villages, who liked Vandal already, saw a friendly face looking back at them. Flot, who was suspicious, only saw suspicion.

In that exact moment, Vandal was having a thought that most people had at least once in their lives.

I wish I was a bird. Someone, give me wings.

Given that he could make the trip back with Flight in under an hour, why was he stumping along on the ground? Of course, there was no real question of leaving Kasim and his companions behind. He couldn't carry this many people, though. It would use too much MP, and Vandal wasn't big enough to carry four people anyway. A strong breeze or a murder of monster crows, and someone would fall to their death.

That meant the only choice was to walk. He had therefore been looking up into the sky, wishing for a way to fly while carrying all of these people.

Then he had another thought.

If I want wings—I can make them myself, surely? Of course, with Vandal's powers, if he wanted wings, all he had to do was grow them. Vandal immediately wanted to give it a try but managed to keep that impulse under control.

I definitely wouldn't be able to pass that off as life magic, he thought. *I'll give it a try after I meet up with Eleonora and the others.*

Eleonora was thinking just how right she had been when she decided that this small dhampir was far more terrifying than Vilkain and the other progenitor species vampires. This wasn't her first time having his thought, but tonight, she had the accompanying question of why exactly her terrifying master had chosen this direction in life.

After all, he had created two-way magical communication using shrunken goblin heads. He could simply sell that device to become a wealthy Baron. She didn't understand why he was so fixated on becoming an adventurer and working his way up.

It wasn't just the communication devices. He could take gemstones, or even magic stones, and use Golem Creation to change their shape and combine them together, turning glittering dust into the kind of stone that would adorn a king's crown. Again, a simple way to become richer than he could imagine. MP compatibility meant that only magic stones from the same rank of monsters could be merged together, but he would still be able to make a gemstone far larger than most would ever find.

But Vandal shot all those ideas down. "The only outcome I can see there is those in power taking me captive to make me their slave and extract more magic from me," he had replied.

Of course, Eleonora didn't believe that everyone in power was a good person. Indeed, she assumed more than ninety percent of them were plotters or bad people. However, she also couldn't imagine that any more than ten percent of them were complete and utter morons.

And only a complete and utter moron would even consider making an enemy of Lord Vandal.

At that thought, massive black wings then gave a flap—wings that were sprouting from her master.

"Now this is flying! Everyone okay back there?" Vandal asked.

"I'm loving it!" hollered Zulan. "The wind is blowing but that's perfect for a summer night!"

"You're the best, king!" Braga shouted. "The people on the ground look like ants!"

Zulan, Braga, and the black goblins were clearly enjoying themselves. Eleonora gave a smile herself.

"Lord Vandal. It does feel most comfortable . . . but is it okay to mutate—no, evolve yourself—to this extent, simply to get around?"

"Huh? I just used Spirit Body to grow some wings. I didn't mutate or evolve anything," Vandal replied.

This reply was hardly convincing, given that he looked like some kind of monstrous bird, with his head struck onto an avian neck and three pairs of tremendous black wings sprouting from his body.

After returning to the Seventh Pioneer Village, Vandal had seen off the priest who was in a rush to get back to town. Then he idled away the time by training with Kasim and the others before spending a night at the General Store. From his room there, he had let Eleonora and the others know that he would head back to them in the morning.

The lodgings at the General Store were bunkbeds for eight people. The owners weren't counting on the income from the inn, and the beds had themselves been cobbled together. Vandal could've stayed longer, even with Kasim and his party in residence. The owner had even forgiven the lodging fee as compensation for his initial treatment of Vandal.

After getting back to his companions, Vandal immediately put his new idea into action. He used Spirit Bodification, Spirit Body, and Substantiation to try and grow some wings. Thinking about it now, the Skeleton Bird—which was now part of Knochen—had flown around by using Spirit Body to grow wings over its bones. Furthermore, Vandal had already been using Spirit Bodification to increase his number of limbs, and even heads, and could turn them into tendrils that branched out as required.

It certainly sounded like he could make some wings. He immediately gave it a try.

He used Spirit Bodification on his back, and then Spirit Body to transform his back into his desired shape, stretching it out and making it larger. Then he used Substantiation in various places in order to enhance the strength of the extensions. All of this eventually resulted in some giant wings.

Each one was about the size of a jumbo jet wing, making plenty of room for Eleonora and the others to ride on his back. And yet, when he flapped them, the wings hardly made any noise at all. That might have been because they were Spirit Body wings, because he had referenced owl wings in the design, or because he was unknowingly activating the death attribute spell Conceal Presence.

Now he was flying at a height no arrow could reach, at the speed of a galloping horse. The black color meant he was almost invisible from the ground, but if someone down there did spot him, they would probably pass out in terror.

"Lord Vandal, what exactly is your intent? To become a living legend?"

"Nothing that grand, trust me," he said. "There are lots of issues with this approach."

"It is lacking when compared to say, time attribute Instant Movement," Eleonora said. "But still . . ."

"You know, Knochen could also fly this many people around, no problem," Vandal replied.

"That's true, but still . . ."

"If I'm the only human who can do this, the only future for me is some kind of hyped-up delivery boy." Vandal couldn't give anyone else wings like this, even if he wanted to. "There are all sorts of drawbacks, too," he continued. "I need to use Mental Multitasking and Rapid Cognition to fly, which drains a lot of MP. I also can't turn for toffee. I couldn't fight an arial battle."

He had wanted to try it out simply as a way to get around. In that respect, it was working. That's all Vandal expected.

"It still burns a lot less MP than Flight, meaning it's a useful trick to have. Ah, we're close to the town. I'm taking us down."

Eleonora seemed to have given up, dropping back a little with a sigh. Lefdia gave her a reassuring tap on the shoulder.

With that, Vandal and his retinue reached the town in a single night, a trip from the Seventh that normally took about three days. Of course, they had overtaken the priest of Divine Alda, Flot, even though he left the day before Vandal did.

At the same time, Kanata was taking his stolen wagon and heading north from his own position toward a different town, one on the other side of Heartner's capital. When he checked his distance to Vandal using the Target Radar the next morning, he was surprised at just how much closer his prey had moved in a single night.

Skill level increased for Spirit Body!

The town of Niakki.

For more than 100 years, prior to the start of the reclamation project, this had been the southernmost city in the Duke Heartner domain. In the last century, it had shrunk down to an urban but still relatively small town of ten thousand. It was ruled by Viscount Niakki and also served as the capital of his territory.

In the market, a boy with silver hair and a rough cloth eyepatch was walking through the crowd. He scanned his surroundings, and then moved over to a stall that his eye settled on.

"An apple," he said.

"One baum each," the middle-aged woman running the stall replied.

The youth searched around in his coin purse. It took him a while to extract a silver coin, which he then handed over.

The woman looked at it intently for a moment, then gave a snort. "That's a fake, for sure. A snot-nosed kid like you has no business with silver. I don't care whether you're a refugee or an orphan; get lost!" Even as she spoke, she tucked the silver "fake" away. She clearly had no plans to return it to the boy.

"Well? What are you looking at? Begone or I'll call the guard on you!" Her shouting attracted attention from other stall owners and passersby, but none of them had sympathy in their eyes. Their eyes held only annoyance, disgust, and hatred.

The boy's face showed no reaction to these looks. He simply left, fading back into the crowd.

"Huh! Little freak!" The woman was smiling, however. She had just made 50 baum.

She also didn't notice that a single apple was missing from her stall.

Meanwhile, the boy—Vandal—was out of the way, eating his apple in an alleyway. He didn't consider this stealing, as the woman had taken fifty times the payment for it.

"This town is twisted." He wasn't trying to look especially dirty, but he was wearing a cloth around his head to hide his identity as a dhampir. As a result, people seemed to think he was a refugee or orphan. Further adding to that impression was his long hair, which also hid his pointy ears. But even if the townspeople saw those, they would probably just think he was a half-elf orphan.

The bigger shock was just how despised the refugees were here. It seemed like the people of the town blamed all their daily strife on them. It was true that, since the Saulon refugees arrived, the economy had taken a hit, taxes had gone up, and overall safety had gone down. There was more competition for day labor jobs, creating conflict among the poor. Vandal wasn't going to mindlessly defend the refugees. However, the economic and taxation issues were because the Olbaum Electorate Kingdom had been defeated in the Saulon Domain, losing that territory and putting the Heartner Domain on the frontlines. That meant an increase in military spending. That wasn't the fault of the refugees but of the politicians who had lost the battles and of the Amidd Empire that had launched the attack. At least, that was the only logical assumption.

"Young people today are so quick to pick on the weak."

"That fruit-selling bitch! I'll curse her to death! Give me some MP!"

"We don't have the leaders like we used to . . . why, it was only yesterday . . . hold on, no, ten years ago?"

"The password is 'ale and moba bean stir fry.' They'll say they're all out, but repeat the order again. Then you can meet with the Night Fangs."

"Hehe, if you're looking for a good time, try Flower Hued Legs to the west. They have the very best whores!"

"I see," Vandal deflected. He had asked the nearby spirits to tell him about this town and the Heartner Domain, and now they wouldn't shut up. As he listened to them ramble on, he considered the discrimination the refugees were facing. This was the kind of thing that would make human rights organizations and the media go crazy back on Earth. He wondered why this kind of thing occurred, even among people of the same nation. There had been similar issues on Origin and Earth . . .

"Oh, of course," Vandal realized. "For the people from Heartner . . . they don't consider those from Saulon as a part of same nation."

In this world, travel by road was still dangerous. Most people lived their entire lives in the villages or towns where they were born. Anyone coming from outside them were outsiders—foreigners, even.

Furthermore, the Olbaum Electorate Kingdom had originally formed from a bunch of small nations. Politicians only governed those in their own domain, and the people from other dukes' domains were considered outsiders. It made sense that people from Heartner wouldn't consider people from Saulon as compatriots.

The pioneer villages are going to have it hard in the future, Vandal thought, taking a second bite of his apple—and he didn't like it much, either. It was, simply put, not a great apple. It tasted like an apple, but it definitely wouldn't have made the shelves in a supermarket back on Earth. It wasn't sweet, but rather sour, and it felt horrible to bite into. Kobol fruit was better than this, although that was more a reflection of how tasty kobol fruit were.

Vandal recalled the flavor of apples from Japan, on Earth. If he could take that flavor, created by long years of selective breeding and the hard work of farmers, and place it into the flesh of a kobol fruit . . . he could sell kobol fruit that tasted like apples for ten Amidd in the Empire, or ten baum here in Olbaum.

"Enough side quests," Vandal declared. "I'm going to sneak into the magicians' guild tonight and search for some older spirits. They keep cursed items there, from the sound of it. There should be some pretty aged spirits—perhaps vengeful ones—hanging around."

He was talking to himself again. He needed to stop spending so long alone.

Vandal set out, still munching on the disappointing apple. Along the way, some thugs gave him some trouble. They had seen him pay with the silver coin. They didn't know anything about Princess Lebia either, but their blood tasted a lot better than the apple.

The small Niakki branch of the magicians' guild was home to a magical text feared for its powerful curse. It held all sorts of forbidden knowledge, granting power to those who read it but also warping their personalities into a totally different ones, crazed and cruel. Some suggested that, rather than forbidden knowledge, the book contained a sealed-away evil god, who crept into the brains of any who opened the tome.

That theory was actually about ninety percent correct.

"Hehe, another fool opens my pages!" The Devil God of Magical Texts, Bubuldoura, cackled with glee. He had been defeated long ago by the hero Gold Farmoun but escaped by turning himself into this book. There was something that he needed to regain his strength: readers.

When someone opened him and read from his pages, he could take over their mind, control them, and suck down their strength like a mosquito, slowly recovering his power.

"I'm about halfway there, at long last! Time to take over another pathetic fool and use them a stepping-stone to my complete revival!" His pages were flipped open. Bubuldoura wasn't about to miss his chance, and he immediately leapt at the mind of the one holding him. "Yes! I'm going to seize control of you! Just like all the foolish prey I've controlled until now!" Bubuldoura's spirit, like some horrible combination of an arthropod and a mollusk, slid toward the mind of his new reader. The reader would be unable to resist and bend instantly to Bubuldoura's subjugation. That was the way it had always been, so he saw no reason for it to differ this time.

"Huh? What's going on? I can't reach him?!"

He reached, and reached some more, but he couldn't arrive at the memories or personality he wanted to touch. Bubuldoura started to panic, stretching and clawing, but he barely felt the lightest touch on the tips of a few tendrils.

The thing he touched puzzled him, as well.

"What's this, now? What's going on? How can such a thing exist? Is this reader really someone from this world?"

Bubuldoura had infected the minds of hundreds, if not thousands of humans. He was, from one perspective, a specialist in the mind. But he had never encountered a human like this.

It couldn't be. The mind had nothing where it was meant to be, and what was there instead shouldn't exist in the first place. It was like a human body, but there was a small intestine shaped like a liver where the brain was supposed to be. It was that kind of impossible-to-understand mystery. Like the entire mind had been cobbled together from random pieces of trash.

Having reached this conclusion, Bubuldoura had a terrifying thought.

"I did hear that a divine being took the souls of the four heroes who were crushed by the Demon King and crammed them together into a single new soul. If that soul was then broken again, for some reason . . . ack?!" In the middle of that thought, Bubuldoura noticed a massive crack appearing above him.

A crack that was moving around.

"Eek, eek, eeeeeek!" The crack opened up a little more, and he saw a massive eye inside it. The mud-colored pupil reflected back the form of Bubuldoura.

"✵〰︎𝔪. . ."

A sound like fragments of metal scraping together rang out behind him. Bubuldoura whipped around to see a deep crack appearing there, too. A tongue emerged from that one, longer and thicker than any of Bubuldoura's tendrils.

"Ah, accck!" The Devil God of Magical Texts shrieked as the tongue wrapped around him, then squished him. At once, Bubuldoura understood the strange sound he heard before.

It had been a short sentence. "Are you trying to tickle me?"

And so it was that the devil god that had escaped death at the hands of Gold Farmoun and concealed himself, consuming the minds of those who would read him for 100 thousand years as he sought to revive himself, was squished out of existence by a certain "reader" as one might swat a fly that landed on one's neck.

Vandal had snuck into the magicians' guild by using Golem Creation to tunnel through the ground and pop up through the floor inside. Then he searched the interior for spirits. He had found some, but unfortunately, they were all old and on the brink of vanishing, only interested in getting a dose of magic or simply crackpot insane. None of them knew anything about Princess Lebia.

The spirits in the town didn't know anything either. Maybe I should be asking living people? Not that I think they would tell me anything useful. Giving a sigh, he decided to search for something else—forbidden knowledge that he might use to bring Dalshia back.

That was when the spirit of a magician mentioned a cursed book that was kept sealed away. Apparently, all who read from the evil book received incredible power but were also fated for destruction. Now that caught Vandal's attention. He used death magic to break the seal on the book and picked it up.

". . . There's a bit of a nasty presence hanging around it but nothing too powerful." He could feel some magical power but Detect Danger: Death barely registered.

It seemed like nothing more than a fusty old book. The sharp corners, reinforced with metal, looked like the most dangerous thing about it. He wasn't expecting much, but he opened the forbidden text and started to look at the strange symbols that covered every page. None of it looked like text he could read.

"Bah. I can't even read it. I'm not going to get any strength like this . . . huh?"

All of the sudden, he felt a tickly sensation, just for a moment. He didn't like it, but it didn't really hurt.

Acquired 5,000,000 Magical Power!

The skill Spiritual Pollution became Spiritual Abnormality!

Acquired the skills Physical Length Change (Tongue) and Spiritual Corrosion!

Skill level increased for Brute Strength, Rapid Healing, Resist Magic, Soul Crusher, God Smiter, Physical Length Change (Tongue), and Spiritual Abnormality!

Suddenly his MP increased, and his skills started to level up.

"Huh?" He checked his status in surprise. There he saw not only the increases from his activities in the pioneer villages, but also the newest round of changes he had just been informed of.

Name: Vandal
Race: Dhampir (Dark Elf)
Age: 7 years old
Alias: [Ghoul King] [Eclipse King] [Unspoken Name]
Job: Poison Master
Level: 20
Job History: Death Mage, Golem Creator, Undead Tamer, Crusher of Souls
Status
Vitality: 184
Magical Power: 378120344 (increase of 5 million)
Strength: 128
Agility: 130

Muscle: 119

Intellect: 761

――――Passive Skills

[Brute Strength: Level 3 (UP!)] [Rapid Healing: Level 5 (UP!)] [Death Attribute Magic: Level 6]

[Resist Maladies: Level 7] [Resist Magic: Level 3 (UP!)] [Night Vision] [Death Attribute Allure: Level 6]

[Skip Incantation: Level 4] [Enhance Brethren: Level 8] [Magical Power Auto Recovery: Level 4]

[Enhance Followers: Level 4] [Poison Dispersal (Claws, Fangs, Tongue): Level 3 (UP!)] [Agility Enhancement: Level 1]

[Physical Length Change (Tongue) Level 3 (NEW!)]

――――Active Skills

[Suck Blood: Level 7 (UP!)] [Limit Break: Level 5] [Golem Creation: Level 6]

[Non-Attribute Magic: Level 5] [Magic Control: Level 4] [Spirit Body: Level 7 (UP!)]

[Carpentry: Level 4] [Construction: Level 3] [Cooking: Level 4] [Alchemy: Level 4]

[Brawling Proficiency: Level 5 (UP!)] [Soul Crusher: Level 6 (UP!)] [Simultaneous Activation: Level 5]

[Remote Control: Level 6] [Surgery: Level 3 (UP!)] [Mental Multitasking: Level 5]

[Substantiation: Level 4] [Cooperation: Level 3] [Rapid Cognition: Level 3]

[Command: Level 1] [Agriculture: Level 3] [Clothing Making: Level 2] [Throw: Level 3]

――――Unique Skill

[God Smiter: Level 3 (UP!)] [Spiritual Abnormality: Level 2 (change from Spiritual Pollution)]

[Spiritual Corrosion: Level 2 (NEW!)]
——Curses

[Unable to carry over experience from previous lives] [Unable to enter existing jobs] [Unable to personally acquire experience]

"Hmm, that has boosted me a little. But why?"

Just reading the book had giving him five million MP, which would indeed be a massive increase—for a normal person. That was equal to the magical power of five thousand elite Magicians; no wonder such power had broken countless minds.

Vandal didn't like the look of the skill Spiritual Corrosion. It also seemed strange that Soul Crusher and God Smiter had leveled up. His Spiritual Pollution skill had also changed to the unique skill Spiritual Abnormality.

"Hmmm, but most of all—what about this Physical Length Change (Tongue)? Can my tongue, what, extend now? Oh—wow, yes it can!"

He tried sticking out his togue, and it just kept on going. It didn't particularly hurt or feel like anything at all. Indeed, it was as natural as extending a limb. His tongue could extend even farther than his arm could reach.

He could also then freely move it around. He could wriggle it like a snake or flick it like a frog catching a bug. He could probably wrap it around a pen and write with it if he wanted to. It was like gaining another hand.

". . . Barbed Tongue." He gave it a try, activating the skill to attack with his tongue. It worked. His tongue shot a shorter distance than its maximum, but at a speed that allowed for rapid fire.

He didn't know what Spiritual Corrosion and Spiritual Abnormality were, but he had definitely gotten stronger.

Perhaps he had also been fated for destruction. Only time would tell on that score.

"Did people who read this book also start swinging their tongues around?" Vandal wondered aloud. "Maybe that led them to be treated as outcasts, ruining their relationships? Is that the destruction they were fated for?"

Someone with a three-foot tongue would be a freak on Earth. Vandal decided he had to be careful with this new power himself, even here on Ramda. He returned the forbidden book to the shelf.

It would be quite a while before Vandal realized that he had destroyed the soul of a Devil God—which had, in all fairness, practically thrown itself into his stomach—and eaten it, obtaining the being's MP and some of its powers. However, he still worked it out long before the Niakki magicians' guild realized that their fabled forbidden text was now just sheets of paper.

It went without saying that the nations and towns of Ramda suffered from the existence of criminal organizations.

They bought and sold stolen merchandise, moved restricted goods like drugs and cursed items, traded in illegal slaves, and carried out contract killing. They were far nastier than the thieves' guilds that appeared in the fantasy works of Earth, and many went far beyond committing "necessary evils."

Niakki, too, had its own such organizations.

One was the Night Fangs. Comprised of around ten

members, this criminal enterprise had been exploiting the economic downturn in the Heartner Domain to buy and sell drugs and slaves. Their boss was Split-Ears Zagi, a man feared for having his ears shredded by a rival organization during torture when he was younger and, yet, never having let out a single scream.

"Speak! What're you doing here?" At the moment, Zagi was glaring at a beautiful woman with red hair and eyes. He was sitting on the sofa in their hideout, a piece of furniture that smelt of blood.

On the sofa opposite him, there was a boy with silver hair and a crazy hat that looked like a human hand, while the woman stood next to him. Everyone else in the room was either bleeding on the floor or cowering in the corner.

"I'm here—"

"I'm not asking you. Shut it, brat. Lady, I don't know what kind of joke this is, but if you're trying to make me think this kid is yer boss, it ain't working. No way a woman who can beat the snot out my guys in seconds serves a ba—!"

As Zagi was running his mouth, a fist smashed into his face. The hand-shaped hat from the boy's head had jumped over and whammed into him.

It's not a hat! It's a real hand?! The surprise hit him as hard as the physical impact, walloping him back in the sofa. Then the red-haired woman grabbed the front of his shirt and lifted him up.

"What are—gwaah?!"

Before he could finish his question, the woman smashed her own fist into his solar plexus and then threw him down onto the floor. *It's like she's handling a child! No normal woman can do this!* Taking blows to the front and back, Zagi couldn't even breathe, let alone pick himself up, and he rolled in pain on the floor. There were tears in his eyes, but he was still able to see the hand trot in front of him, using its fingers like legs.

"Gwah!"

The woman proceeded to stamp down on his chest with one beautiful leg. Some people may see this situation as a life goal, but Zagi wasn't so far gone as to enjoy the sound of his ribs creaking. The last of the air in his lungs burst out, but the lady pressed down harder, like she wanted to shatter his ribcage.

The boy, however, had recovered the severed hand and then indicated for her to stop.

"Eleonora, calm down."

"But Lord Vandal, these measly lifeforms who denigrate your greatness have no right to breathe the same air as you. They need to be tortured to death—as slowly and as quickly as possible."

"Now you're just contradicting yourself," the one called Vandal chided her. "I don't want them to die yet. Please, calm down."

". . . Of course. You should be grateful for the mercy of Lord Vandal, human."

"Ah, I've been meaning to mention that. You can't use 'human' like that. Me and you and Lefdia and Zulan, we're all humans, okay?"

"Yes, of course. We are all humans, all humans." She turned back to Zagi. "Be grateful, you ball of hair."

"There we go. Much better."

Zagi still couldn't breathe, even after Eleonora removed her leg. He also finally realized, listening to the bizarre conversation going on, that the child really did hold all the power. He was also relieved to realize that the child didn't want to kill him—at least, not right away.

From the abilities this Eleonora had already displayed, it was clear than even if the other guards or Night Fangs members were here, they wouldn't be able to lay a finger on her. Zagi could see the best of their bodyguards from where he was on the ground: a former Rank C adventurer, who now had a big sword wound right in the chest.

My only way out of this is to buy some time for the boss to get here, Zagi thought. Hopefully, the "boss," the one behind not only this organization but all the activities that went down in the shadows of Niakki, would come to sort this situation out. Zagi had already sensed the presence of one of the boss's familiars; he was sure that the boss himself would show up. The only issue was whether his arrival came before or after Zagi was dead.

"Ngh . . . so? What do you want? Were you paid to do this? Is it the drugs? Don't tell me, this is about revenge?"

"The last one. Revenge. But we're here on behalf of someone else."

At this reply, Zagi felt something of a surge of hope. There was still a chance if they weren't here for personal revenge.

When it came to revenge, most didn't think in regular terms of risks and rewards. If money or women were going to make them think twice, they wouldn't be the sort to go against a crime boss in the first place. But the fact that they were here on behalf of someone else meant there was hope.

"What did they give you? Money? We can match it. Beat it.

Why don't you change to our side?"

"No, thank you. We'll help ourselves to your money once we've killed you."

"What?!" Zagi shouted. "Hold on! I thought you were here for revenge?!"

"That's right. All your money and your entire organization will be a little bonus." Vandal's voice was still emotionless, empty.

Zagi shuddered a little at his words. If what he was saying was true, it meant Zagi was going to die after all. He still didn't understand any of this.

"Hold on—who are you here to avenge? This has to be some kinda misunderstanding! I'm not saying I'm a good guy— but I don't kill without cause. Only to survive. Everyone I've killed was a bad guy! We have our code, even in the shadows—"

"If you are lying, you will suffer for it."

Of course, Vandal knew that Zagi was lying. The spirits of Zagi's men who they had already killed were spilling all sorts of beans.

"About whom we are here to avenge," Vandal continued. "Do remember a tavern called the Scarlet Dream?"

"What—are you talking about?" Zagi tilted his head. That name rang no bells for him at all.

"We're here to avenge a woman who was swindled by a bard and conman who used to sing at that tavern fifteen years ago."

"What? What the hell? Fifteen years ago?! A swindler? Why are you coming to avenge something as petty as that?! Are you that stupid—gwah!" Zagi's eyes were wide with disbelief at what he was hearing when Eleonora kicked him in the side again.

"Watch your mouth, you pile of mucus," Eleonora said.

Zagi rolled on the ground, spitting up blood. Then he heard Vandal speaking again.

"Maybe I can explain. It was earlier today . . . "

Something big was going to happen.

Mother Milan had been a fortuneteller in Niakki for a long, long time. Tonight, she was sure of this particular fortune. Her Job was Medium, and she was a good one. Anyone with her level of talent would have been able to tell something was up.

"There you are. You've been bad for business, boy." She was speaking to the new customer coming into her small establishment.

"What do you mean?" The boy in question had silver hair and a patch over his eye.

Mother Milan's wrinkled face split into a smile at his question. "Are you asking if I knew you were coming? Or why you've been bad for business? I would think you can work out the answers to both of those. You've taken away every spirit in the town, right down to the mice and bugs. What's a Medium like me meant to do, eh? With all those spirits following you around, I'd have noticed you from miles away." As a Medium herself, Mother Milan could see the large number of spirits gathered around Vandal. Hundreds, even thousands of them, flocking like insects around him. She was amazed his sanity was intact.

"Some of the spirits told me that you know about the past here," Vandal told her.

"Maybe. I'm an elf, and I've lived a long time." Mother Milan dropped her hood to reveal her pointy ears. "Not that I'm really hiding it. It's just that being a mysterious old woman who's been wrinkled for decades gets me more work if I'm just an old elf."

It seemed that the atmosphere of a fortuneteller's shop was important, even in a world where one could actually talk to the dead.

"What do you need to know?" she chirped. "I don't make a living from selling information, but I can give you a story or two on the cheap."

A Medium could tell a few fortunes and talk to the dead, but it wasn't all that much use apart from solving the odd murder or receiving reports from spies killed in the line of duty. Older spirits had bad memories and shattered personalities, so they tended to fixate on things from life or lose all memories other than the object of their spite before they faded away. This could happen in only a few days. At most, they lasted a few decades.

Even if they maintained their memories and personality, spirits could still lie. In the past, criminal investigations that relied on Mediums had led to innocent people being executed. If the victim was related to the killer, they might protect the culprit, even in death.

However, Mother Milan was herself an elf with a 500-year lifespan. She remembered the past and remembered the things spirits had told her.

"I need you tell me what happened to Princess Lebia from Talosheim and her retinue approximately 200 years ago."

"How do you know about that?" Mother Milan asked. "Do you have dealings with that kingdom of giantlings? Ah, no, maybe I won't ask."

"I can tell you, if you like," Vandal offered.

"I think not. The spirits around you look quite angry. I'm not sure you'll like what I have to tell you, but please, don't shoot this old messenger."

According to Milan, the tunnel in the Boundary Mountains had been found 200 years and some decades ago by Duke Heartner, a militaristic and passionate believer in Vida. He therefore proactively sought out trade with Talosheim, a country of giantlings who worshipped Vida as well. This trade brought wealth to his domain, changing the impression of him as an earthy man of battle to a man skilled in economics and politicking, greatly increasing his standing with the people.

However, his successor was a devout follower of Alda. He believed that it was Alda, the victor in the battle between the two, who could provide protection in battle, not Vida, the loser. That wouldn't have been a problem if he followed the conciliatory precepts, but his adherence to them was just a front. In truth, he was a hardline fundamentalist.

He wasn't a fanatic, however. He was also a shrewd ruler. Trade with Talosheim had many benefits, so he kept the arrangement going. Personally, he hated it, but he kept that to himself.

That was when it happened: the Milg Shield Kingdom's invasion of Talosheim. The new duke took advantage of this situation. When Talosheim requested aid, he stalled his reply, and let them get wiped out. He said he would take in the Princess Lebia and the 500 she brought with her, but that was also a lie.

He poisoned her guards, and then framed the princess for planning to murder him and take the domain for herself, leading to her execution. As a result, he obtained all sorts of treasures that Talosheim had wanted to keep from the Milg, including a box that could hold an infinite inventory. He packed off the remaining kids and elderly giantlings to the mines as criminal slaves.

The town that had served as the portal to trade with Talosheim, where the people knew the giantlings best, was abandoned. It could no longer serve as a trade city anyway, as there was no one to trade with. The tunnel had been filled in, meaning there was no worry about Milg continuing the attack beyond Talosheim. As a result, Duke Heartner got the treasures of Talosheim and hundreds of new laborers, without having to lose a single fighting man. That worked out incredibly in his favor, to say one possible alternative was sending in their own forces to aid Talosheim and losing them all.

"But I thought what happened to Talosheim was used as justification for the war between the Olbaum Electorate Kingdom and the Amidd Empire," Vandal said. If what Mother Milan was saying was true, a few other things Vandal had been told didn't add up, especially the part about going to war to avenge Talosheim.

But Mother Milan simply shrugged. "Boy, I'm just a Medium. I can tell you what the dead tell me. I don't make assumptions, and I don't do investigations. What I can tell you is that only a handful of folks know the truth: those of the ducal household, their aides, the top Olbaum brass at the time, and perhaps no one else. They could easily set up a substitute for the princess to deceive the people and then, once the war ended, say she died of sickness." Mother Milan shook her head. "Even an old lady like me can think of a way to make it work." There were fewer giantlings than humans in the world, perhaps, but there were still a reasonable number living in Olbaum. It wouldn't have been too hard to find a convincing substitute for the princess. Lebia was well known in Talosheim, of course, but in the Olbaum Electorate Kingdom as a whole, only a few would have known her real face. Meanwhile, public attention would have been on the fighting and its outcome. People would have accepted that the poor refugees had arrived and probably not questioned things beyond that—or had the means to confirm it themselves. What Milan suggested sounded possible with enough high-ranking individuals working together.

"... Does that mean the refugees from Talosheim are still in the mine today?"

"Probably. Giantlings are tough. They might have been imprisoned as criminal slaves, but since that's not really the case, they're probably getting worked not quite to the brink of death. The old folks may be gone, but the ones who were kids at the time are probably still alive—although maybe not all of them. The mine is like a village for slaves, operated by the military. One of the spirits around you told me that."

"... Where were Princess Lebia and her guards interred?"

"Got all the questions, don't you? We're still out here away from the capital. Spirits who know secrets like that rarely reach us. However, if someone wanted to really bury something—the truth along with the bodies—there's a perfect catacomb. They say one of the heroes sealed away a piece of the Demon King there, long ago. That means any evil is unable to escape once placed inside."

"Where is it?"

"Below the ducal castle. Take care on your visit, okay?"

"Take care? You make it sound like I'm going to visit this place."

"I've been doing this even longer than it looks," Mother Milan said with a sigh. "I can tell just from the spirits around you that you're close to boiling over with rage."

Vandal was indeed seething. The spirits around him were basking in that anger, raging and rioting. After all, if what she had just said was true, what other response could there be besides anger and cursing the names of all who took part?

He wanted to leave the fortuneteller's place and tear apart every living thing that he saw. He was incensed to the brink of mass murder.

However, the calmer part of him knew that such an act would be meaningless and that it wouldn't make him happy.

Yes, the people of this domain had abandoned the refugees from Talosheim. None of them—not even the old elf in front of him—pleaded for them to be saved. That said, the Olbaum Electorate Kingdom was another feudal state. The regular folk didn't have a chance to get involved with politics. Almost no one alive today would even know what happened back then, anyway. To top it off, the people of Talosheim—Nuaza, Borks, Zulan, and the others—didn't believe in pushing the crimes of the parents onto their children. Vandal agreed with that. It was wrong to ask the people of today to pay for crimes from 200 years ago.

At least, for crimes that had actually taken place 200 years ago.

"Okay," Vandal said. "Let me ask you this. If the slave mine were attacked and all the slaves were to vanish, would you sell information to the people investigating the incident?" Instead of avenging those crimes, the first thing Vandal needed to do was free the giantling slaves—regardless of the laws of this nation.

But freeing them wasn't enough. They needed to move the hearts of these giantlings and get them to come to Talosheim. And they needed to trick Duke Heartner concerning their true purpose.

Mother Milan watched Vandal for a moment. "No. I value my life more than coin. But I will warn you about revenge, as one old woman—actually, forget that, too. As soon as I started talking to the dead, I realized the living have little perspective on that topic."

The ideas that the dead no longer wanted for anything, or that they only wanted the living to be happy, were horrible and foolish delusions. There were some spirits like that, but Mother Milan also knew of far more that longed for and celebrated the destruction of those they had hated in life. It would be especially silly to try and sell any other idea to Vandal in particular.

"I'll be leaving this town tomorrow. Is there anything I can do before then to repay you?" Vandal asked, pushing down his anger. He managed to sound like the lady had just given him a nice fortune.

"Payment for this information? I've got quite a nest egg, don't you worry. I could live out my days in comfort if I quit today. But there is one thing I might ask of you."

With all the spirits around Vandal, her business as a Medium was on the rocks for now. Mother Milan had been thinking she might shut up shop for a while, or even move to another town. With that in mind, there was a fragment of something lodged in the corner of her memory.

"This would have been about fifteen years ago. One of my regulars fell in with a bard who would sing at a place called the Scarlet Dream. I warned her that he was a conman, and she told me she'd break things off. But then . . ."

"Three days later, that woman appeared again—this time as a spirit, with a sad look on her face—then promptly vanished. My client just wants to know what happened. We followed up on the incident and got a good line of information, leading us to you. You did it, didn't you?"

Vandal's voice was light as he explained, but Zagi was dripping with sweat. *This freaky kid is going to kick something off in this domain*, Zagi thought. *And we're going down as collateral damage!*

"Actually, most of you are still alive. Apart from your bodyguard and a few others. The rest are just bleeding a bit. Their hearts are still beating."

Did he just read my mind?! Zagi was too surprised to even speak. In fact, the spirit of his bodyguard had spilled the beans to Vandal, chuckling about how dumb his former employer was.

"Well? Do you know what I'm talking about?" Vandal asked again.

Zagi didn't reply, but actually, he did have some idea. The details had come back to him as Vandal laid out the story.

It happened 15 years ago, when Zagi was still just a grunt in the organization. He had been blessed with a violent nature, criminal skills, and good luck even back then, and the boss at the time had taken a liking to him.

One of Zagi's jobs was to go after a foppish bard who had

been tricking women out of their money without paying his dues. However, Zagi screwed things up and let the conman get away. In order to cover his mistake, he had snatched one of the conman's marks, killed her in a horrific fashion, and dumped her body in the room the conman had been using. That made it look like the man had killed the woman and fled to escape his crime.

He bought off his companions and turned in the money from the women that the conman left behind, saying it was the conman's payment. That should have been an end to it.

If I admit it, I'll be killed for sure! Zagi thought. *No! I'm not going to die for the sake of that pathetic woman!* "I don't have a clue!" he yelped. "It must have been . . . the work of the bodyguard you already killed! He loved to kill women. A real headcase!"

"He's lying! I killed five people, maybe, but they were all men!" the dead man's spirit quickly reported.

Zagi was trying his best to wheedle out of this, but his efforts were in vain due to Vandal's ability to talk to the dead.

Gah! Where's the boss?! Zagi thought. *Why isn't he here yet—ah!*

The door suddenly opened from the outside with a creak. A man with red eyes and pale skin entered, accompanied by a giantling with his face covered by a black mask and a number of smaller individuals.

"Boss! You made it!"

The man leading the newcomers was a vampire. He had been posted here as the resident agent of the progenitor species vampires who worshipped the Demon God of Living Pleasure Hihiryu-Shukaka. He was the one backing Zagi and his criminal dealings. Zagi had become the vampire's lapdog, and in return, he got to play the big boss of this small city, without any interference from other organizations. Zagi didn't recognize the giantling or any of the others, but they were probably other subordinates.

"Boss, please! Kill this shitty brat and his shitty woman! I'll do whatever you need me to do!"

"Zagiiiii! You have been loyal and worked hard for me. I always thought highly of you . . ." The vampire continued forward, looking for a moment like he would do as Zagi requested.

But then he walked right past Vandal and Eleonora, only stopping to stare down at Zagi. "But look at you now, worthless mongrel dog! How dare you speak ill of these exalted ones!" Then he kicked Zagi in the chest with his pointy heel and proceeded to stomp on him.

"Gwaaah! Boss! What are you doing?!" As he listened to his ribs cracking—not for the first time today—Zagi spotted something. The clothing of the man he thought was his boss was stained with dark red.

"Enough," Vandal said. "We aren't finished with him yet."

"Of course . . . my master."

Seeing the vampire bow his head to Vandal and then kiss his feet, Zagi realized what was going on. This man, this undead vampire, was the source of Vandal's information. Zagi's only hope of salvation had been removed from the table before Zagi's hideout had even been attacked.

"This can't be . . . can't be! My organization, my life, for that worthless, worthless woman!" All hope lost, Zaki's face looked more like a corpse than the actual corpses littering the floor.

Vandal tilted his head as he replied. "She was a worthless woman to you, and you didn't care whether she lived or died.

But you're a worthless thug to me, and I don't care whether you live or die. That's all we're dealing with here."

With that, Zagi, boss of the Night Fangs, died.

However, the following morning, he was seen giving orders per usual, without a single mark on him.

Zagi was a lot more cheerful than before, and ruled the shadows with a fairer, more even hand. It would be some time before the activities of a certain adventurer revealed that he was actually undead.

The Death Mage

CHAPTER FOUR
KING. THE ADVENTURER?

M arie, betrayed by her stepfather and sold into slavery, had fallen into crushing misery.

"King! I've finally got a girlfriend!"

"Huh?" Vandal exclaimed. "When did that happen?"

Her real father had died when she was small. Her mother remarried but passed away from sickness. Her stepfather had decided to ignore her mother's final request that he take care of her daughter and, instead, sold her as a slave. This betrayal from someone she had loved like her true father plunged her into despair.

Young girls like her, in their early teens, would only be purchased by brothels if they were exceptionally pretty. She was more likely to be sold off cheap and expended on rough manual labor in a mine.

"Heh-heh, my beautiful bride. Tell me your name, my flower . . ."

So when she discovered that she was being sold to a vampire, she was actually relieved. At least it would be over quickly. Even if a decent buyer had miraculously appeared and released her, she had no family who loved her left in the world. Having to live the rest of her life with this pain was more than she could bear.

"You don't wish to speak? No matter. I will soon taste all of you with these fangs and tongue, my dear." The handsome face of the vampire turned beastly as he flashed his fangs. Those same fangs closed in with her neck—

One of the precious, expensive glass windows exploded.

"What? Ugah!" A black shape darted across the vampire's back and around his sides, blood erupting from the vampire's body with each pass. Marie could hardly believe what she was seeing. This was a vampire in front of her. The very essence of evil, something that only adventurers and heroes could kill. And yet something was slicing it up, completely one-sidedly.

"Curse you, coward! I'll heal this damage in seconds—!"

"No, you won't. These daggers are blessed with the Child's Zero Heal magic."

"And covered with Virulent Poison, too. Powerful enough to work even on vampires."

"That can't be! No, impossible . . . blagh!" The vampire spat blood from his mouth and then stopped moving.

The vampire that was supposed to end Marie's life had been killed instead. A giantling wearing a mask carried the body away.

What am I meant to do now? Marie wondered vacantly. She was filled with fresh terror. She grabbed a piece of the glass, hardly even thinking.

"Wait!" As the shard approached her neck, however, one of the small assassins grabbed her arm.

"Why are you stopping me?!" Marie wailed. "Please, just let me die!"

"No! I can't let you die!"

"Why not?! I'm not special! Anyone could be used like me!"

"No! No one can replace you!"

"—Huh?" Marie's arm relaxed a little at the sheer strength of these words, at this rejection of her chosen fate.

In that moment, Braga snatched the glass away. Then he treated the cut on her hand that it had left behind.

"Everyone is worried about you. Don't throw your life away."

Their king, Vandal, had told them to rescue and secure as many of the people being held by the vampire as possible. Braga and the others were therefore scrupulously ensured to keep them all safe. His words were 100 percent honest.

But in her weakened, exposed condition, in that moment Braga became Marie's black knight on a white steed.

"And so, King, this is my girlfriend, Marie!" Braga announced proudly.

"Please, will you bless our marriage? Please!" The girl at his side looked like a teenager.

You never know where love will blossom, Vandal mused. "I'm happy to give my approval, but you understand that Braga is a black goblin. Are you okay with that?"

Black goblins were closer in appearance to humans than normal goblins and had much nicer personalities. Choosing one as a friend was one thing; marrying one might cause all sorts of impediments in life.

But Vandal's concerns seemed unjustified. "Of course I am," Marie replied. "The only person to even treat me this well was my dear departed mother. Braga and the others saving me just before that vampire killed me—it has to be fate!"

"I-if you say so," Vandal stuttered. "But once we leave, we won't be coming back to this country for at least a decade. Are you okay with that too?"

"No problem!" she replied brightly.

"Then the only thing left to do is offer my congratulations," Vandal said. Back on Earth, such a marriage would be unquestionably immoral; on Talosheim, not only did many women get married in their early teens, but more importantly, Vandal was flabbergasted at how to put a stop to the situation. And most importantly, bringing Marie to Talosheim would ensure her a much safer life than here.

"Hey, Child, what about the prostitutes and other women being put to work by these bad guys?" Zulan piped up, with a catch in his voice.

Behind Zulan's mask, Vandal could tell he was having some kind of issue. "What's up? I was planning on using my Spiritual Corrosion skill to stop them from talking about us—a gentle push, nothing more—then pay them off and let them go."

Vandal's group had taken over the Night Fangs organization, but they were only going to be using it for a few months at most. There was no need keep operating certain branches, like the brothel, and Vandal certainly didn't intend to do so. The nasty women who ran the place had been disposed of, but Vandal intended to silence the rest and then release them.

"Ahem," Zulan said. "You see, the issue is, after what happened with Marie, the goodtime girls have got the idea that they won't get killed if they can get us to . . . like them. The black goblins are having the time of their lives right now, let me put it like that."

". . . Oh boy."

"None of them have much experience, either. They are like putty in the hands of these women."

". . . Never say you can keep a good woman down."

"Lord Vandal, what shall we do with them?" Eleonora asked.

That was a very good question.

"We'll have a chat with each of them, and I'll give them a health check, to start," Vandal decided.

"Oh, dear, you need to tell him about Linda as well," Marie said.

"That's right!" Braga exclaimed. "King! I've also got another girlfriend!"

". . . Congrats."

In a quiet part of the manor annex, conspirators were meeting to give their reports. These individuals sought to bring an end to the settlement project that was the brainchild of Belton, the second son of Duke Heartner.

"You're saying that this dhampir child completely ruined all of our plans?" This from Carlkan, a knight from the Lucas faction, who sounded suspicious of this development.

"Exactly, Sir Carlkan!" Flot, the fake priest of Alda, replied, having just completed his report.

"I hear what you're saying, and I trust you, sure I do. But still . . ." A little healthy skepticism on Carlkan's part was perhaps to be expected. After all, the details of the reports were pretty hard to believe.

This newcomer had flown to the Fifth and cured everyone of poison. Appeared from the sky and slain all the orcs. Built a well in mere moments. The Second had been slated to be abandoned by spring next year; Carlkan had previously had his own knights deliver a load of poisoned pesticide. Now this child had taught the villagers how to make emergency rations from goblin meat. The bandits that his agents had worked so diligently to point toward the villages were also missing, and Flot was adamant that this child had something to do with that as well.

This child was, apparently, a dhampir. That was a big part of why Carlkan was suspicious.

"Master Carlkan, I saw the incident with the orcs for myself," added the Bestial Magician who had tamed the orcs. "With my own eyes, I saw the orcs I had unleashed wiped out in seconds by this dhampir!" Bestial Magician was a Job that used magic to create bonds with monsters in order to get them to do the Magician's bidding.

"Not to mention breaking down the poison I created," added one of the younger agents. "I made it so that it would kill slowly, and no normal detox magic or potions can stop it. This dhampir has significant skills." He had used a disguise to pretend to be a middle-aged merchant.

The details revealed that this was not a carefully constructed ruse to avoid responsibility for their failures. Carlkan decided the best course of action was to consider this the truth—at least as these men saw it—and proceed from there.

He was responsible for his own unit of knights, after all. After being a knight for a long time, he had seen for himself that people were sometimes capable of feats that didn't match their appearance or age.

"This child was a dhampir, eh? It's hard to believe, but that also makes it possible. At the very least, we have a Magician in the villages at least as strong as a Grade D adventurer, with powerful healing magic."

Defeating three orcs was not a feat to be sniffed at, but the first had pretty much been a surprise attack, and so swinging that into a second and third was possible, even for a Grade D.

"But this child doesn't seem to be setting up base there, like those refugee adventurers. Indeed, it sounds like he already left to become an adventurer in one of the towns. So, get the job done while this wonder kid isn't there."

"Do you think it's that simple, Master?"

Carlkan laughed. "You worry too much. What, you think this dhampir has set watch here? Traps?"

"No, that does seem unlikely."

Of course, Vandal had put Lemures on watch and defensive Stone Golems by the dozen at every pioneer village.

"If this dhampir child plans to become an adventurer, he will need to spend at least a year at the adventurers' academy," Carlkan said. "We can use that time to wipe out the villages, making it look like the work of bandits. I will lead my forces, myself, to do this."

Flot and the others all gasped.

"Are you sure, Master? If this were to get out, regardless of the fact that they are refugees, you would be hanged or sold as a slave!" Flot exclaimed.

"That is the risk we must take. Everything I do is to scour these festering Saulon parasites from the glorious Duke Heartner domain! For the people and for Prince Lucas!"

Carlkan was motivated by more than just disgust for outsiders and pride in his domain. He had yet to really achieve anything for Prince Lucas. If the prince became duke at this point, Carlkan would be in no position to bargain for any kind of seat at the table.

"My unit is scheduled for training maneuvers next month.

When that happens, we will start with the Seventh, and then proceed to attack all of the villages. Sir Flot, you will join us."

"Me? Why?"

"In your guise as the priest, you have spent the longest among these people. We will need you to confirm that each location has been completely eradicated. If we can do this, your own position as a minister will be assured. I'll be counting on you."

"Yes, Sir Carlkan." Flot felt that he was getting dragged into this a little too deeply for his liking, but it was also too late to turn back now.

At that same time, the one who had unknowingly been thwarting Carlkan's plans was heading through the market to the adventurers' guild.

His purpose, of course, was to finally register as an adventurer.

The situation has changed a little, with all this new information, but this is still the perfect time to register, Vandal thought. Learning of the Heartner house's betrayal of Talosheim had given Vandal and his team a new objective: to rescue the giantling slaves still being held in the mines. He had sent word of this to Talosheim, and Borkz was so mad that he was ready to attack the domain at once. Vandal was pleased to hear it.

The main reason Vandal was still registering was because if he missed this opportunity, it might literally be years before he got another one.

I just need to register real quick, then I can leave town and meet up with Eleonora and the others. We'll wait until night and then fly to the capital.

They had to wait until it was dark if he was going to be flying again, anyhow. He had time and the opportunity.

What he didn't need was a tropey encounter with some punk low-level adventurers looking to haze the newbie. After learning about the crimes that the Heartner house had perpetrated on Princess Lebia and the others, Vandal was feeling pretty stressed out and pissed off. All it would take was some smartass making a comment about "go home and suck Mommy's titties, little baby" and he might unleash his full power to shut them up. Give them not just his fists but his claws.

"I just have to remember what Kasim and my other adventurer comrades taught me," Vandal said. "Adventurers need courage and belief in themselves." When Vandal first encountered then, Kasim had been leading his party against goblins with almost no chance of victory. The young man had even been trying to hold back the goblins so that Zeno and Fester could escape and warn the village.

This was the same thing. He needed the bravery to overcome the fear of getting picked on and the belief in himself that he could keep his murderous rage under control.

"It's also been useful to learn about everything else I'll need in order to be an adventurer. I'll definitely need a house, for example."

Normally, an adventurer wouldn't need a house. Newbies would take cheap lodgings, and veterans might have a particular inn that they used as a base. But Vandal had Borkz, Zadilis, Sam, Eleonora, and all the others to think about. They wouldn't be treated as humans but rather as subordinate monsters that Vandal had tamed.

For that reason, he wouldn't be able to make use of an inn. Just like restaurants and lodgings on Earth didn't allow pets, inns did not allow monsters that were far more terrifying than the most feral beasts. Lefdia or small pixies was one thing; those from humanoid races like Eleonora and Zadilis might be admissible depending on the place. But strolling in with Knochen and Skeleton would never work. Of course, there were Tamers among adventurers, but when they used an inn, they would stable their monsters. Goblins, kobolts, even ghouls—their place was in the stables. And all of Vandal's subordinate monsters would receive the same treatment.

I can't let them suffer such a slap in the face. When Vandal had realized all of this the previous night, Eleonora got the wrong end of the stick, saying, "I never imagined anyone would see me so humiliated—other than you, Lord Vandal—but I'll sleep in the filth with the horses if need be!"

"All this means," Vandal muttered to himself, "I need to attend the adventurers' academy before I become an adventurer, but before I even do that, I will have defeated bandits and criminals, visited dungeons to collect treasure, and even bought my own large house. Hmmm. It feels like I'm doing things in the wrong order."

It did sound strange. Still, he couldn't make it alone because his curse prevented him from earning experience, and the loneliness would just crush him anyway. He certainly didn't have the confidence to find a party at the academy.

So he needed more money.

"Even after I get a house, I'll need collars or necklaces for everyone to show that I've tamed them, or we won't be able to walk the streets unmolested. It's not easy, becoming an adventurer." As he had that thought, he passed a dilapidated Vida shrine and arrived at the adventurers' guild.

It was a two-story affair that looked like dozens of the entire General Store from the Seventh Pioneer Village, guild branch and all, could fit inside. It was clearly one of the largest buildings in Niakki, rival to anything apart from the lord's manor. In a proper city, the building for a guild branch in a town was going to be even larger; Vandal had seen that for himself in Talosheim. He offered a brief prayer that the adventurers wouldn't give him grief.

"Let's do this." Firming his resolve, he opened the door to the adventurers' guild.

It was past the time of day when adventurers crowded around looking for new postings, so there weren't many people inside. There were the receptionists at the quest counter and some other workers doing paperwork in the back. Vandal proceeded quietly forward, arriving at the counter without incident. His prayers were being answered.

Naturally, this assumption was flawed. Most of those present hadn't even noticed him. Even if they did, none of them were going to start something with a child. Any children who came to an adventurers' guild were either first timers coming to register, Grade G adventurers, or students from the academy. Grade G adventurers took on day labor around the town and kept the guild clean. The only thing to be gained from asking if they could hope to succeed as adventurers was laughter at asking such a silly question.

If they were students at the academy, giving the kid grief would look even worse. Becoming an instructor there was a popular second career for adventurers after they stepped away from active duty. Berating a student with good cause was one thing, but threatening them for no reason would piss off a bunch of veteran adventurers and possibly jeopardize a future teaching career. The trope of adventurers getting picked on by those with more experience only therefore occurred after newbies had graduated and were heading out on their first real quest, or if the ones doing the bullying were also children.

Of course, in all walks of life there were those to whom common sense did not apply, but they weren't exactly stationed on purpose in every guild branch. Vandal's prayers had indeed come true, in that the Niakki branch did not have any such problem elements.

"Hello. I would like to register as an adventurer."

"Ah! H-hello." The girl on reception looked surprised for a moment—probably not having noticed Vandal until he spoke up—but then quickly restored her smile and offered a paper and pen. "Please, fill out this form with your name, age, race, and any special skills you have. Do you need someone to fill it in for you?"

"No, I can handle it. But what should I put for special skills?"

Borkz had told him about the process from 200 years ago and Kachia about the modern one in Milg, but different times and different countries probably meant differences in the process. It didn't hurt to ask.

"You can mention any training you received, any attributes you are particularly skilled with, and any unique skills you have."

"Unique skills? I thought you see skills when you issue my guild card?"

"Yes, but anything seen by our staff at that time is protected information that remains secret. Anything you write on this form will mean you don't mind other people knowing about it. We can use it to help find you work."

There were unique skills that allowed for additional damage against specific monsters, such as Goblin Slayer and Dragon Slayer. Making that information public could help the guild find work that suited those skills or help people who needed adventurers to find the right party. However, if the adventurers wished to keep things secret, in principle, staff who saw all their skills would need to keep that information to themselves.

I bet there are some exceptions, Vandal thought. *Like telling the guild master.* The adventurers' guild was still an organization run by fallible humans. It probably wasn't best to bank on their obligation to secrecy. For example, although Vandal didn't know it, the guild master of the adventurers' guild in Milg had promoted Green Gale Spear Raily without due cause, simply on the word of Count Thomas Palpapekk. Of course, there were guild masters who ran everything above board, as well as those who didn't.

In that case, I should leave the space for special skills blank. As soon as he was done registering, Vandal planned to make a break for the town limits. Vandal filled in just the name, age, and race boxes and returned the paper.

"Let me see . . ." The girl took the paper and the narrowed her eyes a little, before looking back at Vandal with something like pity in her eyes. "According to this, you are a seven-year-old dhampir, correct?"

Those details would come to light when making the guild card, so he hadn't seen the point in lying about them now. "Yes. That is correct."

Dhampir were probably pretty rare. He lifted the cloth to reveal his concealed eyes. Seeing his two different colored eyes, one crimson and one violet, the girl flinched.

"In that case—we can't register you."

Vandal blinked a few times at this unexpected reply, confused.

The girl's face didn't change, and she didn't take back her comment.

"Why not?" Vandal asked. "I thought those under the age of ten could still register. We just have to take a simple exam." If they passed that exam, proving they had intellect and facilities comparable to those of a ten-year-old child, they could be registered as a Grade G adventurer. Achieving Grade F or higher involved the same process as other underage adventurers, requiring one to graduate from the academy.

"That has recently been changed, in the name of Prince Belton and the Heartner Guild Master. Now, those with mixed linage that includes lamia, centaurs, and other Vida races with monster roots are not allowed to take the exam before the age of ten. Of course, that includes dhampirs."

Kasim hadn't mentioned anything like this, but he probably hadn't kept quiet on purpose. All three of his party were humans, and it wasn't even beastmen, giantlings, dark elves, or their mixed-race children that would be affected. It was only those born between humans and those considered monsters, such as vampires and lamia, who would be affected—a tiny minority compared to the greater whole.

Furthermore, Vandal realized he hadn't even told Kasim his age. He had lopped off that Goblin Barbarian's head and cured Iwan with (what everyone believed was) powerful life magic, so they probably all considered him older than seven.

"I see . . ." Vandal said.

"My apologies. There has even been talk of changing the regulations again, within this year, to prevent such individuals from taking the entrance exam for the adventurers' academy." She did look sorry to also be breaking this further bad news. If that happened, he wouldn't just be waiting three years.

"I . . . see . . ." That was a further shock to Vandal. It was like Prince Belton and this guild master were ganging up on him specifically. First the betrayal of the Talosheim giantlings and now this. He would not forget this.

However, it was also pointless to fight a desk minion over it. All he could do was give up and leave the town. Once their other business here was finished, he could go to one of the other domains and register there. What he certainly couldn't do was wait for years and years. He needed to do it next year. The year after, at the latest. It wouldn't be easy in this world for a normal child to move between these domains, even between two trading cities located close to each border. But with Vandal's upgraded powers, he could make the trip literally like the crow flies. This was annoying, for sure, but it wasn't a big setback.

"Can you hold on a moment there?" Someone spoke up behind Vandal.

The girl on the desk, the other guild staff, and the scattering of adventurers in the room were all murmuring and watching the speaker. Vandal turned around to take a look as well, and then his eyes opened wide.

He had heard this voice before.

The adventurer came briskly toward the counter where the stunned Vandal stood.

"This is the first I've heard of these changes. Can you explain them to me?"

"I'm sorry, sir. I'm dealing with this child at the moment—"

"And I'd like to discuss how you're dealing with him. Could you call the Guild Master?"

"I don't think I can. If you wish to discuss guild policy, you have to first voice your concerns with someone here on the desk. After waiting your turn, of course."

"And I'm Heinz, a Grade A adventurer. Again, I wish to use my authority as a Grade A adventurer to speak with the Guild Master."

Heinz. That Heinz, right here.

Vandal's head turned with a rusty stutter, taking in the adventurer who was standing right here, right next to him. He looked like a handsome young man in his mid- to late twenties, with fine features, blonde hair, blue eyes, and an air of determination about him. From the way he handled himself and the gear he was carrying, it was clear he was no newbie. His voice was a little different, but Vandal still remembered it from Evbejia. His description also matched what Raily had told him.

Another of my mother's killers! Blue Burning Blade Heinz! Vandal had heard that Heinz had moved his base to the Olbaum Electorate Kingdom, but he hadn't dared hope he would be in this domain or that he would encounter him during this trip.

Reviving Dalshia was an absolute condition for Vandal's "pursuit of happiness." He had to remove anyone who got in the way of that. That was why he had to kill Heinz.

It didn't matter to Vandal that selling his mother to those Alda fanatics had simply been a paying job for Heinz or that what he had done wasn't illegal. It also didn't matter how Heinz might have changed, or what he thought about his deeds now.

The problem was the future, right, the future! Heinz had given Dalshia over once to those fanatics. What was to say he wouldn't do it again? Even if he changed his mind once, he could just as easily change it back. *So he must be eradicated!* Vandal thought.

This was also the perfect chance to do it.

Of course, Vandal couldn't be too open about it, with so many people watching. He understood that much.

He just had to poison him somehow. Infect him with something. *Maybe I can alter my breath? Turn the tiny water droplets into poison that would enter through his skin?* Or maybe he could pretend to bump into him and use that contact to infect him.

Vandal considered various plans, but whatever he thought up, Detect Danger: Death went off like alarm bells in his head.

If he tried poison, he was the one to die. If he tried a disease, he was the one to die. Whatever Vandal did, the one to die was not Heinz, but himself. *This is crazy! What is he, invincible or immortal?*

It was light and day compared to when Vandal had faced High Priest Goldan. Vandal was surprised, but he also couldn't deny the reality that was right in front of his eyes. And death attribute magic had never steered him wrong.

This is what Borkz was talking about, Vandal recalled, *when he told me how easily Divine Ice Spear Mikhail killed him. The strength of a Grade A who, for all practical purposes, is already a Grade S.* Grade A were already considered superhuman; Grade S was a superhuman who surpassed other superhumans. Someone living in a completely different dimension from Raily, whom Borkz had defeated before Vandal crushed his soul. Not to mention, Heinz had reliable friends and allies.

Vandal moved his eyes to look beyond Heinz and saw a party of five other men and women. Two of these matched up with information he had extracted from Raily: a female dwarf with blue hair, the Shield Bearer Delaiza, and a male Scout with black hair and eyes, Edgar. Then there were two newer members: a female elf in monk's attire and armed with a mace and a young woman who looked like some class of fighter. Vandal assumed they were Grade A, B, or C at the very worst. That made this the new Five Hue Blades, filling in the gaps created by Raily's departure and the female elf with elemental magic who had apparently been killed in a dungeon.

There was a fifth person who looked as young, if not younger, than Vandal. Delaiza was protectively standing in front of this young girl. She couldn't be a member of the actual party. Probably someone's kid sister or something like that.

Oh, I get it. This is my problem right here. The little girl aside, he could tell by looking at the other four. They were the reason he wasn't going to get to kill Heinz in this setting.

The women were sighing about Heinz throwing his weight around. But if anything were to happen to their leader, they would react instantly, and with appropriate force. If Vandal fought Heinz while his party was around, they would all work together and likely succeed in punching through even Vandal's incredible barriers.

Poison and disease were not going to work. These adventurers weren't like those easy marks among the Milg Shield Kingdom expedition. They had experience fighting high-ranking monsters with all sorts of malady-inducing attacks. They weren't like Raily, puffed up on their own bullshit. They were the real deal.

They were incredibly strong. The volume of Magical Power didn't matter. If Vandal was a massive elephant, these were the ants who could sting him to death.

That's it, then. I just have to bear it. I can't get myself killed here—I've got things I need to do. I just have to be satisfied with having seen their faces. I can kill their leader once I'm stronger. I should just get back to Eleonora and the others . . . huh? What are they doing? What's Heinz doing? Vandal had even turned on his Rapid Cognition skill in order to rationalize his way out of his feelings of powerlessness and humiliation. He ran back over the information that was coming in through his ears.

"Please, hold on a moment. The Guild Master is currently out—"

"Then a submaster should be here. Regulations state that when the Guild Master isn't present, at least one of the two submasters must be. Or have those regulations changed as well?" Heinz wasn't talking to the receptionist anymore, but now a man who looked like her boss. They were arguing, and the other man didn't look to be holding his ground.

"I'm afraid that's—"

"I know, okay. It's pointless to say this to you. To even the Guild Master of the Niakki branch. I just want someone here to write a letter, that's all. A letter of introduction to the Guild Master at the Heartner guild HQ."

"But if we do that—it will give the impression that our guild master agrees with what you are saying!"

"So? You can't write such a letter, is that it? Even though you can easily follow along with this meaningless change?"

"That isn't something a guild employee like me can comment on!"

"And you don't have to be a guild employee to see what's really going on here," Heinz said. "I worked it out right away. With the troubles in the ducal house, Prince Belton doesn't have access to the duke's army. But he wants to bring the noncommittal Alda lot and all their shrines to his side, so he's trying to win their favor with policies like these that amount to little more than bullying."

The highest ranks of the Alda faith in Duke Heartner's domain were currently stacked with fundamentalists, apparently.

"Children with monster blood are too dangerous to ever test, is that it?" Heinz continued. "They might lose control, meaning it's too dangerous to let them into the academy? Is that that what you really believe?" Every word Heinz said made the man pale further.

He turned his face away. Inside, he probably agreed with what Heinz was saying. The other employees, and the original receptionist Vandal had talked to, looked the same way.

"What does it matter? At least run it up the ladder!" The other adventurers who were present started to shout their agreement.

"That's right! The adventurers' guild opens its doors to all, right?"

"You gonna kick beastmen like me out next?"

The new voices seemed to help the man make up his mind.

"Very well. But the only thing I can do is send it on to the Guild Master."

"I understand that. That's enough," Heinz replied.

"One word of warning . . . Yes, Grade A adventurers have more clout than petty nobles. But what you have said here will reach the ears of our princes. I do not know how they will react to it."

"I understand that too. I'm not motivated by my position as an Alda conciliator. I'm just an adventurer, saying that the guild should not be bowing to political pressure when making policy. That's all. 'The door to adventure is open to all races.' Are we going to ignore the words of our founder?"

"I also like that quote myself," the man said. "Very well. I will send a messenger to the guild master at once." He looked down at Vandal with a smile. "Looks like you got lucky today, kid."

That comment finally got Vandal's brain working again. *Lucky? Why?* Because he got to see what his hated enemy looks like and how strong he is? No, that wasn't it . . . *Hold on . . . Heinz is helping me out? No! No way!*

He glanced at Heinz to see the adventurer giving him the most reassuring smile. Like he was saying, *Leave everything to me.*

The smile didn't reassure Vandal, however. Instead, he felt something more like—insanity. *Why is he helping me? Why does it have to be him?! No! This must be a trap! There must be something else here! There must! Something is strange! Something is wrong! I can't accept this!* It felt horrible, like his brain and spirit and even his soul were all being churned together.

He could barely think. Using Mental Multitasking and Rapid Cognition only confused him more.

"Oh boy. Who's the one always going on about not being interested in politics? We complete an escort quest and return to town, just to walk right into this. We'll have to show ourselves in front of the prince and the HQ Guild Master at this rate."

"But Edgar, you know what Heinz always said. All of Alda's faithful need to be more like the conciliators. Heinz chose to come to this nation, even at the cost of parting ways with Raily."

"I thought our main goal was to complete the Wandering Dungeon called Zakkato's Trial."

"Don't be like that, Jennifer. Or do you think Heinz is in the wrong?"

". . . That's not what I meant."

From what Vandal could hear from the party chatting, it sounded like Heinz's companions weren't entirely surprised by this, nor did they particularly oppose it.

"Hey, Heinz is an Alda conciliator?" Vandal could hear other adventurers were whispering nearby.

"You bet. He witnessed the tragedy of a dhampir and his mother in the Milg Shield Kingdom. That's what brought him to this country."

"Wow. That's why he's helping out the dhampir. Grade A really is something else."

Putting it all together—after handing over my mom and seeing her burnt at the stake, he became an Alda conciliator, and moved his base of operations to the Olbaum Electorate Kingdom. And now he's helping dhampirs out? He's . . . helping us out? Inside, he was in turmoil, but externally, Vandal looked like he was just standing there.

"It's okay." This from the girl who was with Heinz and his party. She even took his hand as she spoke. "Heinz is nice. He'll help you out. He'll protect you. Like he did for me!" The girl gave him a smile.

Then Vandal saw her eyes. One of them was crimson-colored, like blood.

"Ah . . ." His hands started to shake. "Ooh . . ." He felt like throwing up. His head ached. Unpleasant feelings surged through him to an extent he had almost never felt during his third life.

Unable to withstand it, Vandal knocked her hand away, and the girl yelped. He kept himself under control as best he could, keeping his claws in and restricting his strength, to make sure she didn't get hurt. That was the best he could do.

"What's wrong?!" Heinz reached out in surprise, but Vandal simply needed to get away. He kicked off the floor with both hands and feet, activating Flight so hard it squeezed his internal organs.

"Hey! Hold on!"

"What's going on?!"

Vandal ignored the surprised shouts, smashing into the guild doors and flying away for all he was worth.

Vandal crouched down on the ground, staring at his hands as they shuddered and shook. He was already on the outskirts of Niakki, in some kind of woodland. He probably hadn't traveled all that far. After leaving the guild, he had no idea how he got out of town. He might have punched holes through the town walls, for all he knew.

"Ah . . . nnghhh . . . oooh . . ." Vandal's mind was in such turmoil that he couldn't bring himself to care about the circumstances of his departure. What he could definitely feel was overwhelming anger, humiliation, and powerlessness that threatened to consume his entire being.

He had been powerless in the face of his enemy. Completely defeated before he could even make a move. He would have thought *that* would be the greatest humiliation he could expect to experience.

But greater humiliation had waited just beyond it.

That enemy had offered him sympathy. Had tried to help

him. He had taken Vandal's pride and trampled it. More than anything else, it was the reason why Heinz had tried to help him that hurt the most.

Because he was a dhampir.

Because, after accepting a job in the Milg Shield Kingdom and handing over Vandal's mom, Dalshia, to a bunch of religious fanatics, Heinz had watched her get burnt at the stake—and changed his thinking, becoming an Alda conciliator as a result.

Vandal groaned. "You've got to be . . . joking me!"

Some rational part of him could see how it had happened. Heinz probably didn't even know that Vandal was alive. He must have considered Vandal to have died along with his mom. The only people who knew about Vandal's existence outside of Talosheim were a scattered handful in the Milg Shield Kingdom and Amidd Empire and a small number of vampires.

That's why Heinz was trying to make up for things. A common story back on Earth, in both fiction and non-fiction: someone choosing to live in atonement for the lives of people they had killed. To save more lives than they took. To try and resolve the guilt they felt for, for example, killing enemy civilians during warfare. It wasn't rare in the slightest.

In Vandal's mind, he associated such a path with fiction. He could imagine the kind of story in which someone had died because of a mistake the main character made, but it wasn't something that could be punished by the law. Still free, that individual wrestles with their actions, saying something like, "Then I'll help other people until I can forgive myself." Or maybe the hero says something like, "You can atone for the past by what you choose to do in the future," to a former bad guy.

That's what Heinz was doing, trying to atone for what he did to Dalshia and Vandal. He was following the beliefs of the conciliators and had saved that girl, another dhampir. Neither Dalshia nor Vandal had asked him to do this, but they were no longer a part of the equation. He was doing it all on his own.

"You've got to be joking!" Vandal shrieked. Was he meant to forgive him, then? Stop blaming him? Stop wanting to kill him? *Out of the question!* It made no sense to Vandal at all.

If that were acceptable, all hell would break loose. If a serial killer went on a rampage, were the families of their victims supposed to forgive them if they saved as many lives as they killed?! If Vandal saved as many people in Olbaum as he had killed from Milg, would the families of those soldiers simply have to let him off the hook?

That wasn't how it worked. He understood that much. Even if some might feel that way, all of them certainly wouldn't.

And yet, if the people of Olbaum Electorate Kingdom knew the whole story, they would surely tell Vandal that he should forgive Heinz. That Heinz had saved many people, done great things, was a hero. That he deserved to be forgiven. That he was going to save many more in the future, reducing the suffering and increasing the joy of thousands and thousands of lives.

That he was only of benefit to this nation, regardless of what he might have done elsewhere. A single dark elf was killed—that was all. They would tell him—forgive.

That sounded like the right thing to do, the correct thing, regardless of the world in which it took place. He should forgive the fact Dalshia was killed. He should quell the hatred and anger that burned within.

All because of the fanciful story that they were building around Heinz, the flawed hero. He was helping other dhampirs he had never even seen before; he was spreading the word of the Alda conciliators. Forgiving him was best for everyone. And that act itself would become another shining part of that same story.

. . . I'll never forgive him!

Skill level increased for Spiritual Abnormality!
Acquired the skill D◆■ge □■◊□■•tr◆♍♦♓on!

But, for now, he had to hold it all in.

The deeds he was doing for the sake of atonement were making him more liked and more popular. Vandal couldn't compete with that. Even if he used death attribute magic and all his skills and brought in Eleonora and the others, there was no way to win.

This was revenge. A process Vandal was going through purely for his own selfish satisfaction. It wasn't about the end result. It wasn't worth it if it cost him his own life or the lives of his friends.

Skill level increased for Spiritual Abnormality!
Acquired the skill D◆nge□■◊o ■•tr◆♍♦ion!

However, he also couldn't control his hatred. That was a fire he was unable to quench, even as a chill of terror threatened to freeze his heart.

"Hey! There she is! Found her!"

"Grab her, then! That's the kid with the silver coin. She must have more!"

"I'm on it, Auntie!"

That was why he had run away. Why he had fled the town. Why he was out here, like this. He hadn't wanted to get anyone else caught up in his agony.

"I can't believe we found her so easily! Luck is on our side, Auntie!"

"This is because we live good, clean lives. Don't think badly of us, little one. Selling fruit doesn't cut it in this economy. You've got nothing to worry about. With your looks, whoever buys you will take good care of you, I'm sure."

"Auntie, I dunno. Now that I look more closely, I'm not sure if the kid is a boy or a girl. I don't think we'll get much for a girl this young."

"But look at the eyes. If we say she's a dhampir, we can boost the price for sure."

"No, that's a bad idea! We shouldn't attract the Grade A adventurer who goes around helping out dhampirs."

"I did hear the Savior was in town. What's his name again? Heinz?"

Yes! Heinz! Heinz is the one Vandal hated!

"Stop blabbing and start tying the kid up! We need to get out of here!"

The middle-aged apple seller from the market was closing in on where Vandal was kneeling on the ground.

Acquired the skill Scream!

"Aah . . . ☥ ♑ . . . ☠ . . ."

The child let out a strange yelp that sounded like some kind of curse. The woman and her male accomplices gave a start of surprise.

Then they quickly moved in to grab him. That was their final mistake.

If they had tried to run away, with all their strength, they might have made it to a safe distance. Maybe.

Vandal let out a terrible scream: "☠ ♑ ♒ ♋ ○ ⌘ ■ ♑!"

Skill level increased for Scream, Spiritual Corrosion, and Dungeon Construction!

"Hyaaaah!"

"Hnnngaaaaaaaaaah!"

Vandal's would-be kidnappers responded in kind to his scream. Their hair bleached white and the light of sanity left their eyes.

"⊗□◆ⅶ☒□◆□○⊬■♎!"

The woman and the thugs didn't die. Nothing of the sort: they were filled with energy. They stuffed their fingers into their ears, chewed their tongues, and gouged out their eyes, desperate to escape.

That still wasn't enough. Somehow, despite their blindness, they latched onto their nearby companions and started to fight and kill each other, like wild animals.

"Hatred! Hatred! I hate—something!"

"Kill me! Kill them! Kill—kill who?!"

"My ears, eyes, tongue, hands, my flesh, my organs, I hate them all!"

"⊗□◆ⅶ☒□◆□○⊬■♎!"

Vandal felt something black and terrible that he had been bottling up inside spill out all around him. Then, with a strange feeling of liberation, he collapsed.

When Vandal woke up, he felt pretty good.

Looking up at the sky, it seemed to be just after noon. He visited the adventurers' guild in the morning, so that was only one or two hours ago. And yet it felt like he was awakening after a night of incredible sleep. He was in great mood.

"But I feel kinda exhausted too. Like a—comfortable feeling of exhaustion?"

He tilted his head and checked his status. His remaining MP was close to zero. He wondered what he had been doing while he was asleep. There were bloody stains on the ground nearby, but no undead.

"Lord Vandal, are you okay?!" That was when Eleonora dropped down from the sky. She picked Vandal up at once.

"Ah, yeah. I don't have much MP left, but I'm fine otherwise. Can you tell me—what happened?"

"That's my question! You said it wouldn't take you long, so I hid myself to wait. Then you suddenly exploded out of the guild and flew off over the walls! I lost sight of you, and you didn't contact us! You've no idea how worried I was!"

"I'm sorry. Sorry for . . . worrying you."

For a while, he just let Eleonora hug him tightly.

After using the shrunken goblin head communicator to call in Braga and the others, who had been searching elsewhere, Vandal explained everything that happened.

"Lord Vandal, we should wipe out this domain and take its territory for our own."

That was the first thing Eleonora said. From the look in her eyes, she wasn't kidding around.

"That won't work. We can't defeat Heinz at the moment. Even if we could, we shouldn't be wiping out or taking anything," Vandal said.

"Why not?! Let's kill them all!"

"Child! They aren't even human! They are feces in human form! Living pestilence!"

"Rahhhh! Let's slaughter them all, boy!"

Many of the others agreed with Eleonora, including Zulan, Nuaza, and Borkz listening on the other end of the communicator. Lefdia couldn't talk, but she was repeatedly hopping between all five fingers, suggesting she agreed as well. Sam and Zadilis probably wouldn't resist the idea either. After Borkz and the other giantling undead learned of Heartner's betrayal 200 years ago, their appreciation for the region hadn't just fallen to zero; it had pushed down into a negative value.

"I'm happy that you're all angry for me," Vandal replied. "But there are good and bad people both in the Heartner Domain. Right, Braga?"

Eleonora, Zulan, Braga, and the black goblins all looked a little shocked at that, as they looked at the "friends" they had made here.

"We've left our homeland behind," Marie said.

"Don't worry about us."

The other women had all decided to come along with Braga and the black goblins, even when Vandal offered them a big chunk of money and their freedom to keep what they knew about Vandal's secret. They were deeply grateful to Vandal already; he had cured their various drug addictions and used magic to remove their slave collars and tattoos. Of course, it might also be that they didn't believe he really would set them free.

Still, they had chosen to come to Talosheim. Even though they had been born in the Heartner Domain, these women were now residents of Talosheim. About a third of those working at the brothel were refugees from the Saulon Domain, so they weren't that attached to Heartner to begin with. That said, talking about killing and living pestilence in front of them probably wasn't the best idea.

". . . Sorry. I got overexcited," Zulan said.

"Me too. I'm sorry," Eleanor added. "I know things aren't so cut and dried in your position."

Braga nodded. "I went too far. Thanks for your understanding, King."

"It's fine. I've gotten mad and screwed up plenty of times," Vandal said, standing up. At least it seemed like everyone had calmed down. "But if we take this lying down, then we're nothing better than prey waiting to be eaten by beasts. Beasts who won't hold anything back, even if we don't resist. They will gobble our flesh, chew our organs, and crunch our bones. We need to take back what was taken from us and make them see the error of their ways. Regarding Heinz . . . we'll let him be for a while. Build our strength while waiting for a proper chance to strike. And as for the Heartner Domain, I'm giving up on it."

That final comment, almost offhand in its delivery, made everyone give a start in surprise.

"By which I mean that I'm not going to register as an adventurer here or undertake any activities here or trade with them in the future."

Heartner had committed a complete denial of Vandal and Talosheim. There was no need to cling to ideals of peacefully dealing with them.

"Ah, hold on. I'm not including the new villages in that."

That comment got pleased smiles around the group.

"One thing, Lord Vandal," Eleanora said. "What is this rock here, exactly? I don't think that was there when we arrived."

"It doesn't look like a naturally occurring phenomenon," Zulan said.

The two were looking up at a massive rock rising up behind Vandal. It was much bigger than any of the trees in the forest. But more than the sheer size, it was its strange shape that caught the eyes. It looked like a giant skull, with a wide-open mouth big enough for a wagon to drive into. The interior appeared to be connected to something—or somewhere. Warm air flowed out, almost as though the skull itself was breathing.

". . . It isn't anything harmful to us," Vandal responded. "I'll tell you that."

Skill level increased for Dungeon Construction, Scream, Magical Power Auto Recovery, Death Attribute Allure, and Limit Break!

Name: Vandal
Race: Dhampir (Dark Elf)
Age: 7 years old
Alias: [Ghoul King] [Eclipse King] [Unspoken Name]
Job: Poison Warrior
Level: 20
Job History: Death Mage Golem Creator Undead Tamer Crusher of Souls
Status
Vitality: 184
Magical Power: 378120344
Strength: 128
Agility: 130

Muscle: 119

Intellect: 761

———Passive Skills

[Brute Strength: Level 3] [Rapid Healing: Level 5] [Death Attribute Magic: Level 6]

[Resist Maladies: Level 7] [Resist Magic: Level 3] [Night Vision] [Death Attribute Allure: Level 7 (UP!)]

[Skip Incantation: Level 4] [Enhance Brethren: Level 8] [Magical Power Auto Recovery: Level 5 (UP!)]

[Enhance Followers: Level 4] [Poison Dispersal (Claws, Fangs, Tongue): Level 3] [Agility Enhancement: Level 1]

[Physical Length Change (Tongue) Level 3 (NEW!)]

———Active Skills

[Suck Blood: Level 7] [Limit Break: Level 6 (UP!)] [Golem Creation: Level 6]

[Non-Attribute Magic: Level 5] [Magic Control: Level 4] [Spirit Body: Level 7] [Carpentry: Level 4]

[Construction: Level 3] [Cooking: Level 4] [Alchemy: Level 4] [Brawling Proficiency: Level 5]

[Soul Crusher: Level 6] [Simultaneous Activation: Level 5] [Remote Control: Level 6] [Surgery: Level 3]

[Mental Multitasking: Level 5] [Substantiation: Level 4] [Cooperation: Level 3] [Rapid Cognition: Level 3]

[Command: Level 1] [Agriculture: Level 3] [Clothing Making: Level 2]

[Thrown Projectile Proficiency: Level 3] [Scream: Level 3 (NEW!)]

———Unique Skill

[God Smiter: Level 3] [Spiritual Abnormality: Level 4 (UP!)] [Spiritual Corrosion: Level 3 (UP!)]

[Dungeon Construction: Level 4 (NEW!)]
——Curses
[Unable to carry over experience from previous lives] [Unable to enter existing jobs] [Unable to personally acquire experience]

"So, it isn't going to harm us . . . and? It looks like a dungeon," Eleonora said.

"Just leave it," Vandal said.

"Are you sure?" Zulan asked. "You don't want to check it out?"

"We're still close to the town," Vandal replied. "If we go inside and then some adventurers come out to investigate it, we don't want know what might happen. Also, we need to prioritize Princess Lebia."

"All true," Eleonora said.

Vandal gave a nod, deciding to tell them about his new Dungeon Construction skill later. It wasn't something they should be experimenting with this close to a town anyway.

The day after the minor incident in which a dhampir child mysteriously fled from the adventurers' guild, everything was normal in Niakki. Apart from for a few junkies looking for a fix and a few men visiting their favorite brothel, it was the same "today" that most lived through yesterday.

Denuh's life had been a string of minor but unfortunate events. Her father had fallen sick, forcing her to work in order to support her family. Once he recovered enough to work again, she was almost immediately married off. In her new home, her mother-in-law used her like an indentured servant, and when the woman finally died, Denuh's husband didn't last much longer. No matter what was going on, she was always run off her feet.

Her son had grown up into a man with no intention of caring for his mother. When he got married, Denuh thought she might finally catch a break, but her son and his new wife simply moved out. The only one who listened to her was her dumb nephew.

There was nothing good to be had in life anyway. I'd grow apples, sell 'em, rinse, and repeat . . . Denuh was walking along, dragging her feet, leading the horde. She had just been selling those apples, when she spotted the kid with the silver coin passing by again . . .

But I never thought my life would continue after death! That he would give me such an important mission. My whole life . . . I lived it all for the purpose of dying yesterday. That's the whole reason I was even born . . . She felt a sense of satisfaction like nothing she had ever felt in life. She felt pride at having become a part of something so much larger than herself.

She continued along the narrow, dark passageway and then came out into the forest. She knew this place. It was the forest where she had died, along with her nephew and his thugs.

If they continued straight, they would reach Niakki. Denuh urged her companions to follow her. As they murmured their new mission, not in life, but in death.

"Ki . . . ei . . .

"Kill . . . He . . . z . . ."

"Kill Heinz!"

Denuh, who had sold apples from a market stall until yesterday, moved forward. Today, she was part of an undead horde of more than one thousand.

A dungeon had suddenly appeared in an ordinary forest. A horde of monsters, mainly undead, flowed out from within, rampaging toward the town of Niakki.

"I'm the cheerful mercenary! Another exciting day of thrilling, thrilling fun!"

Flark, the criminal slave who had belonged to Green Gale Spear Raily in life, was singing to himself as he hoed the ground and spread more fertilizer around.

"What's that? Some more of the crushed-up shell? Leave it to me, my honey!" He was currently tending to the monster plants and going about the task with aplomb.

Since becoming a zombie, one would expect him to have moved on from things like "excitement," "thrills," and "fun," but for some reason, he always behaved like this. He was always singing, even in the middle of the night. He actually managed to creep out the other zombies.

For some reason, Flark was also able to understand immediately whatever the monster plants needed, even though they had no eyes or mouths to communicate. When asked about it, the zombie himself had a rotating selection of answers. The one he gave the most often was that he could hear the voices of the fairies.

"Hey! Flark! You handle these fields while we're gone, okay?"

A bunch of giantling undead came along, all of them

seething with anger. They were apparently about to start some kind of operation to save their children, who had been taken by—someone. No one told Flark much of anything that was happening, but he didn't care.

"The Child said to let you care for the monster plants! Don't let him down!"

"Of course I wooooon't!" Flark howled back happily. Vandal trusted him and expected big results from his zombie farming. That knowledge was all it took to blow his blues away.

Not that a zombie got the blues, either.

He skipped happily around the fields, gathering produce, harvesting wheat using a Tractor Golem, and checking in on the Immortal Ents.

"Oh my! Oh me!" In the Immortal Ent forest, he found a big gate, created from a number of trees all twisted together.

It looked like a dungeon had popped up. Flark had no idea why.

Kanata was sitting in the driver's seat of his wagon, proceeding along the paved road. He was slowly moving toward Vandal's position, as relayed to him by his Target Radar, but there was something odd about the proceedings.

"What tricks is this undead-loving dickbag using?"

The radar gave him precise details on Vandal's position. Not just the distance but also things like his elevation in relation to Kanata. That information had told him, the previous night, that Vandal had been proceeding through the air at a height of around 300 meters. Kanata didn't have an accurate timepiece, so he couldn't be entirely sure, but based on what he could estimate, Vandal had likely been traveling at thirty or forty miles per hour. That continued for hours, with him only returning to the ground when dawn was almost breaking.

Kanata also didn't have an accurate map, but he presumed Vandal's destination was here, the capital city of the Heartner Domain. But his means of travel was the far bigger concern.

"His Divine Holiness mentioned his ridiculous volume of Magical Power, but I thought he could only use death attribute magic. How is he flying around, then? There are no jets or helicopters in this world, more's the pity."

The only things Kanata knew about death attribute magic came from the materials that had been left on Origin and more incomplete information from Rodocolte. From his data, Kanata's analysis was that—whatever it was called—death attribute magic specialized in the medical field and could be handled fairly easily if measures were put in place to avoid poison and sickness. It seemed to have nothing but the kind of abilities that would be considered fringe in a video game. Niche, but not nasty.

His understanding did *not* allow for flight like a bird.

"I know he didn't get any affinity for other attributes. So how is he flying around? Did he build a plane or something?" Kanata considered that Vandal had somehow used his knowledge from Earth to create a vehicle of some kind, but that also felt like a stretch. Kanata had been trained hard by the military and obtained all sorts of useful skills. If he had the materials, he could probably fashion a decent glider, or use magic to make a hot air balloon. However, a glider could only do that—glide. It couldn't move at car-speed. That was even more true for a balloon.

Kanata therefore considered that Vandal had built some kind of aircraft, but that seemed improbable as well. In theory, sure, it might be possible. But he would need to make not only every nut and screw, but the tools to make them all first. If he was an aircraft geek of the highest order, he might be able to fashion a propeller aircraft, given a few years; Hiroto Amamiya hadn't seemed like an aircraft geek to him.

"Ah, but this is a fantasy world, isn't it? I keep thinking I'm just back in the dark ages. They have gods and dragons and all that shit here. Maybe he's friends with a monster that can fly or has some flying undead. What do you think?" Kanata turned to look into the wagon bed and at the half-naked women lying there.

After taking the first wagon from the merchant, Kanata had gathered food and equipment in the closest town. That said, he didn't fancy the "leather" armor made from the skin of some crazy monster, nor did he want to encumber himself with heavy metal. So he ended up only buying some shoes and beast hide gloves. For weapons, he selected a knife and arrows coated with silver to provide anti-undead properties. He also purchased a short staff, which was useful as media when casting magic—all the while muttering about how, on Origin, they had used rings, gloves, or even implants embedded in the arm for that purpose.

He wanted a crossbow, but he needed to provide identification to make that kind of purchase here in Heartner, so he had given up on it. He also wanted to give himself a little hero treatment with a nice meal and clean bed, but even a large town on Ramda couldn't provide him with the kind of pampering he craved. He had no interest in eating monster meat.

He had therefore turned his attentions to women. The prostitutes on offer were beast girls, dwarves, and giantlings.

"Does everything on this world have fur or a beard?" he despaired. All the more human-looking whores had happened to be already occupied, as the madam told it, but Kanata wasn't about to pay to screw something with a tail. He left the red-light district behind.

The following day, just before his departure, Kanata happened to see an adventurers' guild. He remembered what Rodocolte said and decided it was worth registering after all. He figured that it might allow him to purchase that crossbow.

Things went well at first. When he saw the elf on the reception desk, he had even had the leeway to recall that he hadn't ever watched the third movie in that popular fantasy series about a ring.

That leeway vanished when he found himself surrounded by soldiers and adventurers.

As it turned out, the stolen stuff Kanata had been selling off included items only handled by one merchant—the guy Kanata had killed. That had put an unwanted spotlight on him.

The soldiers closed in, presumably to seize and interrogate him. So Kanata muttered the word "Fire" and activated a fire magic attack all around himself. The soldiers and adventurers had likely considered him no more of a threat than a regular bandit; they paid for that mistake by burning to death, along with the unlucky elf at reception, all while Kanata used Gungnir to pass through the building, ground, and castle walls to escape.

Those back in the town would probably still be looking for him, locking down the gates with the assumption that he couldn't have left the town so quickly. Kanata got back on the road and stole another wagon from the next merchant who came along. The women in back were the adventurers who had been protecting that merchant.

"That was a bit of a surprise back at the adventurers' guild, sure, but it wasn't any trouble in the end. I was one of the Bravers, for all my faults. I guess I can handle myself."

Kanata had the stats of a Grade D adventurer, the skills of a Grade C, and the magic of a Grade B or A; he certainly wasn't invulnerable. Without Gungnir, it would have been bad. Indeed, even with it, if he had stuck around in town to fight, the Grade C adventurers or knights would have picked him off once his MP ran out. He didn't know anything about battle techs, non-attribute magic, or the effects of different skills.

"No reply for me, ladies? Oh, crap, did I kill you all? I don't remember killing that one . . . ah, I guess she bled out after I cut her ligaments to stop her from fighting back. Should've tried harder to stop the bleeding."

All the adventurers had expired. Kanata had already enjoyed his time with them, anyway. *Fur and beards and whatnot aren't so bad when you don't pay*, he thought.

Kanata would already be a wanted man and considered a dangerous criminal. He had unleashed powerful fire magic inside of the adventurers' guild and left a trail of carnage in his wake. The guild would be highly invested in hunting him down. Even with Gungnir, it was only a matter of time before he was caught and killed.

There was a question of why Kanata acted this way. Why he didn't feel guilty or scared of being punished for his crimes. Why he could be unthinkingly vicious at the drop of a hat.

It was because he had literally just been reborn into this world and saw no value at all in his third life here.

Previously, Vandal thought that if he obtained a certain social standing in Ramda, it would shield him when Hiroto Amemiya and the others were eventually born here. That thinking assumed that the newcomers would have families and their own place in society on this world and would have to live their entire lives on Ramda. They wouldn't be able to afford to do anything too extreme if they had family, friends, and partners to worry about.

But someone without any attachment to Ramda had directly appeared here, fully formed. Such a person could kill people who pissed them off on a whim, steal whatever they liked if they needed money, and rape and kill anyone they pleased, without any cause for concern so long as they could make their escape into the next life. Even if they were caught and executed, they didn't have to worry about upsetting their friends, or ruining their family name. No one in this entire world could emotionally leverage anything against such a person.

Kanata was, strictly speaking, one of the reborn. But as he had arrived on Ramda at the same age, in the same body from his previous life, it was much more like he had been teleported over. That also meant he didn't know anything about the social norms and values of this world, which the other reborn would naturally absorb as they grew up here. That was how they would learn that the people of this world were, for better or worse, the same as them. That they had the same humanity. Kanata didn't understand that, and he had no desire to learn it.

For Kanata, this third life on Ramda was nothing but a bridge into his fourth one. He thought as little of the people on this world as the dirt on his boot. They were primitives, living on a ball of mud far inferior to Earth or Origin.

Indeed, he may not have even considered them as living things. Not in the same way as himself. All this status and skill stuff, the elves and beastmen and dwarves—Ramda felt more like a video game to Kanata than real life.

"If he's heading to the capital, hopefully he'll settle down for a little while rather than fly off again. I don't need the hassle of trying to work out how he's getting around," Kanata muttered.

Rodocolte's information was full of holes. So while Kanata knew that Vandal's base of operations was on the other side of a large mountain range, he had no idea how Vandal had crossed those mountains to get here. He also knew almost nothing about that base of operations itself.

"I'm fated to kill him or whatever all that stuff means," Kanata sighed. "It'll be fine. First, I need to dispose of this wagon and these corpses."

The capital of the Heartner Domain, Neinland, was basking in the hot summer sun. The marketplace of the sprawling city was bustling with life despite the heat.

Heartner was landlocked, so almost all seafood products were dried, salted, or pickled. There was a small amount of fresh goods, the transport of which required magic items. But aside from seafood, the overall range of produce was exceptional.

"I've never seen these spices before," Eleonora commented.

"I'd think not! They are special to our country! You won't find them on sale in any other domain!" The storekeeper sounded very pleased with himself, to which Eleonora responded with a smile and then a purchase. "Great! Thank you. Don't you want them powered up, though?"

"No, thank you. I'll take the seeds."

"You sure know your stuff," the merchant said with a smile. Eleonora took her bag of spices and moved to another stall.

"Hey there, pretty lady! Take a look at my wares?" A merchant selling accessories tried to strike up a conversation, but she didn't even glance in his direction. Vandal had asked her to buy spices, vegetables, and fruit. That was it.

She chuckled to herself. "Lord Vandal's magic will have us growing your special spices before you know what hit you!" Death attribute magic could push away the specter of death from even the most difficult-to-cultivate plants. They would still need water, of course, but such magic would even allow alpine plants to grow in a desert.

On Origin, while death magic was successfully used to get plants to grow, it had been a lot harder to make them flower or fruit. On Ramda, living creatures were far more prone to mutation. If they planted these seeds in Talosheim, they would definitely turn into monster plants or Immortal Ents and provide fruit. Once the bags carried by Eleonora passed to Vandal and returned to Talosheim, the Heartner Domain would lose its agricultural edge forever!

Of course, such schemes would only really play a role once Talosheim started to trade with ducal domains besides Heartner. So Eleonora didn't really understand exactly how terribly what she was currently doing would one day impact this domain.

"Honestly speaking, I was hoping for revenge to be a little more . . . visceral," Eleonora said to herself. "But Lord Vandal said it would be a calamity, so I'm sure that's what he will bring."

Vandal's Spirit Body wings had allowed Eleonora and everyone to travel in one night a distance that would normally take a month to walk on foot. They therefore knew nothing yet of the incident involving monsters in Niakki.

"What next . . . ?" Eleonora looked around. "Oh, I've never seen this fruit before either."

"Lady, you a traveler? This fruit is a specialty of our domain. It only grows here! You can taste our pride in every bite!"

"Well then! How could I possibly turn that down?"

"The society you have here is excluding me. I knew it," Vandal stated.

"*D-d o y o u . . . t h i n k s o?*"

"I do think so."

"*Y-y o u d o . . . t h i n k s o.*" The guild master of the magicians' guild was stuttering ghoulishly, his eyes rolled back white. Vandal may as well have been talking to himself.

Vandal's reason for this assault on the guild leadership was because this particular master was a progenitor vampire sympathizer. Vandal and his allies had extracted that piece of information from the vampire they killed in Niakki. Upon their arrival in Neinland, their first order of business was to track the man down and attack him. The first part had been easy, thanks to the countless spirits that had approached Vandal upon their arrival, revealing the location of the Guild Master's mansion.

Then, they attacked it.

Vandal simply created a Magic Sucking Barrier that covered

the entire building, and the man promptly collapsed. He would have been a powerful foe, if allowed to use his magic. Without it, he was just an old man with a fancy title. Admittedly, covering the entire building with a barrier after a long Spirit Body flight drained Vandal's own magic.

Braga, Zulan, and Eleonora defeated the other powerless Magicians and the mansion's hired guard. The bigger challenge was getting the Guild Master to actually talk: the man was strong-willed and had a high level of Resist Poison, so Vandal decided to try out Spiritual Corrosion.

He increased his number of heads and looked at the man straight-on while whispering into both of his ears. Not for very long—an hour at most. That was all it had taken to break the man completely. Vandal's original plan had been to simply kill him and move on after getting the information he needed.

"Not that I have any sympathy for you, after all the horrible things you've been doing in exchange for forbidden knowledge from Tehneshia," Vandal chided the man.

"*I-I am . . . s-sorry . . .*"

"Hmmm, this Spiritual Corrosion skill is powerful, but hard to control. I definitely need more practice."

The issue was more with Vandal's own personality than the skill itself, namely his inability to take it easy on anyone he saw as a threat.

"At least this got us access to your secret library."

Vandal gained access to the restricted areas of the magicians' guild by using Possession. This involved using Spirit Bodification on his entire body and controlling the fleshy remains of the broken Guild Master. Possession was a death attribute spell he had only created recently. He couldn't fully control the beings he possessed—it was more like riding along—which meant he couldn't command someone in full control of their faculties. However, if someone's mind had been completely broken, he could puppet their remains around as he saw fit.

Thanks to this nasty new technique, he walked right into a veritable flea market of forbidden knowledge.

"Hmm, none of this knowledge looks like it will be useful right away," Vandal commented. "Oh, here's a way to make homunculi. But you need to make a contract with a Demon or Devil God first."

He perused further. "A way to control the minds of others? Hm, but it's a complex procedure, and we don't need that with Spiritual Corrosion around. Let's see, let's see. This poison . . . a downgrade from what I already use, with a higher MP cost."

In fact, while the label of "forbidden" made the library sound appealing, it didn't have much useful stuff. Many of the skills were inferior versions of things Vandal could already do. Of course, there was no helping that; death attribute magic was itself "forbidden knowledge" of a sort, just for the entire population.

"Using magic to mutate monsters is forbidden, apparently. That sounds like what I'm doing in Talosheim could be a problem." Vandal scratched his head. "Eh, it's probably okay if we're not a member of the magicians' guild. Like we could even join anyway." Vandal read further. "These guilds are real gatekeepers, sheesh. A shame."

The adventurers' guild here would be the same as in Niakki, of course. Getting into the magicians' guild required approval from a Guild Master and a letter of recommendation from a high-ranking member or noble or graduation from the magical academy. The artisans' guild required working experience with a master or other artisan; the merchants' guild required a product ready to sell and the admission fee; the tamers' guild required training by a member or a recommendation from them and being able to prove that you could actually tame monsters.

The guilds all had different names, but they all needed pretty much the same thing to get through the doors. Among them all, Vandal thought he might currently have a chance with the tamers' guild. But the issue would be showing off his tamed monsters. If he wheeled out Eleonora, a noble vampire, it would probably tip off the agents of the progenitors that were still in the city. Meanwhile, demonstrating his zombie ninja giantling and black goblins would cause no less of a panic. Lefdia would probably get him tarnished as a freak serial killer. He could make some golems and show them off, but those would likely get labeled as alchemy.

"The best idea is still to wait for things to calm down and then register with an adventurers' guild somewhere else," Vandal decided. "I can think about becoming a tamer or merchant or whatever after that." He clapped. "All right, let's pack up and move out!" Vandal had adopted a divide-and-conquer approach for his library search—by literally dividing his body.

Now he collected up a pile of texts and cursed items and prepared them for transportation. He had already used the highest-ranking members of the establishment, also vampire sympathizers, to practice his Spiritual Corrosion. He simply used the guild master as a puppet and asked them to speak alone, one at a time. Once they were away from prying eyes, he had moved in close as though to whisper some juicy secrets in their ears, ended his Possession, and used his new elongated tongue to stick some poison in their ears. The capture was simplicity itself.

Then he subjected them to Spiritual Corrosion until their minds broke.

"I thought Magicians had a little more mental fortitude than this," Vandal breathed.

Now, he could order them to carry all the forbidden texts and cursed items out from the restricted library for him. After all, they were the bigwigs around here.

"At least we have the location of the crypt. I'll start digging a tunnel down there tonight."

Gaaaaaaah!

The final monster had been a Rank 7 Poison Zombie Giant, comprised of multiple Poison Zombies all mushed together. Heinz chopped it down with his burning blue blade as it bellowed, checked to make sure no new foes had appeared, and gave a sigh. This last monster had been significantly stronger than any of the others, formed around the core of a zombie who looked to have been a middle-aged woman.

"That's the end of this undead rampage. Everyone still with me?" Heinz called out.

"Yeah, still here. Worn out but alive."

"Not a scratch on me . . . but worn out for sure."

Heinz and his party had been put to the test. The monsters in the rampage were mainly between Rank 4 and 5. There were also fewer of them than average for a monster rampage, somewhere between a few hundred and one thousand. It should've been no challenge for the Five Hue Blades. In fact, normally, such a horde would hardly be worth the time of day for them. The fighting should have been totally one-sided—that was the power level of a Grade A party.

However, the monsters that had swarmed into Niakki had not been normal.

More than seventy percent of the horde were undead, with the remainder made up of plant and bug monsters. All with the capacity to speak repeated just one phrase, like some kind of curse: "Kill Heinz." A horde of monsters led by one with the "King" title could sometimes move almost as a single organism, but this was a hundred times more extreme.

On balance, though, it could also be called a good thing. The horde hadn't been interested, specifically, in entering the town of Niakki. The guardsmen, knights, and adventurers present gathered to form up an emergency force, but the horde ignored them and the town completely, instead charging directly for one particular individual standing on the frontline of the defenders: Heinz himself.

Even if there were wounded, immobile soldiers within reach, and even if there were exhausted adventurers practically dropping their shields, the monsters ignored them to strike at Heinz instead.

The monsters were also far stronger than their Rank would have suggested and continued the attack, regardless of the numbers they lost—and regardless of whether or not they died. When the living bug monsters were slain, they promptly turned undead and pressed the attack. The bones of the defeated undead gave off bacteria and mold, in turn creating plant-type monsters like Poison Mushrooms and Venom Molds. When the plant types were chopped down, bugs emerged from their bodies and turned into new monsters.

Faced with this endless cycle of monsters, Heinz and the other defenders had in actuality faced a horde more than ten thousand strong.

"Someone really hates you, that's for sure," Jennifer said. She was the human fighter who had joined Heinz's party after he moved his base of operations to the Olbaum Electorate Kingdom. "What did you do to deserve this?"

"We do kill a lot of monsters in our line of work. Plenty of reasons to upset someone somewhere. But this still felt pretty extreme," said Diana. She was an elven priestess of the Sleep Goddess Mirl.

Before Heinz replied, he turned to look back in the direction of Niakki.

Because the monsters had only targeted the Five Hue Blades—only targeted Heinz, to be exact—the town walls were untouched. The same could not be said of the defenders, of course. But while there were some serious injuries, only a handful of unlucky ones had died.

It was a while before Heinz responded. "If I had to make a guess, I'd say that dhampir kid," he finally said.

"The one who suddenly flew out of the adventurers' guild?" Jennifer asked. "Can you think of any reason you might hate him?"

"I doubt that boy and this monster rampage have any connection at all," Diana added.

Heinz wasn't sure how to explain this to them, but he opened his mouth to try.

"I agree, for the most part. It's just . . . his name was Vandal."

The two women didn't understand what his answer meant and just blinked.

Heinz honestly wasn't sure himself. However, the dark elf "witch" he had helped captured in Milg had been named Dalshia. That incident was about seven years ago, too. On the sign in sheet at the adventurers' guild counter, there had been the name Vandal and the age 7.

"I think he might be—"

"You're overthinking things, Heinz."

"Edgar?"

"There's no way the non-vamp parent of that dhampir was a dark elf," Edgar said. "His skin was white as snow. Impossible! Heinz, it's just your guilt making you feel that way."

"You . . . might have a point."

The classic characteristics of a dhampir were their different-colored eyes, with one of them always blood-crimson in color, and their freely retractable fangs and claws. Everything else about their appearance was derived from their parents, like any other child. With a parent as a dark elf, that wax-like white skin made no sense.

Furthermore, there was no way an infant could hope to survive alone, out in the wilds. And definitely no way such a child could have managed to cross the Boundary Mountains and reach the Olbaum Electorate Kingdom.

"Yeah. I'm overthinking it. Thinking a kid like that had something to do with this rampage—I guess I'm worn out too. It's not like he's the Demon King reborn or anything like that." Heinz muttered the rumors that had been on the lips on many devout to Divine Alda in recent times.

Edgar gave a chuckle, nodding along. But, behind his

agreement, he had already decided to check into Vandal some more once they got back to the town.

The flow of information in Niakki is handled by that group calling themselves the Night Fangs, Edgar thought. *I'll have to reach out.*

This decision by Edgar would eventually lead to the shocking Night Fangs Incident, in which it came to light that the head of the organization and other key figures were continuing to run it even after dying and becoming undead.

"More importantly, after getting back and resting up, we need to come and check out the dungeon those monsters all came from," Heinz said. "The horde didn't come from the direction of any known dungeons in the vicinity, meaning there must be a new one out there. It might even be Zakkato's Trial."

Zakkato's Trial was the only confirmed so-called "wandering" dungeon in the world. It was first confirmed around 100 years ago, and it would appear somewhere on the continent, without any warning, and then vanish again after about one month. It was impossible to rate or classify, and one had never returned from it alive—excepting Heinz and the Five Hue Blades, although doing so was a feat that had reduced them to four. It was said that Zakkato's treasure, along with the undead Zakkato himself, lay on the bottom floor and that the one who defeated him would become the true successor to the Hero Bellwood.

"If that's the case . . . we're going to clear it this time," Heinz declared. "For Malti's sake, too. First things first, though. We need to get back to the inn. Seren will be worried."

"No, first we need to report to the guild . . . Okay, okay, I'll do that. Just don't blame me when the guild girls start to only look in my direction." Edgar gave a wry grin at his leader, who, he knew, was anxious to return to the dhampir girl's side.

The Death Mage

CHAPTER FIVE
THE GUY WHO FINISHED ON HIS THIRD LIFE

Vandal groaned. "Haah . . . oooh . . . this is nasty stuff!"

"Lord Vandal, whatever is the matter?"

"Unforgiveable. Punishable by death!" Vandal was currently in the middle of digging a tunnel from the house of the magicians' guild master to the crypt beneath Duke Heartner's castle via the simple method of turning the ground into golems using Golem Creation and having them open a path. Braga, the other black goblins, and their girlfriends were staying behind in the house. Meanwhile, the members of the guild whose minds Vandal had already broken were preparing something of a parting gift.

The guild master's mansion was home to some pricy artifacts, such as magical staves, but Vandal was still empty-handed. If he tried to use wands or staves created for human magic, he had to be incredibly precise and careful or the item would simply tear itself apart, rot away, or crumble to dust. Using a wand to help him cast magic required concentration akin to writing on grains of rice, so Vandal hardly cared to try. He did wonder, though, if there might be a wand out there more suited to his needs.

And although he was unarmed, he did have an extra hand along in the form of Lefdia, although he could hardly be said to have equipped her.

Regardless, in the middle of these earthworks, Vandal suddenly started to mumble to himself.

"A party of adventurers called Western Calm. The receptionist Aria. Hanna and her father."

Zulan, undead himself, could see the spirits that were crowding around Vandal. "They are some of the countless spirits around the Child. All of these seem like folks who died recently."

It had been just like when they arrived in Niakki: a horde of spirits almost overwhelmed him as soon as they entered the capital of Neinland. There were so many, Zulan couldn't make out what any individual one of them was saying. However, the spirits that were currently talking to Vandal seemed a little different from the others.

"Eleonora, Zulan," Vandal said. "If a man who looks around thirty, black hair and eyes, by the name of Kanata Kaito should appear before us, I want you to let me handle it unless I say otherwise," Vandal said.

"Kanata Kaito? That name sounds like—"

"One of the scum who killed you in your previous life, Child?! If he does appear, perfect! We can kill him, turn him into a zombie, and pump him for information!"

As it turned out, the spirits of the people Kanata killed had already tattled on him. They told him that Kanata was in Neinland and closing in on Vandal. They had no idea how, but it seemed like he was aware of Vandal's location.

The spirits told him that their swords, spears, and magic hadn't been able to so much as touch him, while his own attacks simply passed through their bodies and armor. He was also skilled in Brawling and Dagger Proficiency and had powerful fire and wind attribute magic.

This ignoring-defenses trick must be the cheat ability Rodocolte gave him, Vandal thought, *along with his affinity for fire and wind, clearly enhanced on Origin. I guess his combat skills come from his experiences there too. This is what happens when you don't curse a guy, Rodocolte!* He thought about how painfully unfair it was that he had been forced to start over from scratch.

But he also needed to talk down Zulan and Eleonora, who looked ready to kill the guy on sight. They were tough enough to handle reasonably strong adventurers or knights, but when a cheat ability was thrown into the mix, it was hard to tell what the outcome might be. That was why they were called cheats, after all.

"You need to let me handle it," Vandal said. "If we're going to kill him . . . okay, we're definitely going to kill him; the guy is a sick jerk, but I want to do it."

"I can tell from those spirits that he's not a nice guy . . . but is he really that dangerous?" Zulan asked.

"He really is. I think he might be insane."

Upon first learning about Kanata, Vandal had felt confusion more than hatred. To put it briefly, he wondered what the hell the guy was playing at.

Everything he did was inhuman, for certain, but also completely reckless and unthinking. He immediately resorted to killing, raping, and pillaging the second things stopped going his way. Even with his cheat ability, he wasn't going to last long if he kept that up. There were other, more pressing issues as well: Vandal was supposedly the first of them to die on Origin, and yet, this guy was showing up as an adult much older than him. And how did he seem to know exactly where Vandal was? Vandal could only assume that it was Rodocolte's doing.

"In any case, he's definitely coming to try to kill me. I'm

going to keep Detect Life running on a regular basis going forward."

Vandal heard that Kanata was talking about a "job" that he needed to do, presumably killing Vandal. He wasn't sure why it was happening now, but it was still something he had to deal with. If Kanata was coming straight for Vandal, at least it meant Braga and the others waiting back in the house wouldn't be in danger.

"I thought they were all heroes on the side of justice in their world," Eleonora said.

"Hardly what I'd call them," Vandal replied. "It's like how Bellwood is a hero to the faithful of Alda but not to us. Same thing."

"That makes sense."

At that moment, Vandal and his allies reached the deepest point in Neinland. Detect Life got no hits from the dark stone passageway or anywhere it led. However, Detect Danger: Death did sense something.

"Traps?" Zulan asked.

"No, from the shape, I think it's a barrier. Must be left down here by the hero," Vandal said.

They had entered the passageway from the tunnel they burrowed open, proceeding with caution. Vandal fired off a weak Death Shot down the passageway. The empty tunnel was suddenly filled with a glimmering wall, throwing off sound and a glaring flash as it repelled the Death Shot.

"A barrier left by the Hero Neinroad!" Eleonora breathed.

"What!" Zulan exclaimed. "Your Death Shot bounced off it!"

"Time to turn that off, then."

"Huh?!"

Eleonora and Zulan gasped. Vandal simply started to use his death attribute magic to break down the hero's barrier.

He wasn't doing anything too difficult. He was simply applying a burst of pressure, more than the barrier could take, smashing through it. Neinroad's barrier held up for a respectable number of seconds, but in the end, it shattered with a sound like breaking glass.

"Phew," Vandal said. "It was tougher than Ice Age's ice, I'll give it that. I used 300 million MP on that. Ah, can I have my snack now?"

"Uh, oh, sure." Zulan still looked surprised as he fished out the flagon from his pack. It contained the fresh blood from one of the Guild Master's bodyguards. The Guild Master had benefitted in many ways from working with the progenitors, which in turn had rolled downhill to his men. Their blood was delicious.

"Ahh! Nothing like a fresh pint after a hard day's work."

"Lord Vandal, I'm not entirely sure . . ."

"I know, I felt it. I'm only seven."

"No, it isn't that. You looked very cute, is all, like a child playing at grownups."

"I see." He slumped his shoulders a little and carried on without waiting for his MP to fully recover.

Kanata was on the way here, but Vandal's Magical Power Auto Recovery skill gave him more than ten thousand MP back every second. It wouldn't be a problem.

After passing through the barrier, they came into a wide underground crypt, quite unexpected from the narrow tunnel that led to this place. There were bones and husks all around in hollows large and small. It definitely didn't look like a holy place. The air was unpleasantly damp and had something nasty about it. Detection magic did not indicate any life down here, and yet, there were soft moans that echoed about the cavern.

"Hmmm. I don't see the princess yet," Eleonora said.

"Hey! Princess Lebia! It's me, Zulan! We have Princess Zandia . . . well, her hand here with us, the Lady Lefdia! Please, come out!" Zulan called out as well, taking Lefdia from Vandal and holding the hand aloft.

There was still no sign of Princess Lebia or any other spirits.

"There might be another barrier," Eleonora suggested. "When sealing something in, people often use a double or even triple barrier, don't you think?"

So they searched around some more, and they found what appeared to be exactly that. There was a silver coffin with a whip wrapped around it. That appeared to be the center of the barrier.

" . . . Someone's got a fetish," Vandal said.

"Ah, Neinroad is said to have had Whip Proficiency. That's probably what this is."

"What do you think is inside that coffin?" Eleonora mused. "If it's a progenitor, it might become a powerful ally for us . . . and it might not. It might be on the side of the Demon or Devil Gods."

"We would get in trouble if something really nasty pops out," Vandal agreed, still deciding to give it a go. He checked with Detect Danger: Death, but there was no real response. "It might just be empty. I'm going to try, anyway."

He used the same method as he had on the first barrier.

Before he was even finished, however, the coffin shredded the whip and opened from the inside.

"Lord Vandal!"

"No!" Eleonora and Zulan were quick to grab Vandal and fall back. Something that looked like a crimson amoeboid popped out the coffin, neck arching as it leered down at Vandal, and then closed in with the speed of a slithering snake.

Glug, glug, glug, glug . . . buuurp!

Just for Vandal to drink it down.

The two of them were stunned. Vandal licked his lips and put his hands together in thanks for the delicious meal.

"Lord Vandal!" Eleonora shouted. "What was that? And why would you drink it?!"

"Why? It practically climbed into my mouth."

"One would normally, I would think, spit it out!"

"It's wrong to waste food. Although I'm not sure I'd normally call blood that was sealed away by a hero 100 thousand years ago 'food,' exactly."

"That's what that was? Blood?"

"Could it have been—a part of the Demon King?" Eleonora exclaimed.

The Demon King Gudranis had famously been chopped into pieces after he was defeated by the heroes, who then sealed away each part. If this seal had been for nothing but a coffin of blood, the only possible source of that blood could be the Demon King.

Indeed, he had heard the announcement **"Sucked the blood of the Demon King!"** in his head. The two of them were so surprised, however, he wasn't sure he should tell them.

Skill level increased to 10 for Suck Blood! Became the higher skill Drain Blood!

Skill level increased for Drain Blood, Death Attribute Magic, Brute Strength, Rapid Healing, Magical Power Auto Recovery, Resist Magic, Poison Dispersal (Claws, Fangs, Tongue), and Physical Length Change (Tongue)!

Acquired the Alias, Demon King Reborn!

Vandal really wasn't happy about that last Alias there. He most certainly was not the Demon King reborn! However—

"Throw it up, Child! Throw up!"

"Spit, Lord Vandal! Spit it out!" Zulan was currently holding him upside down by the legs and shaking him around, while Lefdia was continually slapping him on the back. But Vandal had other things on his mind.

"I can't, I mean, I really, absorbed, it, ah, hello, there." As Vandal was still being shaken up and down, his upside-down eyes saw a horde of ghosts appear. Probably because the seal had been broken.

Phantoms. These were like the spirits that Vandal, undead, and Mediums could see, capable of only manifesting a spectral image. Phantoms may not have a physical body, but they were dead people who had turned into actual monsters.

They were Rank 2, and while almost all physical attacks were unable to affect them, they didn't have physical means of attacking either. However, many of them did keep their personalities or memories from when they were alive to a pretty large degree.

"Who are you?" Zulan asked. "From Duke Heartner's house? But no, what's this terrifying but somehow reassuring presence . . . ?"

"Look at the giantling and that hand. They are undead."

"What are undead doing here? They have broken the barrier? We have been freed?"

The phantoms—semi-transparent with a wispy outline and missing their bodies from below the knees—were muttering amongst themselves. They didn't appear to be hostile, but they did appear to be scared of something.

"Oh! Princess Lebia, are you here? It's me, Zulan from Talosheim!" Zulan unthinkingly let go of Vandal's legs and then started to shout toward the phantoms. Eleonora caught Vandal without missing a beat, as he saw a female phantom with long hair down to her waist emerge from among the horde. "Princess Lebia!"

"Zulan. I remember you. A scout and warrior; the best among our people with a short sword."

Princess Lebia and Zulan hadn't been close, or even really had much contact, but in Talosheim, there had only been a population of around five thousand and a lax hierarchy; an excellent warrior would have opportunities to meet with a princess. Zulan was a scout, rare for giantlings, so that had probably helped him to stick in her memory.

"You remained in Talosheim with Zandia and the others and fought bravely to the end. What are you doing here, pray tell? Ah, but now that you are here, you have joined us as prisoners, I fear. We will never be able to return to the goddess, never able to have our vengeance on this mortal plane, forced to wander here for eternity—"

"Excuse me, I broke the barrier," Vandal piped up.

"Yes, unless that double barrier is ever somehow brought down—" Lebia paused. "Sorry, you did what?"

"I broke it. My apologies for my rudeness, Princess. I am Vandal, the current king of Talosheim." Vandal gave his greeting while still being held upside down by Eleonora.

Princess Lebia proceeded to listen to Vandal's explanation and then look at Lefdia. "I'm sorry to say, but just from the left hand I can't really confirm if this is my sister," she said.

"I understand completely," Vandal assured her. "What about this rock salt?" The left hand of her sister had not been sufficient proof. However, the rock salt they had carried in from Garan Valley in Talosheim couldn't be found anywhere else, so that served as enough proof for the princess to believe what Vandal was telling her.

He breathed a sigh of relief. If she hadn't believed him, things would have been much more difficult.

"I see," the princess said. "Those who remained in Talosheim made a brave account of themselves. You have my heartfelt thanks for showing your guidance to Borkz and the others and protecting the nation of my forebears. In comparison, I did little to protect my own wards . . ."

"That wasn't your fault, Princess!" Zulan proclaimed heatedly. "The duke betrayed you! He's the bad guy here!"

When Lebia arrived from Talosheim, with her small retinue of guards and other countrypeople, they were welcomed to Heartner not only by its people but by the duke himself. However, when the duke presented a feast to welcome the giantlings, the food was laced with poison. The princess and her companions had believed Duke Heartner's house to be their allies, and none of them suspected a thing as they ate the tainted food. Upon realizing the truth, they did attempt to fight back, but the duke's knights and magicians captured them. They killed her guards on the spot, framed Princess Lebia for attempting to kill the duke and burnt her at the stake. They then buried her body inside the barrier in this crypt.

"I know most of what has happened since, from the people interred here after me," Lebia continued. "The knights and magicians who killed us were also buried here to keep them quiet."

The duke at the time certainly knew how to pull off some shady stuff. It sounded like the information passed to Vandal by Mother Milan in Niakki was coming from someone who had managed to avoid the fate of being trapped here and then wandered as a spirit after their death.

"Shall we discuss what to do next?" Vandal suggested.

"Very well," Lebia agreed. "I know this isn't my place, as one already departed from your mortal world, but you are the ruler of Talosheim now. Please, continue to lead my people. Thank you." Lebia gave a deep bow.

Every single movement she made was so elegant, so refined, it was hard to believe she didn't have a physical body. At the same time, there wasn't a hint of pride or arrogance in her. She was regal and lovely, the epitome of the word "princess." Of course, being a giantling, she was still around seven feet tall, even missing the bottom of her legs. Her outline was blurry, too, but Vandal was sure she had been very attractive in life.

"Now all of us here can finally return to the goddess," she said.

"Ah, can that wait a little longer?" Vandal asked. "We would very much appreciate your help in rescuing those of your people still being held at the slave mine."

"You would? Appreciate what, exactly? I fear there isn't much I can do."

"You won't have to do much," Eleonora said. "We want you to cooperate with Lord Vandal and show yourself to the living giantlings, that is all."

It went without saying that the giantlings currently held at the slave mine didn't know anything about Vandal or modern Talosheim. Furthermore, Death Attribute Allure would not work on them, so they probably wouldn't believe him if he said he had come from Talosheim to rescue them.

Even if Zulan, Borkz, and the other undead giantlings tried to persuade them, Vandal wasn't sure how effective it would be. They might believe close family members or relatives, but undead with no deep relation to them could easily be written off as crazy undead.

Showing them Lefdia wouldn't work, as Princess Lebia herself hadn't been able to confirm the hand belonged to her sister. The teachings of the Goddess Vida were lenient on undead, but they also didn't say to love and obey them no matter what.

Of course, they could ignore the feelings of the slaves, force them to go to Talosheim, and resolve the misunderstanding that way, but any unexpected resistance might lead to injuries or even deaths. Vandal didn't want that. He could, of course, turn anyone who died into undead, but it seemed better to find a way that did not involve anyone dying.

That was where Princess Lebia came in. She had led her people 200 years ago. Even as a ghost, Vandal was sure her words would reach them.

"They should at least listen to you," Vandal said.

"The words of the one who failed to save them? I am not so convinced. I also have little, in rage or anything else, holding me to this world any longer. We have been saved. I'm sure your son will be able to free the slaves without my aid—"

"S-son?! Ah, no, I'm not Lord Vandal's mother—!" Eleonora stammered.

Vandal cut Eleonora off and continued. "Are you okay with that?"

"With . . . what, exactly?" Lebia asked.

"Forgiving them so easily? The ones who killed you, killed your guards, and sealed you away for 200 years. The ones who captured your remaining people and have worked them to the bone for those same 200 years. Don't you wish to bring down your anger, hatred . . . your wrath upon them?"

"I mean . . ." Her voice trembled.

The other giantling phantoms looked equally shaken. When they were killed 200 years ago and learned that the living had been taken to the slave mine, they had indeed been filled with anger and hatred and wrath at the Heartner house. They cursed the betrayal, swore to never forget their grudge, and clung to dreams of vengeance. It had been so bad that they had even responded to the scant magical power of the Demon King and turned into phantoms.

"Revenge doesn't—"

"Revenge is justified," Vandal said. "In this case, especially. I'm not suggesting you hit the people living today with your grudge from 200 years ago. I'm suggesting you hit them with your grudge from today."

Vandal looked Lebia and the others right in the face as he spoke. He wanted them to feel the anger, hatred, and wrath that he was feeling; he wanted them to call forth their own hatred and feelings of powerlessness.

"You should be angry and hate them and hold a grudge. If you're a living being, that's how it would be. You were betrayed by someone you trusted. Killed and defiled. Those you cared about were captured unjustly and put to work for 200 years.

You would be insane if you didn't have powerful feelings about that."

"Yes . . . but . . ."

"When you realized you had been poisoned. When your guards were killed. When you were burned. What did you feel?"

"What did . . . I feel?" Lebia groaned. "Ah! What did I feel?!"

"There should still be hatred, anger, and pain inside you. Allow it to flare up again now."

"Inside me . . ."

"Our anger . . ."

"My . . . HATRED!" Even some random phantoms whom this had nothing to do with were getting a bit worked up, but Vandal pressed his point home.

"Please, lend us that strength. Help us to take back what was taken away." As he finished, he heard a grating sound like sparks, and then light and heat burst out in the darkened crypt.

"I remember now!" Princess Lebia roared. "Now anger! My hatred! I cannot pass on without bringing this grudge to bear! Let us sally forth, my people!" She was burning. Not in a metaphorical sense, either—she was literally burning. Her previously frail-looking spirit body was a shimmering red, with clearly defined lines so that even the details of her face could be seen. She looked like a goddess of fire, with flaming long hair and a burning dress.

Acquired the skill Necromancy Magic!

"That's right! They're both right!"

"We cannot fade away until we bring calamity to the Heartner house that so wronged us!"

"They will pay for using me then casting me aside! The maids know all your secrets! Raaaagh!"

Besides the giantlings, others who had fallen victim to Heartner's schemes in various ways were also swearing revenge. Vandal didn't concern himself with that. Still, all the ghosts in the crypt were burning as though on fire.

"Did they rank up? Why?!" Zulan exclaimed, looking around. "Well, no matter. It looks like Princess Lebia and the others are sticking around."

It was Vandal, sharing his own powerful negative emotions via Spiritual Corrosion, who had triggered what the ghosts had themselves felt in the past and caused this vengeance-hellbent explosion. Further affected by Lebia's history of being burnt at the stake, the princess had turned into a Rank 4 Flame Phantom, while the others became Rank 3 Fire Phantoms. If the Magicians and scholars studying magic at the magicians' guild had witnessed this, they would have gotten very excited.

"You continue to impress me, Lord Vandal," Eleonora said. "Well done."

"Your legend only grows!" Zulan proclaimed.

His companions weren't quite as excited but were definitely impressed. Vandal was himself surprised at how they had all suddenly caught fire. He had shared his own burning, boiling rage and hatred with them, but he hadn't expected it to literally ignite something.

Of course, he wasn't so surprised that he forgot what they came here to do.

"Very well! Let's go and save our people!" Lebia shouted.

But rather than taking Lebia's burning hand, Vandal turned and looked back down the passageway they had arrived through. "I'm sorry, after all that, but something has come up that I need to take care of first."

There was a man standing there, around thirty years old, with black hair and eyes and both hands raised over his head to show they were empty.

"Hold on! Hear me out! I'm sorry about what happened! Forgive me!" Kanata Kaito kneeled before Vandal and then pressed his forehead into the dirt in apology.

When his Target Radar informed Kanata that Vandal was heading down beneath the castle, Kanata clicked his tongue in annoyance.

There would probably be limited space down there, making it harder for Kanata to bring his full strength to bear. If he unleashed his most powerful magic, he would risk his own life by potentially bringing the place down. He might be able to pass through rock and soil using Gungnir, but that wouldn't bring him oxygen.

Furthermore, he had been hoping to attack using ranged weapons—what was called Bow Proficiency here on Ramda. But that would be difficult in a potentially obstacle-filled underground crypt. He might be able to use Gungnir to pass his arrows through any impediments, but he couldn't make his eyes see through them.

That was why, on Origin, he had used an infrared scope to spot targets or used detection magic. There were no such scopes on Ramda, of course, and if he took the time to cast detection magic, there was a good chance it would only let Vandal know exactly where he was.

Given all of these issues, Kanata had decided to give up on a long-range attack. There were two reasons why he hadn't decided to simply give up the attack and either wait for a better chance in the future or try to build a better chance for himself with a more refined strategy. First, Vandal was far more mobile than Kanata, and he might get away if left unchecked. Second, and more significantly, Kanata just wanted this over with so he could start his fourth life.

He had taken some holy water from one of the female adventurers he had toyed with, and he splashed it onto himself now in order to remove any spirits that might be attached to him. What he couldn't know was that they weren't there anymore anyway, having already gone over to Vandal.

Then, relying on his Target Radar, he passed through walls and the floor to reach the crypt.

That was when he realized Vandal knew he was coming.

This knowledge wasn't a result of any of the skills he possessed. It was simply his instincts, honed by all the life-threatening situations he had survived during his previous life.

"Hold on! Hear me out! I'm sorry about what happened! Forgive me!" He therefore revealed himself earlier than intended and proceeded to grovel on the ground. *He's a little bigger than the info from his Divine Holiness suggested*, Kanata thought. *He's got a whole bunch of monsters with him I never heard anything about, too. Are those—burning people?* Outside, Kanata was desperately apologizing, but inside he was cursing Vandal for increasing his combat strength and berating his taste in companions.

". . . What do you want to say?" Vandal asked.

Kanata was thrilled that he had chosen to talk rather than simply attack. A touch soft, just like he had surmised.

"You remember Origin, right? I'm Kanata Kaito. I was a student at the same high school as you—back on Earth, I mean."

The spirits had told Vandal the name Kanata Kaito already, so he had already worked this much out. There was no one with the surname "Kaito" on Ramda. Even without all that, Kanata had been acting so strangely that being one of the reborn was the only way to really explain it.

"I was there at the laboratory," Kanata said.

"... Now that you mention it, I think I do remember you," Vandal said. This was new information. His attention had been held by Narumi Naruse and other more familiar classmates, and those like Kanata whom he hardly knew anyway hadn't really held a place in his memory.

Vandal didn't seem as moved as expected, so Kanata hesitated for a moment but kept his tongue moving. "We didn't know you were the same as us. I really am sorry. Please, forgive me! If you can't—go ahead and kill me. But please, just don't kill the others!"

"Sure, okay."

"Please—huh?" Kanata looked up, meeting Vandal's blank gaze.

"I'm saying, I accept your apology for killing me on Origin," Vandal clarified. "Rodocolte is the one at fault. If you're willing to apologize for that, I forgive you. If you leave me and my allies alone, then we don't need to interact with each other ever again. I'm very busy with all my own problems."

For a start, they needed to set out to save the giantlings still working at the slave mines. So long as the reborn didn't bother him, he didn't care about them. Kanata or even the others. That was the truth.

Indeed, it would have been a bigger hassle if they asked to join him or asked him to join them. Their respective systems of values simply didn't align. The only way he would consider it was if the reborn acknowledged the human rights of undead such as zombies and skeletons and showed respect to them.

But that wasn't going to happen. On Earth and Origin,

turning the dead into undead was considered defiling them. In all forms of stories, including religious ones, the dead had to be buried swiftly or terrible things would happen. That was how it always worked. In movies and games on Earth, there were scenes where, when a character was faced with their zombie girlfriend or father, they said, "That isn't them anymore" and shot the zombie in the head. Vandal could see that same thing happening here. The best he could probably hope for was them agreeing to use undead as weapons.

In any case, he couldn't let anyone dangerous close to Talosheim.

"Is that so? Okay then. I'll make sure to let the others know. We won't get in your—barrier." Kanata specified the barrier that he was expecting Vandal to create and then quickly pulled the trigger on his crossbow, which he had been hiding by keeping the floor transparent using Gungnir. No matter how Vandal replied, Kanata had always been planning to find an opening and shoot him in the head.

The arrow indeed passed through the barrier that Vandal reflexively created, whistling past his ear and then plinking off the wall behind him.

But it hadn't missed. Vandal had dodged it.

"I see," Vandal said. "So your cheat ability is to be able to ignore things. Not just matter but also things like my barriers."

Kanata's face tensed up when the surprise attack he had been so confident in failed. To Vandal, of course, Detect Danger: Death had been reacting while the Kanata was prostrating himself on the ground. That was why Vandal had been watching so closely. Kanata had thought he saw an opening simply because he couldn't read Vandal's expressionless face. To top it all off, Vandal had already heard about Kanata's power from the spirits of those he had killed. He had been pretty much ready for what happened, as he had already assumed that taking cover or using barriers wasn't going to work.

"Hold on, please! I'm not doing this because I want to! It's all Rodocolte!" Kanata recovered from his shock and channeled his surprise to start trying to explain himself again. Eleonora and Zulan, who saw no point in listening to him further, were ready to attack at once. But the name of the god he spoke created a moment of hesitation for Vandal. "I got cursed by that scum-sucker too! I can prove it—eat this!"

Kanata lied about being cursed and then threw the set of knives he had also been concealing in the ground with his crossbow.

"Hah! The same trick again?" Eleonora and Zulan moved to knock down the knives even as they passed through the barrier.

The moment they moved, Kanata celebrated. *Got them! Lucky me, stealing these magic items!* He had thrown magic items that he had stolen from the adventurer party Western Calm. Any strong impact on the blades made them explode, scattering fragments and smoke. His plan was to use the resulting smokescreen to rush forward and stab Vandal himself. Eleonora and Zulan would then kill him, surely, but he didn't care about that. So long as he killed Vandal, his job here was done. Getting killed as a result just saved him from having to kill himself, and his fourth life of luxury could begin.

"Hold on! Don't touch them!"

Just before Eleonora and Zulan touched the knives, however, a shadow moved in between them and their target. Some of the burning phantoms took the knives into their own bodies and contained them.

"These knives will explode to create a smokescreen! They come from our belongings! We know what they do!"

It was the same adventurers of the Western Calm, who had been killed by Kanata and turned into Fire Phantoms alongside Princess Lebia and the others.

"What do you want to do next?" Vandal asked. "If you have any last words, you can go ahead. I'm listening."

Kanata's face twisted with annoyance. His surprise attack had been foiled, and his backup had failed as well. "Gah! Belt of Flame, dance!" Kanata cut himself off from Vandal's view with a blazing lash of fire magic and then leapt backward to put some distance between them.

The phantoms started to shout. "Enough games! Stand and fight!"

"You'll pay for this!"

"Everyone, please, do as I said and leave this to me," Vandal said. "Zulan, you take charge of Lefdia. I want to get some idea of how strong the other reborn will be, and I have some new skills I want to try too."

Vandal used Steal Heat to instantly extinguish the raging flames and then followed up by deploying some powerful poison from his tongue and claws. Undead like Zulan, and Eleonora with her Resist Maladies, wouldn't be affected.

"Floor, ground." Vandal was proving faster than Kanata had expected. He quickly used Gungnir to pass through the floor and hide.

"Fall back, Death Shot." Vandal instantly turned the ground into golems to expose Kanata, then used Detect Life to find his location and fired off Death Shots toward him.

"Argh! He's so quick!" Kanata found the ground he thought had been shielding him actively moving out of the way. Completely unprotected, he managed to overcome his surprise in time to avoid the incoming Death Shot, only getting grazed by it. Now it was Vandal's turn to be surprised—there should have been enough magic in that attack to kill him even from just a scratch, but Kanata was still up and zipping around. The poison also didn't seem to be working.

"Based on your speed and the strength of your magic, I'd say your stats are similar to mine, perhaps a little higher," Vandal observed. "But you don't seem to have an unimaginable reserve of vitality, either. I'm guessing Rodocolte didn't curse you. Rather, he gave you resistances."

"Great Immolation, magical power!" Kanata ignored Vandal's theorizing and launched a large-scale fire attribute spell. It was a technique that used intense temperatures to burn everything in its range to ash. *Normally, he'd be able to use his barrier or that heal stealing technique to stop it, but I used Gungnir immediately afterward! There's no way for him to protect against this heat! He's going to roast alive, along with all his crazy creatures!*

Kanata breathed a sigh of relief, assured of his victory. Once the flames died down a little more, he turned off Gungnir and used wind magic to create a vacuum, sucking away the last of the fire. His work was done here once Vandal was dead. He had been planning to kill himself and set off into his fourth life of luxury, but he also wasn't dumb enough to choose death without confirming that the job was actually done.

"That was a bold move, even engulfing yourself."

Vandal was standing there, covered in flames.

"Jesus! What the hell magic is that?!"

"Actually, my new friends are protecting me."

"Who?" Kanata couldn't believe his eyes. The flames around Vandal flickered and formed into female shapes. "No! Those dead bitches?!" He had seen their faces before. "Damn it! I drenched myself in holy water for nothing!"

The fire women were none other than the merchant's daughter, Hanna, the receptionist from the guild, Aria, and all the other women Kanata had killed since coming to Ramda.

"You never made undead like that before!" Kanata shouted. "Not on Origin or here!"

"You know, I just learned how to do this. It's going to need a name. How about Fire Elemental's Embrace?"

Behind Vandal, the Fire Phantoms were protecting Zulan and Eleonora in the same way. The two of them looked pretty pleased at how things were turning out.

"He's no match for Lord Vandal, is he?" Eleonora said.

"Nope. Can't believe I was worried about this loser," Zulan agreed.

The two of them were correct. This was no longer anything close to a fight to the death. It was completely one-sided, and Kanata was on the losing side.

"Can you do this for me?" Vandal asked, providing some MP and intent to the Fire Phantoms.

"Leave it to us!"

They were more like fire wraiths now. And those wraiths started to attack Kanata. Some of them turned into spears of flame, some of them slithered in like snakes, and some turned into giant skulls. All of them sought to burn Kanata with their blazing black fire.

This was the effect of the Necromancy Magic that Vandal had just learned. The name might have suggested the kind of things Vandal already did, such as turning corpses into zombies and skeletons, but it was actually a skill much more like Elemental Magic.

Elemental Magicians provided elementals with MP and the caster's intentions, allowing them to cast spells with more efficiency than normal attribute magic. The principle here was the same. Vandal shared his power and wishes with the phantoms, and they performed the magic for him. The Fire Phantoms were under the influence of Death Attribute Allure, and quite a few of them had been killed by Kanata himself. Their attacks showed no mercy.

Kanata tried to dodge the attacks, at first, but these were Fire Phantoms that had turned themselves into fiery spears, snakes, and skulls. They chased him down no matter how he tried to avoid them.

"F-Fire, Wind—gaaaaah! Why isn't it working?" Kanata turned on Gungnir and tried to fight back with wind magic. He had expected the black flames to just pass through his body, but that wasn't what happened. When he started to burn, his screams cut off his attempt to cast magic.

"Ground!" Next, he tried to escape down into the ground, but his feet didn't sink at all. "Why?! Why won't Gungnir activate?!"

"It's working," Vandal told him. "It's that ability of yours. Gungnir, did you call it? You can't pass through spirit bodies."

Kanata's Gungnir was the ability to pass through anything that he stipulated. If he stipulated weapons, for example, then it wasn't just enemy weapons; his own weapons would also fall through his fingers. Vandal had worked most of this out from the information the spirits had told him.

However, Vandal was using something that Kanata couldn't pass through: spirit bodies.

Every living human had a spirit body inside themselves while they were alive. If Kanata were to apply Gungnir to that, it would be like casting his own spirit out from his body. Suicide, nothing less. On a primal, instinctual level, Kanata wouldn't attempt it. That was why he couldn't avoid the attacks of the Fire Phantoms: they were burning spirit bodies.

Furthermore, Vandal had extended his Spirit Bodification body into the walls, floor, and ceiling throughout the crypt and used Substantiation.

"I've got some other attacks you probably can't pass through as well. For example . . . ♦ ♍ ▢ ♏ ♋ ☉!" Vandal pursed his lips and launched off a directional Scream.

Kanata was still trying to fight back, using his Resist Fire Attribute and Resist Death Attribute, but when this new attack hit him, he screamed and grabbed his head. "My ears!"

His Spiritual Pollution could nearly withstand the attack, but Scream wasn't magic, it was just a skill. Kanata was therefore unable to protect his senses from the raging noise, which sounded like glass fragments grinding together.

This was another weakness of Gungnir. If he turned off sound, Kanata would himself be unable to cast any magic.

"You've got one final weakness, too—" Vandal closed in, almost recklessly, as blood gushed from Kanata's ears.

Screaming wildly, Kanata grabbed a knife with his burnt hand and desperately threw it at Vandal. Vandal slashed it away with his claws, almost nonchalantly.

"You little shit!" Kanata bellowed, taking out one more knife and dashing forward. Maybe he had quickly used a potion or something because the burns across his entire body were already starting to heal.

"You're the shit one!"

"We'll burn you as many times as we need to!" Hanna and Aria attacked again, still big burning skulls. However—

"Phantoms!" Suddenly they were unable to touch Kanata, simply passing through him. Kanata had used Gungnir to specifically state "phantoms"—not spirit bodies as a whole, but the monster in particular.

"This is because you just had to monologue everything! You underestimated me, and now—you'll pay!" Kanata had only been able come up with the idea of stipulating "phantoms" thanks to Vandal's running commentary. Kanata smiled at the idiocy of sharing your strategy with your opponents while in the middle of fighting them as he attacked Vandal with the knife. His movements were quick and clean, bringing to bear all of the high-level training he had received.

"I'm not underestimating anyone." Vandal easily avoided Kanata's knife. The man stuttered and gasped but pressed the attack.

Two, three swings. He launched a feint at the face to disguise a kick, trying to hit the kid in the crotch. Vandal remained completely impassive, ignoring the knife and dropping backward to dodge the kick. Kanata swung the knife as fast as he could, launching slashes and thrusts, but Vandal made skillful use of his claws to intercept and deflect the attacks.

"Claws!" Kanata added those annoying claws to his Gungnir.

But Vandal reacted as though he had been expecting this move as well. "Now it's my turn," he said.

He's faster than me and stronger too?! Kanata thought. *And he's got all sorts of techniques! Where did he get all of this from? Was he always some kind of martial artist?! It can't be—he played this world like a freaking video game?!* In the moment he had that thought, the blood rushed to Kanata's head. It felt like he was boiling alive.

"You're joking me! Just how much training do you think I received on Origin—?"

"I have no idea. I spent my entire second life in a laboratory." Kanata's anger had no effect on Vandal. He simply focused his intent to kill and launched an overarm strike.

"Ngh!" Kanata managed to sweep the attack away with his arm, but Vandal's fingers ripped off a chunk of his flesh at the same time.

"In this third life, though," Vandal continued, "I've had plenty of training and practical experience."

"Gaah!" Kanata followed up with a kick, trying to sweep the kid's ankles out from under him. But Vandal dodged that too and, as he did, tore another chunk out of Kanata, this time from his leg.

I'm avoiding his claws! What's going on?! The effects of Gungnir meant that Vandal's claws shouldn't be able to hurt him, and yet Vandal was still causing considerable damage. "Don't tell me—you're only using your fingers to do that?!"

That was exactly what was happening. Swinging his claws around when fighting people and monsters had naturally strengthened the fingers from which his claws extended.

"I have a lot of enemies," Vandal said. "Enemies like you."

"You freaking monster!" Kanata continued the fight, raging inside, but he was on the losing side of this equation. He had to be far more careful of Vandal's attacks.

"No matter the attacks you use, you can't make your opponent's body transparent. Otherwise, you wouldn't be able to hurt them. Which means, I simply need to use my body to protect myself. That's your greatest weakness. However—"

Vandal launched a kick toward Kanata with the sole of his foot. Kanata saw it as a chance to counterattack and tried to stab Vandal in the foot by ramming his knife through sole of the incoming sandal. If he could take out one of his legs, even a monster like this would slow down.

However, Kanata groaned and yelped as his knife not only failed to pierce the sandal, but it snapped with a clear metallic sound. Kanata ate the full force of the kick, which sent him flying backward. His right arm was left mangled, bent in an unpleasant angle.

"You have weaknesses beyond your ability. Did you really think a simple steel knife would pierce these sandals, made by my expert crafter?" The sandals Vandal was wearing had been made from dragon skin as a special order by Talea: the same monster materials that Kanata had scoffed at and refused to consider using. "On that note, your crossbow, the other knives, that armor—they're all just steel and animal hide. Why didn't you get some better gear first? You didn't want to use any materials that didn't exist on Origin, was that it?"

Of course, Vandal had heard from Hanna and the other spirits how Kanata had scoffed about using things made from monster materials. He was bringing all this up intentionally.

"Taunting me, are you?!" Kanata also knew what was happening. He swung his knife, not with the right arm but the left.

"Four limbs!" As he swung it, he shouted to activate Gungnir. The knife passed through his own limbs, through his left arm and flew toward Vandal.

He won't stop this one, surely! Kanata had been in a panic, scrambling for ideas. He finally landed on a throw where the start of the motion passed the knife through his own body.

"Yes, I was taunting you. I wanted to see if you had anything else up your sleeve."

Vandal smashed the knife out of the air using his tongue, even as he talked.

"It looks like that's all your tricks."

Barbed Tongue's level had increased already, allowing Vandal's tongue to extend even further. Kanata watched it writhing in the air and, this time, completely gave up.

"Of course, a knife that size wouldn't do anything even if you hit me with it."

Then, Vandal picked the knife up with his tongue and snapped it.

"You can't beat me at magic, and in terms of fighting, we're fairly evenly matched. Why, then, didn't you get some decent gear, and then attack me while keeping your cheat ability secret? Instead, you flashed it around to anyone you came across. You underestimated me, severely. You were rash and overconfident; that's why you lost. Why didn't you even use any battle techs? You might have done better with a few of those."

If Kanata hadn't killed anyone using Gungnir until finding Vandal, he wouldn't have been so completely countered like this. If he had cast aside his prejudices and selected his gear based on capabilities, his knife wouldn't have snapped like a twig, and Vandal wouldn't have been tearing chunks out of his flesh along with his armor. If he had learned some battle techs, he might have had a better chance of killing Vandal. At the least, his knife attacks wouldn't have gotten blocked by a tongue.

More than anything, if he hadn't been fixated on getting this done quickly—if he had followed Rodocolte's instructions, registered with the adventurers' guild, changed Jobs, boosted his other stats, and waiting for a proper chance—he might have had much better odds.

"Curse you! You freaking monster! Don't you dare look down on me!" Reflecting on these points was far beyond Kanata's capabilities. He didn't consider what was happening now to be his fault. He simply thought it was all unfair. He could do no more than hurl insults at Vandal.

"I see. It appears I was the fool here for attempting to talk to a man incapable of conversation. I think your MP is about to run out, no?" Vandal was shaking his head, clearly bemused. He started to give some MP to all the Fire Ghosts, including Princess Lebia and Kanata's victims. "I'm happy to just kill him with my tongue, but do you want to do the honors?"

"Yes, of course! Everyone, chip in!" Lebia spread her dress of black fire and closed in with Kanata.

Kanata let out a terrified shriek as Lebia changed form in the blink of an eye, seizing Kanata and holding him in place. As Vandal had predicted, his rampant use of Gungnir had drained all his MP, and his cheat was now offline. Lebia held his body tight, crucified in the air, and then the wraiths of burning fire started to crawl up him from the legs. Kanata gave a terrible scream as his body started to burn.

"Funeral Pyre . . ." Vandal intoned, giving this new attack a name. "You appear to have Resist Fire Attribute, but that's only working against you in this situation. This must really hurt, oh boy. I'll make sure you can keep breathing, though. Don't count on passing out from asphyxiation."

As his entire body burned slowly to a crisp, Kanata screamed inside at how unfair this was—and how different from what he had been told. *I received full military training on Origin! How can he be stronger than me? How can he avoid my knife attacks so easily? He isn't scared or even remotely shaken by anything I do! This is a guy who was nothing but a lab rat for 20 years on Origin! After he was reborn, I thought he was playing king of the hill with his undead buddies! Rodocolte said he was far weaker—but he's even more of a threat than when he was that undead! I got a body resistant to poison and disease, and I still can't fight him!*

Kanata had appraised Vandal entirely based on the information provided by Rodocolte. That was his biggest mistake. Rodocolte's information was all out of date and acquired through the eyes of other people. It was like watching a documentary without any commentary. It wasn't live or even recent in some cases. Furthermore, after Rodocolte obtained that information, Vandal had continued to grow more powerful and experienced far more hardships on Ramda than Kanata had ever known.

Compared to Vandal, Kanata had done very little since his arrival on Ramda. He had increased his level from 0 to 100, acquiring minor stat boosts, but that was it.

Kanata's magic was all used up. He couldn't cast a basic spell to light a cigarette, let alone use Gungnir. He couldn't escape. He could only wait to finally burn to death.

Even so, Kanata still did not repent his ways. Because this wasn't the end for him.

"Damn you! Don't get too comfy, you gross little necrophiliac! You're planning on turned me into undead and pumping me for info, huh? Hahaha, bad luck!"

". . . Why do you say that?" Vandal asked.

"The ones like us, when we die, we return to his Divine Holiness before we can be turned into undead! It doesn't matter how many times you kill us! We'll keep coming back! Again and again, reincarnated by a god who wants you dead! We'll kill you in the end!"

Kanata wasn't about to lay down, die, and give up on his reward. He would beg Rodocolte for another chance for revenge on this loser who thought he was better than him. Next time, he would get that wonderful fourth life for sure.

"I won't drop my guard next time!" Kanata screamed. "I won't fight you alone! I'll work with the others, and we'll kick the crap out of you! All I have to do is kill you, and his Divine Holiness has promised to give me a life of luxury! Everyone is going to want a piece of you! Even Amemiya; even Naruse!"

Of course, Kanata didn't know when the others still alive on Origin would expire. Rodocolte, the one reincarnating them, probably didn't know either. Mari Shihoin was a good candidate, though—Metamor, the one who had killed him. If she was caught for his murder, she'd probably be executed. Kanata didn't want to team up with the woman who killed him, but the rest of the group was constantly targeted by the terrorists called the Eight Guidance. At some point, some of them were going to die.

"Don't get full of yourself, just because you saw through my Gungnir!" Kanata continued to rage. "The others have got crazy cheat powers like you wouldn't believe! I'm going to team up with them, and I'll kill you one day. I'll kill you!"

Vandal's tongue had still been outside his mouth for this entire time. As Kanata babbled on, his tongue sagged, and then returned to his mouth. Kanata took that to mean Vandal had been broken by this news. He was filled with such joy, his face twisting with glee, that he forgot the pain of being burned alive.

"You'd better be reaaaaady! After I've killed you, I'm doing to kill your women, your undead, everyone you ever met—blaarrgh—"

"Barbed Tongue."

A wet sound interrupted his shrieks, followed by the sound of something hard cracking.

Kanata looked down to see Vandal's tongue piercing his chest. However, there was no blood. He thought maybe he had activated Gungnir, without even realizing it, but then Vandal recalled his tongue and spoke.

"I just used my tongue and Spirit Bodification to crush your soul. It was my first time using my tongue to do it, so I didn't completely smash it in one go, but I definitely made a big crack. It won't take long to shatter."

"Huh? What? My soul?"

"In other words, you are finished here," Vandal said. "No more afterlife, no more rebirths, no fourth or fifth or any more lives."

"You're bluffing! That can't be—gaaaah!?" Kanata's face paled and he sounded distraught—and then a new pain, something far worse than being burned alive, raced across his body. It hurt so much, and yet he couldn't tell which part of him was hurting.

"It can't be! That holy moron didn't say anything about this!" Kanata's body was still resisting the flames, but something else—something more vital to the composition of Kanata Kaito—was cracking and splitting apart.

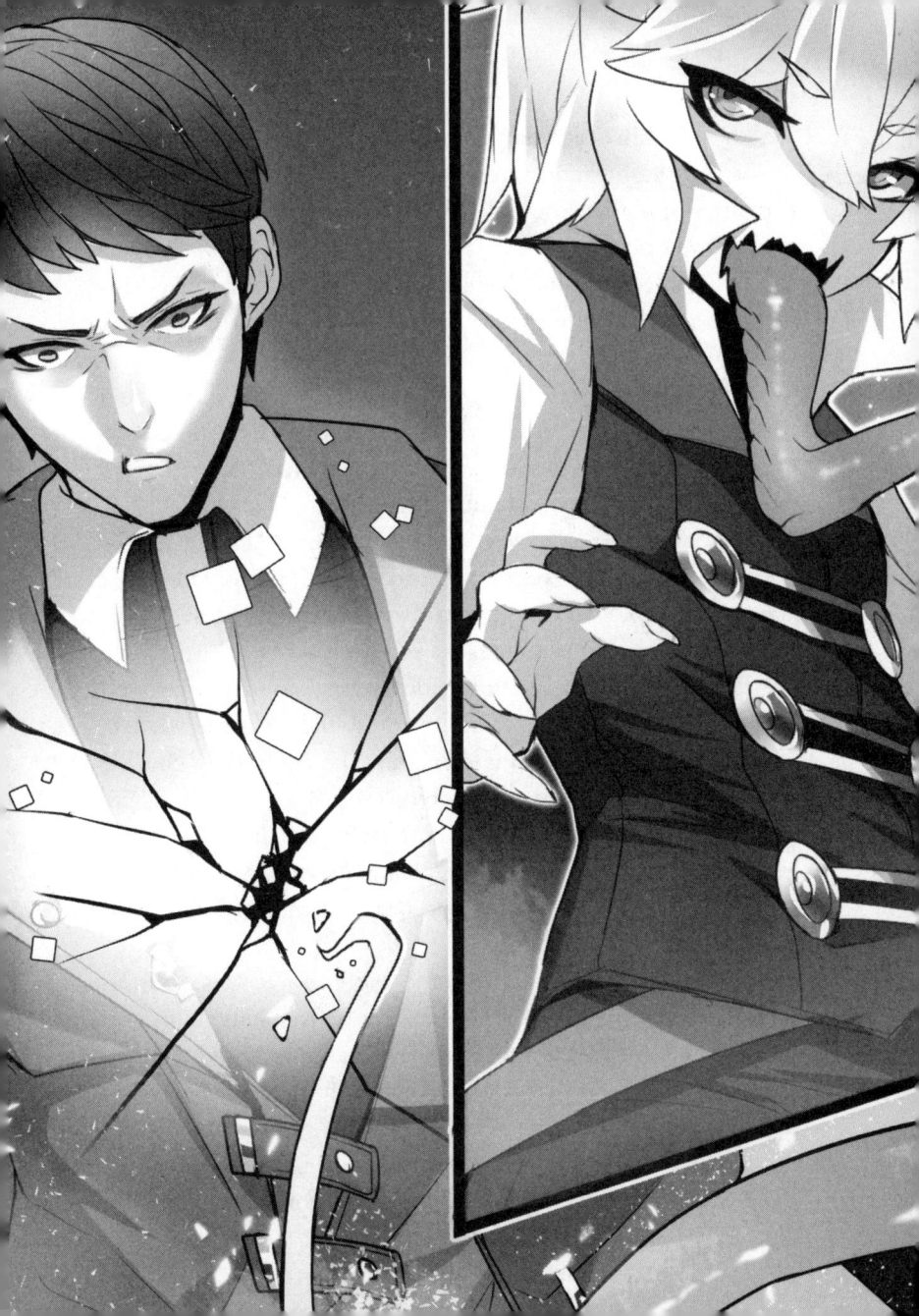

"So he didn't tell you," Vandal sighed. "I thought not. No one in their right mind would have said all those stupid things you just said if they knew about this. I was going to crush your soul anyway, of course."

Up until this point, Kanata had panicked and cursed his bad luck, but he hadn't faced down such pure mortal terror as that which contorted his face now.

"No, please, don't do it!" Kanata yelled. "Why, why would you do something so horrible? No more life?! I've still got so much I want to do! I don't want to die! Spare me!" Kanata cried out at the sensation of his entire being crumbling away.

Vandal gave a deep and meaningful sigh. "That goes for everyone. The people you killed, and the people I've killed too. Life isn't a game you can reset and start over. You should have paid more attention to the reality you were living in."

For Vandal, who certainly didn't want a fourth go around and was living his best possible life on Ramda, the way Kanata had chosen to live here was something he could only chuckle about. Kanata detected this, behind Vandal's emotionless façade, and felt rage surge inside himself, rage that almost made him pass out, overwriting his despair and terror.

"God damn you! I'm going to take you with me, you dropout loser piece of shit!"

Kanata had mocked the game-like status system, but he suddenly made use of his Discretionary Active Skills ability and learned the Limit Break skill up to level 5. He activated it, pushing his body beyond its limits to instantly boost his physical capabilities.

It was the moment, for the first time since dying on Earth and being reborn into other subsequent worlds, that Kanata actually felt alive. He planted his feet on the ground, ready to fight. His heart didn't just rage with selfish anger but also brimmed with a sense of fulfillment. Kanata was desperate to take this strength and smash it into Vandal. To at least get some measure of vengeance—

"—Armff."

He let out a bizarre, pathetic noise, and then his head just slumped down. His heart was still beating but his body stopped moving. The light of intention in his eyes and all expression and life simply faded from his face.

They said that you could always start over. That life goes on.

Of course, that wasn't strictly the case.

"Princess." Vandal provided some more MP, and Lebia used it to chop off Kanata's head, right where he was standing.

His severed head, burnt through at the neck, rolled across the ground.

Then they received the experience from the kill, bumping up their levels. Not just Lebia, but also Vandal.

At last, he climbed his wall.

Acquired the skills Barehanded Attack Boost: Low, Physical Boost (Claws, Fangs, Tongue)!

Skill level increased for Agility Enhancement, Command, Necromancy Magic, God Smiter!

Name: Vandal
Race: Dhampir (Dark Elf)
Age: 7 years old
Alias: [Ghoul King] [Eclipse King] [Unspoken Name]

Job: Poison Warrior

Level: 100

Job History: Death Mage Golem Creator Undead Tamer Crusher of Souls

Status

Vitality: 344

Magical Power: 379120344

Strength: 188

Agility: 251

Muscle: 159

Intellect: 784

——Passive Skills

[Brute Strength: Level 4 (UP!)] [Rapid Healing: Level 6 (UP!)] [Death Attribute Magic: Level 7 (UP!)]

[Resist Maladies: Level 7] [Resist Magic: Level 4 (UP!)] [Night Vision]

[Death Attribute Allure: Level 7] [Skip Incantation: Level 4] [Enhance Brethren: Level 8]

[Magical Power Auto Recovery: Level 6 (UP!)] [Enhance Followers: Level 4] [Poison Dispersal (Claws, Fangs, Tongue): Level 4 (UP!)]

[Agility Enhancement: Level 2 (UP!)] [Physical Length Change (Tongue) Level 4 (UP!)]

[Barehanded Attack Boost: Low (NEW!)] [Physical Boost (Claws, Fangs, Tongue): Level 1 (NEW!)]

——Active Skills

[Suck Blood: Level 10 Drain Blood: Level 2 (NEW!)] [Limit Break: Level 6]

[Golem Creation: Level 6] [Non-Attribute Magic: Level 5] [Magic Control: Level 4]

[Spirit Body: Level 7] [Carpentry: Level 4] [Construction: Level 3] [Cooking: Level 4] [Alchemy: Level 4]

[Brawling Proficiency: Level 5] [Soul Crusher: Level 6] [Simultaneous Activation: Level 5] [Remote Control: Level 6]

[Surgery: Level 3] [Mental Multitasking: Level 5] [Substantiation: Level 4] [Cooperation: Level 3]

[Rapid Cognition: Level 3] [Command: Level 2 (UP!)] [Agriculture: Level 3] [Clothing Making: Level 2]

[Thrown Projectile Proficiency: Level 3] [Scream: Level 3] [Necromancy Magic: Level 2 (NEW!)]

——Unique Skill

[God Smiter: Level 4 (UP!)] [Spiritual Abnormality: Level 4] [Spiritual Corrosion: Level 3]

[Dungeon Construction: Level 4]

——Curses

[Unable to carry over experience from previous lives] [Unable to enter existing jobs] [Unable to personally acquire experience]

Kanata might have been a terrible person, but he was still one of the Reincarnation God's reborn warriors equipped with a cheat ability. He was worth a lot more experience than a regular monster or human.

"Lord Vandal, 99 more to go."

"His cheat wasn't much use against you, Child. I reckon you'll have wiped them all out long before you become a noble, if they all fight like that."

"We will fight for you! Our new king!"

Everyone else was overjoyed, celebrating the defeat of one

of these "cheaters" Vandal had been worried about, but Vandal himself was calm and collected.

"No, no. I might not have to kill them all. Some of them might not want to fight me."

"But that pathetic creature said . . ."

"Pathetic being the operative word. Don't believe everything he said."

Among everything Kanata had spouted, Vandal didn't believe much of what he had said about the other reborn. He didn't know what position Kanata had been in on Origin or what his relationship was with the others. But from the way he spoke and the things he did, Vandal couldn't believe he had been someone especially important. He probably only had a handful of close friends among all of the others.

Of course, the other reborn would probably learn at some point about Kanata's erasure and that Vandal had done it. Still, he wondered how much of a difference that would make to most of them.

Rodocolte didn't tell him about Soul Crusher, but I bet he's also hiding a lot of other stuff from them too, Vandal thought. *The fact I was able to win and wipe out Kanata, in spite of however that divine dunce tries to paint me, will probably make the others think twice about tangling with me.*

Of course, there would probably be those who were mad at Vandal for crushing Kanata's soul. The kind of naïve idealist who would say, "But we're all still human in the end!" when confronted with all the bad stuff Kanata had done. But that surely wouldn't be all of them.

"The general policy for handling that problem will be the same moving forward," Vandal said. "Although I am now a little concerned that they may all turn up as adults."

His plan had been to use his head start to obtain nobility and social standing, creating an environment in which it would be hard for them to act against him. But if that head start was taken away . . .

"It should be fine, Child," Zulan said. "If you become important first, it won't matter if a whole bunch of folks pretending to be heroes show up. Everyone will back you."

"I agree. Who will the people choose: unknown strangers—even if they possess incredible skills—or a renowned member of society? The answer seems clear to me," Eleonora said.

"You already rule Talosheim, but you wish to become even greater?" Lebia asked. "You are ambitious indeed!"

"Our new king wishes to rule the entire world!"

"No wonder the gods send assassins to kill him."

"We are already dead! It is our honor to pave the way for our king's greatness!"

"Hold on," Vandal said, interrupting the excitement of the undead. "I'm not planning on ruling anything." Apparently, Vandal needed to set things straight with them. "First things first. I'm going to cave this place in to cover the fact that the seal of the Demon King's blood was broken. We can put the blame on the dead guy in the room. Then, we should swing by the treasure room and collect the items that the duke's family took from you, Princess Lebia."

Vandal didn't want anyone to know that they had invaded the castle and broken one of the seals of the Demon King, but at the same time, he didn't want to have to kill everyone in the castle. This seemed like the best route to take.

Now the fighting was over, Lefdia chose this moment to leap from Zulan's hands toward Princess Lebia. "Hey! Be careful!" Lebia shouted, catching the hand out of the air.

Then a look of nostalgic calm came over her face.

"This hand . . . I couldn't touch it, when I was just a normal ghost, so I didn't realize . . . I recall this sensation. Yes, it has to be . . ." Lebia was taken with vibrant memories of her homeland and the sister she had parted with when it fell. The dazzling smile of her magically talented younger sister, who had still looked up to her so much. This was the same small (by giantling standards) hand that she had held so tight when they parted, convinced of her dreadful belief that they would never meet again. It even had the same warmth to it.

"Ah, Zandia!" Lebia exclaimed. "Zandia, that's you, isn't it! I remember this warm hand. I remember!"

". . . Warm? I'm pretty sure her flame is just heating up Lefdia—but maybe we shouldn't say that," Eleonora said.

"Let's hold our peace," Vandal agreed.

"Then Lefdia is Princess Zandia, after all!" Zulan exclaimed.

"Unfortunately, Zulan, I can't be sure of that," Lebia said. "Lefdia herself has no awareness of who or what is inside her."

Lefdia was bending her fingers, looking puzzled in Lebia's arms. She was now sure that the left hand that Lefdia inhabited had belonged to her sister, but she couldn't be sure that the spirit inside it was Zandia. Lefdia herself seemed very friendly with Lebia, but also didn't seem to have remembered anything about her life. "But she's definitely taken a liking to me, which makes me happy. I wonder if I could consider her . . . a second sister?"

"I'm fine with that. Lefdia seems happy about it."

Lefdia was bending repeatedly at the wrist, perhaps nodding in agreement. Once they got back the other remains of Princess Zandia from the progenitor vampire Gubamon, they might discover that her spirit was elsewhere, but they could cross that bridge once they came to it.

"Thank you, Your Majesty. I'm very happy to meet you, Lefdia." Princess Lebia gave a smile, to which Lefdia responded with a thumbs up.

The ghosts of Princess Lebia's royal guard all celebrated this new addition to the royal family.

"Oh! The birth of a new princess!"

"I'm not following any of this but that sounds wonderful!"

"Hurray for Princess Lefdia!"

"Yes, yes, hip-hip-hooray!" Hanna, Aria, and the others were just kind of swept up in the excitement, but they celebrated too.

"Okay. Tomorrow night we'll fly to the remains of the town close to the tunnel," Vandal said. "Borkz and the others are already heading there."

"I'm looking forward to seeing Borkz again," Lebia replied. "What kind of undead has he become?"

"He's a zombie like me," Zulan replied. "Half his face is his exposed skull. He's much more handsome than he was when he was alive."

"Zulan, perhaps I'll tell Borkz you said that?"

"Free feel to do so. He's so angry with the Heartner Domain right now, it'll all be in one ear and out the other."

With Lefdia still in Lebia's arms, the hand then proceeded to pick Vandal up by the head. Then Lebia started to float through the air, carrying Vandal along.

"Hey! Give Lord Vandal back!" shouted Eleonora.

"I'm sorry! You naughty little hand! Lefdia, give His Majesty back to his mother—ah, what should I call you, as the mother of our king?"

"I keep telling you! I'm not Lord Vandal's mother!"

"You aren't? Could it be that you're his gran—"

"Complete that sentence and I will seek a duel to the death."

"Princes Lebia, Eleonora is one of my trusted allies," Vandal said. "We are not related. Come on, we can talk while we walk out of here."

They collected the remains of the whip and the coffin that had sealed away the Demon King's blood. Then, Vandal and his party departed the castle.

That morning, the air in Heartner Castle was as tense as ever.

The current duke was almost completely bedridden, perhaps having a few waking hours in total over any number of days. At this point, his successor should have taken over all his public duties, but his two potential successors only continued to bicker over who would get to sit in the ducal seat.

The duke's second son, but his first with his wife, was Prince Belton. He led the political side of the debate, believing that protecting the Heartner Domain from the Empire was the most pressing issue and that the duke's army should be a shield. Meanwhile, the duke's oldest son, born from one of his concubines, was Prince Lucas. He believed in taking the fight to the Empire and striking back over the loss of the Saulon Domain to bring glory to the house of Heartner.

Under normal circumstances, Prince Belton would clearly hold the upper hand. But the Heartner Domain now found itself on the frontline of the conflict with the Amidd Empire. That had given Prince Lucas, who had the full support of the duke's army, a much more commanding presence.

In the past, everyone assumed that Belton would use his cunning political acumen to command the domain, while Lucas dealt with military matters. But now, many suggested Lucas should become duke, leading the army into battle, while Belton remained at home to tend to political matters.

Of course, the chatter meant nothing if the current duke simply chose his successor. This squabble would immediately come to an end. However, every time Duke Heartner did manage to wake up, he said something different. He appeared to be lucid, but the content of his head was a jumble. Even his closest ministers didn't know what to do.

As a result, the domain had split into Belton and Lucas factions, along with those attempting to curry favor with both sides. The whole affair created considerable tension, but the situation had also been going on for so long that most of the castle staff simply worked around it by this point.

"Prince Belton, may I have a word?" Prince Belton was heading to the dining hall for an early lunch when he was called to a stop by Baron Ikks, one of his close confidants. Ikks was a noble priest and diligent civil servant. While he worked under the State Bursar, a man from the Lucas faction who desired to stimulate the economy through the conflict, Ikks had chosen to side with Belton. Of course, his primary motivation was the hope of promotion if and when Belton became duke.

"What is it, Baron Ikks?"

"There is clearly something going on at the magicians' guild, my lord," Ikks reported. "Guild Master Kinap and a few other key figures are clueless, but some of those paid to protect them have completely gone missing."

Prince Belton remained calm while muttering to himself under his breath. The magicians' guild was a key base for his support. Each guild ostensibly professed political neutrality, but he was unable to ignore the support of the magicians' guild in his current situation, with their varied research and development of spells and magic items, and their stable of skilled Magicians.

In particular, Belton was of a mind to use guardsmen and knights to deal with keeping the peace and fighting monsters within the domain, so the adventurers' guild didn't think much of him. He had the HQ Guild Master under his thumb but faced a lot of opposition from those in the regional branches. That was another reason he wanted to maintain support from the shrines and the other guilds.

"Is it my brother?" The agents of Prince Lucas might be throwing around bigger bribes again or be holding something over those in question.

"It doesn't seem so," Ikks replied. "I was unable to confirm any movement from Prince Lucas's men. I have received other concerning reports, however—unsubstantiated for now. I will report further once I have confirmation."

"Very well. I know I work you hard, Baron Ikks. This will all be worth it."

"My Prince." Ikks gave a bow and then dropped back.

Belton knew that Ikks was skilled at collecting information, using a complex network of spies. Surely he would find the truth of whatever was going on and report back swiftly. Belton watched the Baron go, keenly aware how much lay across those broad shoulders.

Then, without warning, he felt the ground shift a little beneath his feet.

"An earthquake?" It wasn't a large one, but still a rare occurrence. Then the rumbling got a lot more pronounced, very quickly.

"Aaaaaaaaagh!" A massive hole proceeded to open up in the floor. Baron Ikks had been walking exactly on top of it and dropped into the chasm without a hope in the world of escape.

"B-Baron?!"

"Prince Belton, please, get back! Get back from the edge!" One of his attendants, someone close at all times, moved in from the shadows and grabbed Prince Belton, dragging him backward to safety.

That was the day that the castle of Duke Heartner started to lean to one side.

Skill level increased for Carpentry, Construction, and Golem Creation!

Guild Master Kinap of the magicians' guild snapped back to himself with a start.

"What—what have I been doing?" He looked around, to see other key members of the guild staff with the same expression.

They all had one glaring thing in common: they were informers for the progenitor vampire Tehneshia, making them not exactly comrades, but definitely coconspirators.

"Master Kinap, whatever is the meaning of this?"

"I can't remember—I can't remember what we were doing. How we got here."

"Calm yourself, everyone. We're in my home." Kinap suffered from the same ailment as the others. He couldn't remember almost anything from the last few days. However, he also hadn't lost sight of what they needed to be doing. "Hold our intent firm in your mind, everyone. You know what we need to do."

"What we need to do . . . yes! Yes, there is something!"

"We can't sit around here talking! We must act!"

"Hold! Do not panic! All we be for naught if we rush into this thing!"

"Everyone! Gather the required proof and then send it via your most trusted messengers," Kinap directed. "Do not use anyone directly in the service of either prince! They might destroy the evidence!"

"Well said. They might be opposed at the moment, but there's nothing to say they won't work together to conceal black spots on the name of Heartner."

"Then we take it to the envoys from the other ducal domains?"

"That seems the only way! Now, everyone, to work!"

Kinap and his colleagues returned to each of their respective homes and gathered up all the evidence they could find of every crime and underhanded deed ever perpetrated in the domain. They then brought it all to the embassies from the other ducal domains. They were obeying a simple order, burned hard into the backs of their brains.

"Confess your evils and bring them into the light of the world."

It was later revealed that the cause of the incident that literally caused Duke Heartner's castle to tilt over and incapacitated Baron Ikks had been a collapse in the subterranean crypt beneath the castle, a place sealed by one of the heroes long ago.

Indeed, it had existed and remained intact for more than 100 thousand years, far longer than the castle above it, raising some concerns about why it would suddenly collapse. One body was recovered from the rubble—one Kanata Kaito—so the blame for the incident was placed upon him.

He had been robbing merchants across the domain, killing a significant number of people with high-level fire magic. The violent and reckless nature of his actions had led many to assume he was a follower of a Demon or Devil God. They assumed he had therefore been planning to revive the Demon King and somehow managed to break the hero's seal. However, perhaps due to a falling out with unknown companions or some accident when breaking the seal, he then passed away.

When the current duke learned of all this, his mental state instantly deteriorated further. Up until that point, at least he was conscious every few days. Now he just moaned and did little else. He wasn't going to make it past the coming spring.

That wasn't all. Key figures from the magicians' guild who had shown strong support for Prince Belton, including Guild Master Kinap himself, had visited envoys from other domains and started to confess all the crimes they had personally committed, both large and small. To make matters worse, they provided proof that they themselves were agents of a progenitor vampire.

This news hit the top echelons of Olbaum hard. The majority of officials had believed, in the end, that Prince Belton would be the one to take over as duke. Now it turned out some of his staunchest supporters were traitors to mankind. The evidence readily provided by Kinap and the others also proved that none other than the comatose Baron Ikks had been in league with the vampires.

Prince Belton swore that he hadn't known this, and there was no evidence that the prince himself was a sympathizer. However, this incident shook the trust placed in Price Belton, not just among the nobles of the Heartner Domain, but also across the kingdom. It looked as if Belton couldn't keep his house in order.

It was also discovered that someone had broken into the treasure vault and stolen a number of treasures. When compared to the size of these other incidents, however, the response was tepid, and the incident hardly investigated.

There were also numerous reports of people seeing a massive bird flying around at night, but those were written off as dreams induced by the stupor of drink.

Alda, God of Law and Life, had a multitude of problems. One of the bigger ones, perhaps, was the fact that Vandal—who everyone had presumed would stay in the south of the Vangaia Continent for at least a few more years—had crossed the mountains and appeared in the east. However, rather than any large-scale plotting, he seemed to simply be spreading the word of Vida, one small village at a time.

"Lord Alda, what do you think he is doing?" inquired Curatos, god of records. "I can't believe he truly plans to become an adventurer."

"I have no idea. Maybe attempting to create a base of operations in the Olbaum Electorate Kingdom?"

Worshippers served as the information network for Alda and the other gods. There was no way for the gods to learn anything that their followers didn't know. They would have sent more divine messengers to gather better information, but many of the gods had lost their strength in the fighting with the Demon King and Vida and had yet to recover. Alda had his hands pretty full simply keeping the world running. They had a growing new generation of gods, such as Sleep Goddess Mirl, but they lacked the numbers they needed.

There was also another issue: if they dispatched messengers to observe Vandal, there was a risk that they would be uncovered, and he would then crush their souls. An impossible feat for a regular human, but that dhampir surely wouldn't hesitate.

Perhaps it was a slightly smaller problem than that, but there was a strange incident that had occurred. The actual events were nothing compared to what Vandal was doing: a rogue criminal hand killed a merchant, his daughter, and the adventurers guarding them and stolen their belongings. A tragic incident, but hardly a rarity on Ramda.

"*What* is this man?"

The issue was the male culprit. The reports from the other gods that reached Alda told of a man named Kanata Kaito. He had a completely unknown unique skill and high-powered fire attribute magic, with hair and eyes of a color never seen in that vicinity, and around thirty years old. Furthermore, there was no record of him other than this incident. And *that* was precisely the thing that was so strange.

None of the gods knew of this man called Kanata or had any record of him. Regardless of how little one cared about the pantheon, everyone prayed to something at least once in their lives. Even if there was someone who had never prayed themselves, it wasn't true for every single person around them. If they spent any time in a town or village, they would have talked to people and been seen by people. But even if that had never happened, a human always had parents. This Kanata didn't even have that.

He had suddenly appeared, and then suddenly started committing crimes. It was a complete mystery what he had been doing until that age and how he had achieved such a high levels for his skills.

There might have been a nearby community who worshipped gods who weren't collaborators with Alda, and Kanata came from there. It was a stretch. There was no indication of such a place. If he had come from afar and quietly crept in to conceal his movements, his sudden and blatant crime spree made no sense.

"Fitun, you seem to have some idea who this Kanata is."

"I do, Lord Alda." The Thunder God Fitun looked a little uncomfortable. "In fact, this one called Kanata Kaito is someone I had taken a special interest in and given special protections."

"What? Even Curatos has no record of him."

"Yet I profess the same. Kanata was born from a pregnant woman who was traveling to her husband's side when monsters attacked her carriage and killed her. The monsters took the newborn away, perhaps as a snack for later, but appear to have ended up raising him to adulthood. Maybe this is why there are no records."

If what Fitun said was true, that kind of birth would indeed leave no records, even with Curatos.

"I happened to see Kanata's existence and took a liking to his raw talents and potential. I admit to giving him special protections, but I also fear that they eventually twisted him."

". . . You're saying his strange unique skill was due to your protection?"

"Yes. I'm truly sorry."

"Some of your own believers were among those slain."

"Indeed. It seems that the blessings from me, and my special protection, twisted him at the very root of his being."

"Why did you never speak of this man, even to Curatos?"

"For fear that you would oppose my protection of him. I made a foolish mistake, that much is now clear."

Fitun continued to capably answer every question, but Alda couldn't shake his suspicions. At the same time, no proof to the contrary was forthcoming either.

"Unfortunately, he moved away from his belief in me," Fitun continued, "meaning I have no idea why he was discovered in the underground crypt with the remains of the Demon King."

"Okay. Enough. Regarding the seal that was broken, we shall have to ask Neinroad."

Neinroad was the hero who had been chosen by Shizarion, a god who had been eradicated by the Demon King. Neinroad was eventually chosen as a goddess herself and now led the wind attribute gods in place of Shizarion. The task left her even more thinly strung than Alda, but as this particular seal had been created by her, Alda had no choice but to get her involved.

"Then I shall take my leave—" Fitun gave a bow and moved to go. "Wait," Alda interrupted. "This Kanata Kaito also had a strange name. Can we be sure he didn't appear from another world?" Alda's suspicions arose from the unfamiliar surname of "Kaito."

Fitun, however, didn't even seem to understand where the question was coming from. "Yes, we can be sure. It seems the monsters who raised him just gave him a random name. You know the kind of random clicks and grunts they make."

"I see. Well, sorry for keeping you."

"Not at all."

Fitun departed, and Alda allowed himself a moment. He was overthinking all this, surely.

"Indeed, Zurwan has yet to recover," Alda concluded. "There would be no way to summon people from other worlds. There are none among the remnants of the Demon King's forces who possess strength to such a degree."

If there were anyone capable of such a feat, it might be Reincarnation God Rodocolte. All he ever talked about was the need to develop Ramda, and he was also the most powerful among the gods of which Alda was aware. With this authority, it would be possible—easy, even—for him to reincarnate people from other worlds here on Ramda.

"Even if that were the case, though, everything this Kanata did was simply too foolish."

He had killed dozens of people, pillaged, raped, and seemingly broken one of the seals on the Demon King. Nothing he did worked toward the progress that Rodocolte was always banging on about. It pushed the needle in completely the opposite direction.

Furthermore, while Alda and the other gods of this world weren't friendly with Rodocolte, they also didn't stand in opposition. They were essentially colleagues. Regardless of how hard Alda tended to ignore Rodocolte's requests, he couldn't believe the Reincarnation God would start sending in people from other worlds without even discussing it first.

He was overthinking. Plain and simple.

He had two far more pressing issues to focus on at the moment: Vandal, who continued to be an unpredictable wildcard, and the whereabouts of the fragment of the Demon King that had been unsealed. Alda put these issues at the top of his priorities and sent a Messenger out to call for Neinroad.

After leaving Alda and returning to his own divine realm, Fitun gave an ecstatic cry at having so skillfully deceived the other god.

"Hahaha! Things are finally getting interesting!" What a stroke of luck that he had been the first to notice this visitor from another world. He didn't care that it had meant the death of one of his weaker followers. Indeed, he would have praised the fellow for letting Kanata kill him, to say it brought Fitun this wonderful information. "And I'm a genius for covering with the child of that pregnant woman, who actually did die in a monster attack around thirty years ago!" Fitun cackled. "Well then, Rodocolte! This Vandal, the one you so badly want to kill, is still very much alive! When will you send your next assassin?"

In the moment that Fitun had learned about Kanata's presence on Ramda, he created a spiritual form from a piece of himself and observed Kanata in secret. As a result, he obtained information about Vandal that even Alda didn't know. For example, that Vandal was the only possible one who could have broken the seal on the Demon King.

That was why Fitun was keeping this information to himself.

It was around 500 thousand years since Fitun had become a god. All these boring days were finally coming to an end.

"Now, my sweet little foe!" roared Fitun. "The one with the potential to end me—continue to build your power. And you, Rodocolte! No more trash like that last moron! I want you to send someone to this world worthy of my protection and my attention!" He burst out into unrestrained, relentless, thunderous laughter.

In the early morning, behind the General Store at the Seventh Pioneer Village, the party of adventurers comprising Kasim, Fester, and Zeno was training passionately together.

"Huhn, hah!"

"Fester, keep it down!"

"Ah, sorry."

They had often trained like this in the past. They had become more serious about it, however, only a short while ago—after Vandal trained with them, upon visiting the village.

While Vandal had done all sorts of difficult-to-believe, miraculous things, the one thing that Kasim and the others found the most incredible was all the strength packed into his tiny body.

His Brawling Proficiency and Thrown Projectile Proficiency were levels higher than all three of them, and he had mastered multiple areas. His Brawling Proficiency in particular was about far more than reliance on incredible physical abilities; there was a range of techniques to complement it. To them, Vandal seemed like one of their training officers at the adventurers' academy.

"I was in the zone again, remembering what he said. Keep my sides tucked in, watch where I put my feet."

"Yeah, he said the sides thing to me too."

"He told me I need more stamina."

Vandal's advice was on point. He sparred with each of them one-on-one, pointing out their issues while also not forgetting to say that he had had the same problems himself, indicating these three could also overcome these barriers.

"I wonder what his mom was like."

"She must have been pretty amazing if she trained him in brawling and magic. Vampires are something else!"

The three of them had the completely wrong end of the stick. If they met Eleonora, they would probably make the same mistake as Princess Lebia.

"I wonder what Vandal is doing right now."

"It's been a week since he went to the town. He's probably already taking classes at the adventurers' academy by now."

Kasim and his party hadn't been adventurers for long, meaning Vandal was the first up-and-coming adventurer they had met entering the system behind them. They knew he was stronger than they were, of course, but it felt like they had gained a powerful younger brother. When they first met, he had seemed a bit prickly, but he was always friendly, strong but not arrogant with it.

"He reminds me of a cat, you know," Fester said. "I bet he's doing fine in the town."

"A cat? If you're talking about his claws, I'd say bear more than cat."

"No, I mean, sometimes you see him staring off into space, looking at nothing at all. Cats do the same thing."

"Ah, yeah. Good point. That's kinda feline."

Of course, Vandal wasn't staring at nothing at all but rather at spirits that the three adventurers couldn't see.

"Catty or otherwise, I wouldn't be surprised if he skips the academy and gets raised to Grade D right away," Kasim said. "He doesn't just have unique skills—he's got the magic and fighting abilities. He could be a frontliner, backliner, and even healer. I doubt the training officers at the academy would have anything to teach him."

"He could probably teach them a thing or two!"

"Sure, but I doubt they'll just make him Grade D. You know, there's that exam."

To reach Grade D, adventurers had to pass a test seeing whether or not the subject could kill another person. On Ramda, adventurers had to fight dangerous bandits or protect their charges from them. If they hesitated to kill during such encounters, their targets might escape, or the one they were meant to be protecting might be killed. That was unacceptable for adventurers. The only way to reach Grade D was to kill.

"You think he could do that?" Zeno wondered.

"Rather than worry about that, we need to focus on catching up with him," Kasim said. "We need to set an example! We became adventurers first, after all."

"You said it. The next time we meet him, we need to be able to at least score a hit—"

"I'm sorry about all this," said a fourth voice.

"Hey, no need to—" Kasim let out a yelp. "Vandal, how long have you been there?!"

Vandal hadn't been stopped by the guard on the gate (they hadn't noticed him). So he entered the village, spotted the adventurers training, and came over to them.

"Didn't you go into the town to become an adventurer? Did something happen? The old man was worried about the merchant not showing up yet." It seemed that the pioneer villages hadn't heard yet about the monster rampage in Niakki.

"As it turns out, the guild has changed their guidelines," Vandal said. "Dhampirs can't register before the age of ten, so I gave up for now."

"What?" Fester exclaimed. "They changed the guidelines?!"

"Hold on—you aren't even ten?!"

They had overestimated Vandal's age. Every race aged differently, so it wasn't too unexpected.

"There are rumors that the adventurers' academy might stop taking dhampirs completely later this year," Vandal continued. "I'm going to wait for an opportunity to go register in another domain."

Maybe a certain Grade A adventurer would make some waves, but Vandal wanted nothing to do with him and wasn't expecting anything. He definitely didn't want to feel like he had become an adventurer thanks in any part to that guy.

"Wait for an opportunity?" Kasim wondered. "Is it that simple? It takes more than a month to reach another domain. Although I guess you could fly there in a few days."

"Yeah, I guess you can fly."

"Flying over the demon barrens would be safer than going

on the ground, too. And bandits can't fly."

Kasim then turned to Vandal with a glint in his eyes. "Anyway, until you get that opportunity, would you like to party-up with us?"

"I'm just a civilian," Vandal replied.

"There's no rules that civilians can't be part of a party!"

"Because most of the time, there's no real question of them being any use," Zeno said. "But you're actually much stronger than us! I know the offer sounded arrogant, but actually . . . it would be more like we're in your party!"

"Exactly," Fester said. "We're weaker than you, but we can definitely get in your way!"

"Hey! No, that's just a bad joke . . . Fester, if you meant it, I'm definitely not laughing!"

It seemed that these three had really taken a shine to Vandal. He hadn't expected the offer, but he also had to admit that it might be fun to team up with them. It felt like getting together with some friends of the same age and gender and going on an adventure.

Vandal had never had friends on Earth or Origin. He certainly wasn't lonely here on Ramda, but he had still never had male friends his own age. So Kasim's offer felt so fresh and exciting for him.

However, Vandal had something he needed to do first.

"It's a fun idea, but first I was thinking of going back home." He needed to free the people of Talosheim, including Borkz's daughter. However, he couldn't tell these kids that he was going to go free all the slaves at the mine, so he used the backstory he had already established as a cover.

Eleonora and the others were already waiting for him in the

village he had taken back from the goblins. Meanwhile, Borkz was leading a force over from Talosheim.

"You have some wonderful friends, Your Majesty," said Princess Lebia.

"You said it," Vandal responded, but so only they could hear. All the phantoms had concealed themselves but were still nearby. Vandal could still talk with them in his mind, while he chatted with Kasim and the others using his mouth.

"If that's what you have to do . . ." Kasim sounded disappointed. "Can you at least train with us again, next time you can?"

"Of course." Vandal gave a nod, feeling the stress of the city melting away at the simple trust displayed by Kasim and the others. The three of them were a healing presence to Vandal.

"Are you leaving right away?" Fester asked. "We'll be putting up the shrine and having a harvest festival in the fall. Come back around then."

When Vandal had done his rounds of the villages, he only asked that they create shrines to Vida for payment. It sounded like that payment would be completed by the fall here in the Seventh. However, he also didn't remember asking them to do that here.

"In this village?" Vandal asked.

"That's right. The owner of the General Store and the mayor made the decision. Said it's a good opportunity and auspicious too."

"Iwan is super invested too. He was a stonemason, back at home before we fled to the Heartner Domain."

"He's talking about making a statue of you, too!"

Things had certainly moved quickly while Vandal was away.

He welcomed the increased faith in Vida but wasn't sure about becoming another statue. The giantling lich Nuaza back in Talosheim had already started a series of such statues, one of Vandal at each age.

"That sounds wonderful, Your Majesty!"

"Doesn't it just," Vandal sighed internally, hoping that the statue wouldn't look much like him. Then he spoke out loud to the humans. "Do you know what's going on in the other villages?"

All he had done here was save Iwan, and they were carving a statue of him. He had no idea what might be going on in the other villages.

"The other villages? I mean, it isn't rare for shrines to feature statues of saints and heroes as well as deities."

"I'd think so. They aren't going to be massive statues, either. About the size of you now."

Vandal was on his way to literally being carved into pioneer village history. He was the one who had chosen to give up on trying to conceal himself, so he couldn't complain . . . but were statues of him going to pop up everywhere he went in the future? Vandal really didn't want that to happen, even if most of the villages were so far off the main road that they were unlikely to be visited by many travelers.

Acquired the Alias Guardian of Pioneering!

Vandal blinked, surprised to see that his story wasn't just carved into the stone of the new villages but also into his status. Still, this nice-sounding Alias was more than socially acceptable and didn't require any explanation, so he was pretty happy with it overall.

"Ah, I'd also like to use the Job Change Chamber today as well, if that's okay."

"It's in the mayor's house."

The Job Change Chamber was normally located in a guild, but it wasn't just adventurers and magicians who took Jobs. Farmer, Hunter, and Fisherman were also all respectable Jobs that people could take. In small villages like this one, the Job Change Chamber was therefore often located in the mayor's house. Vandal took along a bottle of wine he had picked up from the cellar of the magicians' guild master as a gift and went over to the mayor's house.

After entering the chamber, he saw a crystal a lot smaller than the one in Talosheim. He touched it.

Available Jobs: Insect Master, Big Boss, Zombie Maker, Arborist, Corpse Commander, Plague Demon, Spirit Gladiator, Tongue Whipper, Berserker, Necromancer, Dark Doctor, Dungeon Builder, Demon King's Familiar, Magic Master

"That's a lot more than last time!" Rodocolte's curse hardly made a difference at this point, with so many options. Although since Vandal hoped to live three, maybe five thousand years, he'd probably run out eventually.

Tongue Whipper sounded straightforward, but he wasn't sure about presumably fighting with his tongue all the time. Berserker had to have some twist to it compared to RPGs, to say it was a completely new Job for this world. Maybe it was related to his new skills like Scream, Spiritual Corrosion, and Spiritual Abnormality.

Necromancer clearly involved the use of necromancy. It might allow him to draw further power out from Princess Lebia and other ghosts. Dark Doctor would likely apply modifiers to skills like Surgery and Poison Dispersal. He assumed all the healing he did during his time in the pioneer villages triggered it. Dungeon Builder came from having made a dungeon and Demon King's Familiar from drinking the blood of the Demon King.

He wasn't sure about Magic Master, though. That also sounded like a Job that should already exist, but his curse didn't let him take those. That was suspicious. It almost felt like some kind of trap.

"Anyway, Dungeon Builder and Demon King's Envoy look a bit risky to dabble with," Vandal said. "I'll think about them later in life. Same thing for Necromancer, and I'm just not sure about Magic Master."

Vandal scratched his head. "That leaves Insect Master, Arborist, Spirit Gladiator, and Dark Doctor to choose from. Bah, if I managed to register as an adventurer then I wouldn't need to worry so much about this!" Since the adventurer's guild would see his status when he registered, he still wanted to avoid Jobs that would really catch the eye.

He wondered if he should have registered with the magicians' guild when he had the guild master under his control. But the plan had always been to discredit the man. It might have caused issues later if he had been recommended by someone who was then promptly executed or locked up for life.

"I'll go with Insect Master," Vandal decided.

Acquired the skill Bug Wearing!

Skill level increased for Remote Control, Magic Control, Bug Wearing, and Physical Boost (Claws, Fangs, Tongue)!

Name: Vandal

Race: Dhampir (Dark Elf)

Age: 7 years old

Alias: [Ghoul King] [Eclipse King] [Demon King Reborn] [Guardian of Reclamation] [Unspoken Name]

Job: Insect Master

Level: 0

Job History: Death Mage Golem Creator Undead Tamer Crusher of Souls Poison Master

Status

Vitality: 344

Magical Power: 379120344

Strength: 188

Agility: 251

Muscle: 159

Intellect: 784

——Passive Skills

[Brute Strength: Level 4] [Rapid Healing: Level 6] [Death Attribute Magic: Level 7]

[Resist Maladies: Level 7] [Resist Magic: Level 4] [Night Vision] [Death Attribute Allure: Level 7]

[Skip Incantation: Level 4] [Enhance Brethren: Level 8] [Magical Power Auto Recovery: Level 6] [Enhance Followers: Level 4]

[Poison Dispersal (Claws, Fangs, Tongue): Level 4] [Agility Enhancement: Level 2] [Physical Length Change (Tongue) Level 4]

[Barehanded Attack Boost: Low] [Physical Boost (Claws, Fangs, Tongue): Level 2 (UP!)]

――――Active Skills

[Drain Blood: Level 2] [Limit Break: Level 6]

[Golem Creation: Level 7 (UP!)] [Non-Attribute Magic: Level 5] [Magic Control: Level 5 (UP!)]

[Spirit Body: Level 7] [Carpentry: Level 5 (UP!)] [Construction: Level 4 (UP!)] [Cooking: Level 4]

[Alchemy: Level 4] [Brawling Proficiency: Level 5] [Soul Crusher: Level 6] [Simultaneous Activation: Level 5]

[Remote Control: Level 7 (UP!)] [Surgery: Level 3] [Mental Multitasking: Level 5]

[Substantiation: Level 4] [Cooperation: Level 3] [Rapid Cognition: Level 3] [Command: Level 2]

[Agriculture: Level 3] [Clothing Making: Level 2] [Thrown Projectile Proficiency: Level 3] [Scream: Level 3]

[Necromancer: Level 2] [Bug Wearing: Level 2 (NEW!)]

――――Unique Skill

[God Smiter: Level 4] [Spiritual Abnormality: Level 4] [Spiritual Corrosion: Level 3] [Dungeon Construction: Level 4]

――――Curses

[Unable to carry over experience from previous lives] [Unable to enter existing jobs] [Unable to personally acquire experience]

"Bug Wearing? Not controlling?" Vandal shook his head and sighed. "Well, I can investigate that later. Now, to head to the old town and wait for Borkz and the others. If it looks like they're going to take a while to arrive, I can fly over to the slave mountain to check it out first."

The End

The Death Mage

SPECIAL CHAPTER

INTO THE HEARTNER
CASTLE TREASURE VAULT!

The house of Heartner had existed as minor royalty prior to the founding of the Olbaum Electorate Kingdom and had flourished as one of the ducal domains in the time since. Their treasure vault was therefore protected by some serious security.

Elite knights kept watch on a rotating shift at the doors, alert at all times. The doors were mithril coated with adamantine; it was said that the castle could collapse, and the vault would still remain standing. The only way to open these special doors was with a key given to registered individuals. The floor, walls, and ceiling inside were protected by barriers, making it completely immune to magic.

"Rise."

Of course, the designers hadn't expected the floor with the barrier to start moving on its own, opening up a hole to invite invaders inside.

"And just in case, Silence." Vandal used death magic to stop any potential sounds leaking to the knights posted outside. "That should do it. Come on in, everyone."

"This is the treasure vault?" Eleanora said, looking around. "It's bigger than I expected."

Zulan and Lefdia, who was floating in midair, came in next. "Even a place like this means nothing before your abilities, Lord Vandal. You could become an incredible thief, if you wished—and give the proceeds to the poor, of course."

"Just taking a look around, there isn't much I recognize," said Princess Lebia, making herself visible. She was holding Lefdia to her chest. The items in the vault included works of art, so she was limiting her strength so as not to set anything on fire.

"It's been 200 years since the things were taken," Vandal said. "There must be a lot of non-Talosheim-related stuff in here as well. Let's search as thoroughly as we can."

Vandal and his party had entered the vault to take back the treasures of Talosheim that Princess Lebia had brought with her 200 years ago, stolen from her by the duke.

"Lord Vandal, there's a tome here with an inventory of the vault's contents," Eleanora called. "According to this . . . there's no Item Box." One of the treasures they had most been hoping to obtain was a magic item that had infinite storage space by placing things into another dimension.

"Such a shame," Princess Lebia said. "With your ability to fly around, Your Majesty, you would have become even more mobile if all you needed was to take that box with you."

"Putting it that way, that's not such a bad thing," Vandal replied.

"What? Why?"

"What I've learned from this trip is that traveling alone is far too lonely."

If he was going somewhere, he wanted to go with someone. If Vandal really had to go alone, he'd likely end up making undead along the way to talk to. He could handle having to work alone if necessary. But if it wasn't an absolute must, Vandal would never choose to do so.

"I suppose being able to do everything alone isn't always a good thing."

"Exactly. Although I wouldn't *have* to use the Item Box all by myself."

"I see. I'm starting to understand how you think, Your Majesty," Lebia said. "Eleonora, does that list have anything that was stolen from us?"

"The records include a simple description of the items, but not how they were obtained. Simply the names here won't be enough to work anything out."

"What about a date? Is there anything like that?"

"No, nothing," Eleonora said. "There must be a more detailed record somewhere else, with those kind of details."

"We're pressed for time," Vandal cut in. "We'll have Princess Lebia and the others take a look around and see if they can pick anything out."

"Oh, that sounds like fun!" Princess Lebia was practically clapping. "A real treasure hunt!"

She started to woosh around the vault in excitement. The phantoms and Zulan did the same. If the guards were to witness the ongoing whirlwind of monsters, they would likely pass out on the spot.

"I guess we can make a mess," Eleonora said. "When the castle gets tilted tomorrow all of this will be thrown everywhere anyway."

"Good point. Oh, look at that big cup. Is that a giantling item?" Vandal spotted a magic item that looked like a massive cup. It had a handle reinforced with mithril and a number of gemstones embedded into it.

"Lord Vandal, that is the Infinity Juglet, an item presented to the duke by an adventurer who became a knight of the house around fifty years ago." One of the maid phantoms revealed the truth, however. "If you drink alcohol from it, you will be able to continue drinking as much as you like, no matter how strong it may be, without getting drunk."

"I would've guessed from the name that the cup would've poured out infinite liquor," Vandal said. "Simply not getting drunk isn't so impressive."

"Ah, also, any poison poured into it will also have no effect."

"That sounds more useful. Huh? What's up, Lefdia?" Vandal put down the juglet as Lefdia trotted up at his feet carrying a necklace made from massive gemstones.

"This pendant? But it looks human-sized—"

"That gemstone!" exclaimed Lebia. "That's one of the rubies from the crown of the king of Talosheim!"

It seemed like Lefdia hit the jackpot.

"So they removed the giantling-sized parts and just used the stone to make a new item," Eleonora said. "Lord Vandal, what do you want to do?"

"There might be other pieces made from broken-down items like this, and it will be odd if just a few gemstones go missing. Let's take the entire necklace." They hadn't been planning to take anything other than treasures from Talosheim, but this was an unexpected wrinkle. Vandal took the pendant from Lefdia and put it into the bag.

"That means we'll need to check every single item in here," Zulan said. "Everyone, look carefully at anything using gemstones!"

The ghosts responded in agreement and started to work through every gem in the place. They were quickly rewarded, as well, with gems from the crown appearing one after the other to collect.

"Lord Vandal, what do you think about this one? It looks like a giantling shield. The inventory states 'a large and powerful wall.'"

Eleonora was pointing at a massive adamantine shield leaning up against the wall. Adamantine was the hardest metal that humans could work, only losing out to the so-called metal of the gods, orichalcum. That made it heavy, but a shield of this size could stop attacks even from powerful monsters like dragons and giants.

"While that is a giantling shield, it was received more than 500 years ago, upon the founding of the Olbaum Electorate Kingdom," Lebia said. "I remember seeing it back when we actually got along with Duke Heartner."

Another dud, then. Talosheim was a kingdom of giantlings, but giantlings had long existed in human society as well. They were the descendants of those who hadn't been able to escape with Vida into the Boundary Mountains 100 thousand years ago. The user of this "great and powerful wall" had likely been one of them.

"I see. Just because it's intended for giantlings doesn't mean it definitely came from Talosheim. I might be better at this if I had been responsible for things here in Olbaum rather than Amidd when I still worked for Vilkain," Eleonora sighed.

"A mistake anyone could have made. Don't worry, just keep searching. Princess Lebia, what about this pot? The scene painted onto it looks like something from across the Boundary Mountains."

"Ah, yes! That's a pot we used to carry salt! Ah, to see it again now . . . but what is it doing here? It's just a pot."

"Who knows?" Zulan said. "With the fall of Talosheim,

maybe they thought no more of this kind of item would be made, so it would appreciate in value."

"Hmm. We actually found something, and it still doesn't feel like a home run," Vandal said. It had been a simple household object, back in the day. While it could be considered an antique, for Princess Lebia and Zulan, it was just a pot for salt.

"What shall we do?"

"Let's take it, I guess," Zulan replied. He didn't seem all that bothered about it, but it was something that had been stolen. That was what they were here to do: reclaim objects, regardless of their value.

"This is more difficult than I was expecting," Eleonora said. "Are there other works of art in here? Vases or paintings?"

"No, I don't think so. Just the crown jewels and other pieces like that. We used the pot to carry things, but we didn't bring any works of art."

"Okay. Let's search everything besides the paintings, then. We could also find someone responsible for this place and use my Alluring Doom Gaze or Lord Vandal's Spiritual Corrosion to control them," Eleonora suggested.

"I think finding the person we want, brainwashing them, and bringing them back here is as much as work as just searching the place ourselves, now that we're here," Vandal said.

And so, they continued the search. They did find a lot of the stolen treasures, but few of the items resulted in easy decisions about how to handle them.

"There's a gemstone here with the Talosheim crest etched into it!"

"I'm sorry, Zulan. That's something we sent to the house of Heartner as a sign of our friendship when we first started trading with them," Lebia explained. "It isn't something that was stolen."

"What about this sword, then?" Vandal called. "It looks like Datara's work."

"Indeed, it is, but he sold it to the duke. Again, it wasn't stolen."

"Does that go for this ring and necklace set as well?" Eleonora said. "It's made from polished dinosaur bone and gemstones found in the Talosheim dungeons."

"Borkz gave that to his daughter! A keepsake from his wife, her mother!"

"Jackpot, Eleonora."

At first, everything seemed like such a hassle that Vandal had considered simply emptying the place out. However, as the treasure hunt continued, Vandal found that he was starting to enjoy himself. In the end, they picked up and looked over almost every treasure in the place.

"For the pieces that have been split up and used for other things, removing just the part we're here for would take too long," Vandal directed. "Let's take the whole thing, for now. If they ask for it back, we can throw back whatever is left—as hard as we can."

At Vandal's comment, Princess Lebia and the others imagined for a moment the members of the house of Heartner getting their heads ripped to shreds by flying shrapnel made from unwanted gemstones and pieces of swords and armor.

Of course, Vandal would never do that. If he was going to hit them anywhere on the body, it would be on the legs. That way they didn't die right away.

"Lord Vandal. I've seen armor with this design before somewhere."

Eleonora was pointing at some armor that clearly looked like a magic item. The adamantine-coated mithril exterior offered high defense while keeping down the weight. The parts in contact with the skin used high-rank monster materials, keeping them soft and comfortable. The robust gauntlets, shoulders, boots, and knee protectors all featured detailed work. The details provided the magic for armor while also increasing its value as a work of art.

The main sections of the armor were bikini-style, however. A bikini for a very well-endowed woman.

"I didn't expect to find more bikini armor here," Vandal said. "I guess there's more of it than the stuff we used for Saria and Rita. As you say, Eleonora, the details of the design and coloring is quite similar to theirs. But the quality and size of this is dramatically better. Maybe it's for giantlings?"

"Hmm, oh, I've seen it before," Lebia said. "Borkz and his party found it in a dungeon, and Healing Saint Geena wore it for a while. When we fled, we took as much of the weapons and armor from our own vault as we could, so as not to give them to the Milg Shield Kingdom. This must have been included with that load."

"Do the dungeons in this world have a thing for risqué armor?" Vandal mused.

"You're lucky you became ghosts before Lord Vandal found this," Eleonora chuckled. "Otherwise, you might have become Living Armor with this as your body."

"That sounds like fun, actually," Lebia said. "Although I only have a passing familiarity with the martial arts."

"I was not expecting you to just accept that idea," Eleonora said.

"I'm definitely not letting Mom see this anytime soon," Vandal added. It would be a nightmare if Dalshia saw this and started getting ideas about becoming Living Armor again. Still, Vandal added the new bikini armor to the pile of objects they were bringing back.

In this manner, numerous treasures were stolen (back) from the house of Heartner.

Special Chapter: Into the Heartner Castle Treasure Vault! The End

Glossary

—Skills

Spiritual Abnormality
A skill indicating a mental composition different from normal humans. All magic, special skills, potions, and anything else with effects on the mental spirit are null and void on the holder of this skill. However, the individual does not become entirely emotionless. The only human holder of this skill is Vandal. Others include a select few among the Demon and Devil Gods who appeared from another world and creatures similar to them.

Spiritual Corrosion
A skill that allows the user to influence the mind of the target, altering their personality, awareness, and memories. Use requires communication of some form with the target, such as direct contact, conversation, or meeting their eyes. It can also be used via indirect contact, such having them read a letter or hear a recorded voice. In the case of Bubuldoura, the skill was triggered when someone read from the forbidden text that he had turned himself into. In the case of Vandal, he hasn't yet achieved the same potency as Bubuldoura when it comes to using this skill, such as directly brainwashing and controlling targets. However, it is highly effective when used by Vandal on the dead.

Physical Length Change

A skill that allows a part or all of the body to extend or contract. The volume of change that is allowed depends on the level: double at level 1, four times at level 2, eight times at level 3, increasing exponentially from there. Although the part extends or contracts, it does not take on any rubber-like properties. There are no humans who possess this skill.

Scream

A skill that affects targets using sound. The screams of monsters such as Mandragoras and Banshees utilize this skill.

As Vandal can use this skill combined with Soul Crush and Spiritual Corrosion, he can cause wide-range sensory and magical damage simply by subjecting targets to his scream. Causing sufficient mental damage can even drive the targets insane. He can also use the skill to simply amplify his voice, allowing him to make himself heard and give speeches without the need for a loudspeaker or microphone.

—Aliases

Demon King Reborn

An Alias that indicates that the bearer is the second coming of the Demon King. It takes more than simply being assumed as such: an individual needs to be able to do the same things as Demon King Gudranis in order to acquire it. Such deeds include crushing souls, creating new types of monsters, and building dungeons. It is also possible to acquire it by incorporating, absorbing, or being incorporated into a piece of the Demon King.

Those who do acquire it receive all sorts of bonuses for handling forbidden techniques and evil knowledge. In particular, they get bonuses for creating new monsters and altering existing ones. One example of this is Princess Lebia and the other ghosts ranking up to Flame Ghost and Fire Ghost. However, bearers cannot create or change any type of monster with zero restrictions. There are all sorts of detailed conditions and compatibilities that apply.

Guardian of Pioneering

An Alias given to those who aid people performing settlement work and help solve their problems. The bearer must be perceived as doing so by at least ninety percent of those working in the specific area.

When one with this Alias is involved in pioneer projects, such projects become more likely to succeed. It also makes it more likely that the one with the Alias will happen to be in the vicinity when said area faces a crisis. There are other Aliases with similar effects, such as Goddess of Pioneering and Savior of Pioneering.

—Jobs

Poison Master

A job for people with knowledge of various chemicals and their effects and the capability to make, use, and break them down, combined with a Brawling Proficiency skill of at least level 3. As it requires scientific knowledge, Vandal is the only one on Ramda who can possibly take this Job.

It allows for skills like Poison Dispersal—which involves the secretion of various chemicals from the fangs, tongue, and claws—and Physical Boost, which strengthens the claws, tongue, and fangs. It also offers bonuses to Brawling Proficiency, making it fairly suited to fighting on the frontline. It allows for stat gains in Vitality, Muscle, and Agility, but less gains for Magical Power and Intellect.

Afterword

Thank you so much for picking up the sixth volume of *The Death Mage*. It's nice to meet those of you coming through for the first time, and welcome back to those who already have a Death Mage habit. I'm Densuke, the author.

The year of this book was a big one for *The Death Mage* here in Japan. The second volume of Takehiro Kojima's comic edition was released, along with Vandal coming to life in a collaboration event with the Yurudorashiru game, developed and distributed by Clover Lab and Saga Forest. I'm still stuck with my flip phone, and so I didn't get to play the event myself, but my readers seem to have enjoyed it.

Thinking back, it's been four years since I won my prize at the 4th Internet Novel competition, which made all of this possible. That means year five is about to start. Makes me wonder if everything that happened is due to the auspicious fourth-year factor. In that case, next year is the fourth year since the publication of the first volume, so I hope the miracles keep coming. Of course, I'm aware that I've only come this far thanks to the support of you, my audience.

In this volume, Vandal finally invades . . . er, encroaches . . . ahem, advances into Olbaum. Vandal and his expanding pool of allies have had this as a target since volume #1, but of course, things aren't going to go smoothly just because they finally achieved it. He meets new faces, visits the adventurers' guild, and faces obstacles from interfering deities and the powerful foe depicted on the cover. He even meets a new heroine, also on the cover. This volume also reveals the mystery of what happened to the previous royal family and remaining people of Talosheim. It also features the return of at least one character with a complex connection to Vandal, although much has changed since we last saw him. There's definitely a lot going on, so I hope you enjoyed it. I'm doing my best to enjoy it myself, although my family does complain about me talking to myself. Apparently I do that a lot when I'm writing, without really being aware of it. I need to be more careful of that!

I don't have much room left, so I'll finish with the usual round of thank yous. My thanks as always to proofreader (sorry for all the typos!), editor, and everyone at Hifumishobo publishing. Also, congratulations on your move! I'm a little worried that I'll lose my way the next time I come over.

I also need to thank Ban! for always designing and drawing the bizarre characters I come up with, and this volume was no different. The attractive, characteristic art really helps to expand the world of *The Death Mage*. Thank you to everyone involved in the publication of this book, and all the readers who support it! I look forward to seeing you in the next volume!

—Densuke

The Death Mage Volume 6
(Yondome ha Iya na Sizokusei Majutusi vol. 6)
© DENSUKE 2019
© BAN! 2019
© HIFUMISHOBO 2019
Originally published in Japan in 2019 by HIFUMISHOBO Co., LTD
English translation rights arranged through TOHAN CORPORATION, TOKYO

ISBN: 978-1-64273-458-4

No part of this may be reproduced or transmitted in any form or by any means, electronic or mechanical, including photocopying, recording, or by storage and retrieval system without the written permission of the publisher. For information contact One Peace Books. Every effort has been made to accurately present the work presented herein. The publisher and authors regret unintentional inaccuracies or omissions, and do not assume responsibility for the accuracy of the translation in this book. Neither the publishers nor the artists and authors of the information presented in herein shall be liable for any loss of profit or any other commercial damages, including but not limited to special, incidental, consequential or other damages.

Written by Densuke
Illustrated by Ban!
English Edition Published by One Peace Books 2025

Printed in Canada
1 2 3 4 5 6 7 8 9 10

One Peace Books
43-32 22nd Street STE 204 Long Island City New York 11101
www.onepeacebooks.com